1.25

ACKNOWLEDGEMENTS

I wanted to list all the people who put up with obsessive talk about nuns, who read and critiqued individual chapters, who asked for more, tossed around titles, voted on cover designs, offered computer advice. But since those overlapping categories include all my (smart, generous) friends, many of the staff and faculty at the University of Maryland and elsewhere, students, neighbors, teachers of every sort, strangers on the plane, nuns I have known, members of my book/simplicity/no-limits groups, and everyone in my very extended family (even more egregiously overlapping categories), I opted for draconian editing. Extraordinary thanks, then, to Karen Oosterhous for demanding the manuscript and seeing me through the revisions, to Julian Foley for editing above and beyond the call of kin, to Jakob, Allegra, Benedicta, Julian, Alex, and Jeff for keeping me close, to Seda and Nico for being too young to worry about the sorry state of the union, and, as always, to Rebecca for loving me even when.

AND THEN THEY WERE NUNS is, from beginning to end, a work of fiction. There is no Julian Pines Abbey, nor is there, to my knowledge, any group of monastics — Carmelite or otherwise — who in any way resemble the community at Julian Pines. Alas.

Chapter 1

Nun and Beast

WHEN Sherry died, they decided to sell the calf. None of them drank much milk, they cooked with oil rather than butter, the cheese-making experiments were mildly successful but the neighbors preferred Kraft, and the statistics on cholesterol alarmed them. Donna, they thought (she knew they thought), would be the only hold-out. She had loved Sherry, nursed her until the end, talked to her soothingly while she injected the pentobarbital. And then she began with the calf. Middle of the night feedings, parental pride in the awkward elegance of the wobbly legs, answering gurgles. Marsala, she named the young beast, Marsie for short. Donna, they thought (she knew they thought), will want to keep her.

But Donna voted with the rest of them, simply, surely. We don't need a cow anymore, she thought, and a cow is hard work. She saw their surprise, she smiled at them, to assure them all that it was fine, this decision, that she was happy. It seemed useless to explain, they didn't understand and it was, besides, very complicated, the way she felt about animals. The skin of them, the mottled, spottled fur of them, the shells, quills, fins, wattles, horns, claws, armor, beaks, hoofs, feathers, snouts, paws and trunks of them. She worked in the Sacramento Zoo for two years after she finished vet school. "And what do you want to be when you grow up?" people asked her, in the classroom, on the playground, on the street (she had been a walker, small, and always alone). "A giraffe," she said. "A gazelle." Later, an aardvark, then, an egret or a black swan. She leaned toward the long-necked. She returned often to the gazelle.

Her father had a cat. A long-haired, heavy-bodied creature he claimed was half-dog, named Kiljoy. "Donna," he said every morning of her remembered young life, "it's time for Daddy's coffee." And Donna, at three, five, nine, and sixteen got up and made him coffee on the trailer stove. She tripped regularly over Kiljoy until her second grade teacher insisted that she have her eyes tested. Donna thought everyone had to squat on the bathroom scale to see the numbers. She weighed thirty-five and needed glasses. They could only afford the ugly gray frames, but she stopped stepping on the cat and the coffee tasted better.

She remembered making coffee when she was five but not learning to make it. She remembered the afternoon her kindergarten teacher visited; later (Donna heard her) she bragged about the little tyke who was so handy with a percolator. "Since she was three," her father had said to Miss Murphy, "since her mother died." Kiljoy slept on her father's bed and ate off her father's plate and sat on her father's lap in the evenings when he got home from school. It was a small school, an expensive school, a very pretty school with a very pretty name, Valley of the Moon ("for boys and girls from kindergarten through high school, dedicated teaching, individualized learning"), nestled unobtrusively at the bottom of a hill terraced for avocados. Her father took care of the trees (the oaks and cypresses and palms only needed occasional trimming, but the avocados and oranges had to be attentively tended, sometimes—when a freeze threatened—in the middle of the night) and the flowers and the plumbing and the floor scrubbing. He was handy, a handy man, and Donna didn't have to pay to go to the pretty little school. No one invited her to birthday parties, but she got good grades, and her teachers said—to her father— "hardworking," "industrious," "serious." Among themselves they said "poor Donna" (she heard this at nine), when they said anything at all.

She didn't like being called poor Donna, but, after all, she didn't have a mother and she didn't live in a house and she didn't get invited to birthday parties and she had to wear glasses and she had never been to Hawaii or Los Angeles. She did, however, know more about lizards than anyone in the school and when she once said "Zebu" in response to the ubiquitous question about what she wanted to be, her teacher had to look up the word in a dictionary.

She never wanted to be a cat even though Kiljoy got to sit on her father's lap and she didn't.

There were twenty-four twenty dollar bills and two tens inside a wool cap in her father's closet, but Donna didn't find them until three weeks after his funeral. They let her stay at Valley of the Moon because she only had three semesters left and it was *their* furnace that exploded and killed him even though he was drunk at the time. Miss Kerry invited her to dinner twice a week and made sure that the school sent her an allowance for food and clothes. "You should sue," Miss Kerry said, but there was the drinking and the matter of a lawyer. And Donna felt rich enough, with invitations, unlimited asparagus, new jeans, and chamois shirts (one blue, one green) from Miss Kerry's catalogue. "Call me Joann," Miss Kerry said.

The five hundred dollars, they agreed, should be seed money for college. Donna gave Miss Kerry $250 of it for her 1960 VW squareback that only had 23,000 miles on the new engine and used the car to find a job in town and to get there and back every day after school. $2.50 an hour, three and a half hours a day, eight on Saturdays. Gretta's Grooming and Pet Shoppe. When a Samoyed puppy lost all her fur, Donna took her home and nursed her back to health and Gretta never asked for her back. Donna named her Bjorna. She slept in Donna's bed and ate from Donna's plate and sat in Donna's lap even when she was full-grown. Bjorna cost a lot to feed but Donna didn't care, and the vet Miss Kerry recommended was a young woman named Dr. Thorpe, "call me Becca," who had gone to college with Miss Kerry and who said to Donna, "You run like a gazelle." Donna loved her. After that, Miss Kerry invited Dr. Thorpe to dinner, too. Sometimes she was on call and had to leave in the middle of the soup, but usually she was back by dessert ("When will these people learn to take out ticks?") and always stayed longer than Donna. They talked about Miss Kerry's classes—she taught general science to the youngsters and biology to the sophomores—and the teachers, heaping scorn on Mr. Trainer who taught Donna's English class and who had never in his life read an unassigned book (he told her that with some pride, Miss Kerry said, the night he made a pass at her). Becca (it was easier to call Dr. Thorpe "Becca" than it was to call Miss Kerry "Joann." Probably, Donna thought, because Miss Kerry had been her biology teacher) talked about her patients, mostly dogs and cats but several valley horses, cows and goats, two boa constrictors, dozens of guinea pigs and rabbits, and, her favorite, a six-year-old red bantam, who had long since given up egg-laying but who ran a nearby chicken coop with admirable efficiency. "Just like Little Red Hen," Donna said, one of her rare contributions to conversation.

When Donna went to UC Santa Barbara, the sixteen units, the twenty hours at the pet shop (she was now getting $3.45 an hour and only working three days a week) and the forty-five-minutes-each-way commute exhausted her, so she began to beg off some evenings at Joann's (now Joann and Becca's). Besides, the hen died, and Becca stopped doing house calls and started specializing in house cats, and Joann told stories about students and teachers unknown to Donna (a small scandal in 1968 that involved several schools in the Ojai Valley occasioned a large turnover). Since Donna said so little herself, loss of interest in the conversation of the others spoiled some of her pleasure in the evenings. But she still liked to watch the way Becca's small hand brushed across Joann's back when Becca cleared the table and the way Joann's long fingers rested tenderly on Becca's forearm when Joann was trying to make a point. Donna wished they would touch her.

All three women assumed that Donna would go to vet school and she did. She took Bjorna, of course, even though most of the For Rent ads said No Pets. She drove up to Davis in her new, used Datsun (the square-back having betrayed her too many times of late) and found, without undue effort, a trailer in a pleasant sort of park, populated by students and their beasts. She liked it there. And she liked vet school. She liked all the classes and she liked all her jobs, except for the one at the primate center. She worked there for one day and then, unable to stop staring at the monkeys with half their brains exposed, unable to ignore the high-pitched screams and the low-pitched moans, she refused to go anywhere near the place. Until she read about the demonstration. She carried a sign. ANIMALS ARE PEOPLE, TOO. She knew it was a silly sign, but someone thrust it at her and it was better than no sign at all. Only one other vet student showed up. The others were angry at the "fanatics."

And that's when the complications began. Oh, as complications go they were minor, no one knew about them. She never could talk as the others could. She heard them, sometimes late into the night, outside the library. Vet students, professors, Students for Animal Rights, Citizens United Against Animal Experimentation, passers-by. They talked about nature and technology and suffering and global interdependence and kinship and grantsmanship and greed. They talked about dolphins and monkeys, vegetarianism and work horses, bee-keeping and Zen. When Donna got new glasses (her fifth, and first flattering, pair), she could hear them more clearly and follow their arguments more closely. She was confused and stimulated, exhilarated and defeated. She read everything she could find on animal issues, she made the library borrow books and journals from Arkansas and Iceland and Argentina, she read around the topic in a wider and wider circle, she read all the time. After that she thought. She thought about animals and about the books and about the journals, she thought around the topic in a wider and wider circle, she thought all the time, until she was barely passing Canine Immunology.

And then, after some months, she wrote The Article, "Feminism, Vegetarianism, and the State." In it she argued ("in cogent and lucid if occasionally halting and over-earnest prose," wrote the first reader) the similarity between the construction of "woman" and the construction of "animal" as subjects of biological, philosophical, and political discourse, and she demonstrated ("by numerous and luminous examples as well as near impeccable logic," wrote the second reader) capitalism's investment in the perpetuation of said discourse. It was forty-seven typed pages. It was (to use Dr. Landowski's rhetoric) a work of art, a labor of love.

Donna showed it first to the woman who taught Large Animal Physiology, because she seemed intelligent and kind. Dr. Landowski called Donna that very evening. "My God," she said, "I never would have guessed. Send it to *The Journal of Veterinary Medicine*. Send it tomorrow." The logistics of its journey from that eminent publication to its appearance as a reprint, eight months later, in a prestigious philosophical journal were predictably circuitous and coincidental and unpredictably swift. The replies piled high on Donna's desk and appeared for almost a year thereafter in the journals' letter columns, "penned (wrote one editor) by a hearteningly and delightfully diverse readership," like an oncology researcher dismayed that a movement he abhorred had found so insidiously persuasive a spokesperson; a heretofore meat-eating feminist contrite over thirty years' participation in her own oppression; a Marxist philosopher offended at the author's heterodox use of the Master; a vegetarian veterinarian disgusted by Ms. Smith's inability to say what she meant in plain English; an English professor delighted that a scientist could produce prose not only literate but comprehensible to the layperson; a member of the California assembly hurt by her suggestion of government collusion in oppression; a German-born Hegelian saddened by Modern

Woman's loss of the ability to forge links of peace in a world already awash with violence and friction (he typed "fiction" but Donna was not a cynical reader and the editor, who was, opted for the emendation anyway); a lesbian separatist grateful for the appearance of such a piece in bastions of male hegemony but concerned that that very appearance ultimately compromised an otherwise unassailable position; a journalist offended by feminists' humorlessness; a high school biology teacher sick of incessant male-bashing; and the abbess of a monastery appreciative of this thoughtful and really quite brilliant contribution to her community's on-going discussion of their own vegetarianism and feminism.

Donna didn't answer any of the letters, but she saved the stamps.

There were many job propositions during this time and several persuasive lunches and dinners (all at intimate restaurants with healthy potted plants and a generous selection of vegetarian entrees), but Donna could see the disappointment of her future employers in her inability to sustain a conversation or discriminate among the fruits of the latest enological experiments. The zoo manager, on the other hand, eschewed the meals, invited Donna for a visit, introduced her by name to her own most intimate acquaintances among the inmates, and didn't offer the job (Associate Zoo Physician) until the oldest zebu nodded her approval. Donna started the next day. She liked the zoo and was happy that she and Bjorna could continue living in the Davis trailer park. Now that she had, however, embarked on this philosophical journey, she was so racked by the anxiety of her own participation in the colonial nature of the zoological garden enterprise that she didn't sleep for weeks. She listened to Bjorna's breathing for hours at a time, while she tried to sort out the strands of her concern, and suddenly there was Bjorna herself, "her" dog, her responsibility, her possession. Colonialism in the bedroom. She cried. The months passed.

One spring the strange thing—or more accurately the strange chain of things—happened that changed her life more than the money in the cap or the loss of the Samoyed puppy's fur or The Article. She was on her way to the snake house to check up on a lethargic young rattler named Othello, when she saw, on the path leading off to the gazelles, three women in jeans, obviously together, laughing. They didn't talk much; at first Donna thought they might be deaf. But then she heard one say, "Gazelle, gazelle, I've loved that word all my life." She was small, older than herself, Donna guessed, deep voice, light curly hair with a few strands of gray. "Yes," said one of the others, older than the first, taller, short-haired, sturdy (in the manner of a willow tree) "a lovely word, but not you. You are an antelope, ancient and fierce." They were teasing with their words, (Donna could see that, though she herself never teased), they were wrapping one another up with them, jostling each other with them, nuzzling and rooting each other with them, sparingly though they used them. The small one, yes, an antelope, but not a gazelle. Donna had all her life been assigning animal names, so she recognized the justice of "antelope ancient and fierce." But it wasn't quite right, she recognized that, too, and it bothered her that she had no better phrase. She followed them. She watched and listened. The third woman was very tall, six-feet perhaps. She had crooked teeth, short brownish hair without gray, though she looked older than the small one. She put her arms around Almost Antelope. She spoke her name. "Anne," she said, "Antelope Anne, I love you." The sturdy one smiled and pointed to a young gazelle hidden behind its mother.

Antelope Anne took the sturdy one's hand and moved to her side. The tall one stood between and just behind them, one hand on each of their outer shoulders. They stood there, the three of them, touching, silent, for a long time and watched, Donna guessed, the tiny movements of the young gazelle. Donna watched the tiny movements of the women. The way they swayed, ever so slightly, in time to some distant or silent chant; the way Anne lifted her shoulder and tilted her head as though to caress the tall one's palm; the way the sturdy one moved her eyes slowly from Anne to the gazelle, happily, it seemed to Donna, calmly, like the way Bjorna moved her eyes from her, Donna, to a small animal sound outside, one she knew she wouldn't answer.

"Animals," Donna thought. And then she voiced the amazing word softly, over and over. "Animals. Animals." They were three animals at play, and at love. Oh, she had believed it all along, she had written about it in The Article. She sometimes wore a button that said, "People are Animals, Too." But she had never seen it so purely, she had never known it in her body, she had never felt it move her arms and legs. She walked over to them. She broke their silence. Her heart flopped about in her chest, her breath came in spurts, her voice crackled and croaked, but she spoke. She said, "I'm Donna Smith. A zoo physician. The young gazelle is Lita and her mother is Harana."

"Nuns," thought Donna on her way back to the Snake House. "Nuns." She repeated the word several times, as though it represented a new type, a new class, a new species. "Nuns." Beatrice, Karen, Anne. Those were their names. Beatrice, Donna realized but did not say, must be the abbess who had written her a letter about The Article. It was her favorite letter. She remembered the return address (Julian Pines Abbey), the postmark (Sheep Ranch), and the stamp (a gray wolf). She remembered a sentence, the postscript: "There are six of us now, living a silent and simple (which means, ironically, exceeding complicated) life in the Sierra foothills; we would be pleased if you visited." Donna liked the sentence and she thought about the invitation for a long time. But no, she could never visit, she decided, because, well, it would be like all the dinners and lunches. They would expect things, these women, like intelligent conversation, philosophical discussion. Besides, she wasn't a Catholic.

Now, though, it was different. They had said, "Visit us." They had given her a phone number and vague directions. They hadn't realized she was Donna Smith, D.V.M., Ph.D., University of California, Davis, author of "Feminism, Vegetarianism, and the State." She was just Donna Smith, zoo doctor. They hadn't expected conversation. They had just let her stand with them and watch Lita and Harana. Three animals, four animals, six animals. Donna had wanted to burrow among them. She loved them all.

But no, she thought, as she reached for Othello, I could never visit. She laughed at herself. I just never visit, she thought, I only make house calls. She wondered if monasteries ever had ailing beasts. Five seconds later Donna Smith, D.V.M., Ph.D. was herself an ailing beast. She had nuns on her mind when she examined Othello. She did it mechanically. She wasn't paying attention. She didn't like him anyway. He bit her. She didn't panic (though it hurt badly); she stayed as still as possible and called for help. Within a minute, the snakekeeper had arrived with a snake bite kit and began pumping out the venom. The ambulance came quickly, too, and Donna was in a hospital bed before the end of the hour. Her hand and arm swelled and pained her horribly, but she was in little danger. The nurses said two days in the hospital, just to make sure, and then some rest. "Go to the beach," one of them said. Or to the abbey, Donna thought, vaguely, as the painkiller took effect. Before she fell asleep, she remembered Bjorna and had the nurse call a neighbor to feed her. Donna hoped she'd be all right. Her twenty-four-hour sleep was spotted with dreams of a white dog who was really a wolf, of Beatrice-the-nun, of her father and his half-dog cat, of Joann and Becca, of someone else, a shadow, who woke her up to sheets drenched in sweat and tears.

"And your mother?" Beatrice asked. "Do you remember her?" Donna's arm began to throb for the first time in several days, and her face heated up, and she thought for a second that she would burst into tears. "No," she said, "no. Nothing." Beatrice didn't press her, just sat there in her cabin, in a sturdy pine chair, facing Donna, in another pine chair, this one painted blue. A long time passed. Beatrice leaned forward and put her palms on Donna's cheeks.

"We had a rocking chair," Donna said. "She held me in her lap. No one touches me now."

"A couple of years ago," Beatrice said after a while, a silent while, "I read an article, a long article, quite brilliant, I thought, and wonderfully passionate. A good friend, actually a woman who used to live here, sent it to me." She closed her eyes. "'Feminism, Vegetarianism, and the State,' it was called. Written by a woman at UC Davis, a professor I assumed, though it now occurs to me she might have been a student. A colleague of yours perhaps. Her name was the same as yours, Donna Smith. I invited her to visit but she never wrote back. She taught us something, she touched us."

"I can't talk," Donna said. "You see that, don't you?"

"I see that," Beatrice said.

"Please don't tell the others," Donna said.

"No," Beatrice said. "I won't tell the others."

"Every morning my father said, 'Donna, it's time for Daddy's coffee.' He didn't say much else. He never touched me."

"Maybe," Beatrice said, "it's just as well."

"Yes," Donna said, "I thought of that, later, after he died."

"And your mother?" Beatrice persisted.

"She was American Indian. Half. Her mother's father was Chumash, her mother's mother Mi-wok. That's what my father told me after she died. I said the words over and over. Chumash. Mi-wok. Chumash. Mi-wok. I said them slow and then fast, slow, fast. They were my friends. Like the animals."

"What was her name?" Beatrice asked.

"Marcy. Marcy Hill. That's what my birth certificate says. Daddy just called her 'your mother.'"

"What did you call her?" Beatrice asked.

Donna blushed. "I made up a name for her when I was little. 'Shining Wolf.'" Beatrice held her hands while she cried.

Later, nodding at the beast asleep all this time on her rug, Beatrice said, "Bjorna seems to be at home here."

"Yes," Donna said, "but they need me at the zoo." For a few minutes

Beatrice let the words wander around the room, doing their proper work. Then she said, "The nearest vet is in San Andreas."

"Yes, I know," Donna said. "I looked in the Yellow Pages."

"Would you like to come back?"

"Yes," Donna said. "Yes." She liked the abbey. She liked the garden and the chapel and the chanting and the silence and the laughing and the cooking. She liked Sherry. She liked all the animals. She thought they needed a dog.

"I'm not a Catholic," she said.

Beatrice shrugged. "Are we? The bishop writes at least once a year to assure us we're not." Donna laughed; the sound surprised her.

"You could stay," Beatrice said, "if you wanted. We met last night, Kathleen, Louise, Anne, Karen, Lynn, and I. We'd like you to stay, you and Bjorna."

"Yes." Donna said. "We'd like that, too. But Bjorna's old."

"A neighbor wants to give us a puppy. The mom looks a little like Bjorna."

"We'd like that."

"When do you think you might come?" Beatrice asked.

Donna paused to figure out how long it would take to search for, hire, and train a replacement. "Two months," she said, "maybe three."

"Do you know," Beatrice asked, "that the Mi-wok lived in these hills?"

"Yes," Donna said, and she smiled, a huge shining smile that made hundreds of tiny lines in her cheeks, at her temples, around her mouth. It seemed to burn out of her, to light up this sweet, warm animal house with its desk and couch and chairs and bed and stove, with its sturdy (in the way of a willow) dweller—Beatrice, nun, animal. The smile stretched Donna's skin until it ached, but she let it ache, because there was so much pleasure in the aching, pleasure that filled her pores, swelled her veins, and washed in gigantic, noisy waves over her heart.

"Yes," she said, again. "I think I've heard them."

Chapter 2

Letters from Sister Sharon

1984

28 JUNE

Dear Kurt,

You wouldn't like it here—too many hills, too many bushes, too many snakes, too many women. Those were my own objections when I arrived two weeks ago, and that was even before I discovered that half of these crazy nuns live in cabins without indoor plumbing. I, fortunately, am occupying the guest quarters which include—new additions they tell me—both toilet and shower. Slowly (the pace seems to be about one every three or four years), they're outfitting the cabins with similar amenities. Kathleen, who must be about sixty, and Jan, who looks like the youngest (though it's hard to tell with these healthy, outdoor types), are at this very moment over at Teresa's trying to figure out the logistics of her bathroom-to-be. She says a hot tub would be nice, but I think she's joking (though it's hard to tell with these holy, hermit types).

I haven't seen a skinless chicken breast, a closely trimmed piece of sirloin or a fish filet since

I've been here, and given that they were the trinity of my month-long diet before I arrived, my poor body is still in shock, which manifests itself in stomach-aches, heartburn, and, I fear, weight gain. It's not that I don't like the food; even you would like the food. I'll bring back recipes. They take turns cooking and so far every meal has been different and delicious except for the vegetarian moussaka that Beatrice made the night before last. All, including Beatrice herself, pronounced it a failed experiment. Most thought it should be expunged forever from the recipe file; Louise, however, argued that the eggplants this year are bitter and have too many seeds and thus need more camouflaging treatment (like eggplant parmesan or well-garlicked baba ghanouj), but that some year's more successful eggplant crop would yield a more successful moussaka. Beatrice then admitted to using more eggplant than the recipe called for in an attempt to use up the surplus, so the recipe was partially vindicated. She served it with a garden salad and a freshly-baked whole grain herb bread, which prevented anyone from going away hungry.

My favorite dish has been Anne's green enchiladas with Brazilian black beans, but I think you would prefer Louise's quiches—one broccoli, one caramelized onion, both made with Emmenthaler cut from an enormous round sent by a grateful guest. I'll have to think of something equally elegant and useful for my parting gift.

Parting leads me to the immediate occasion for this letter, though I have been intending to write to you anyway for several days. I've decided to extend my stay for two more weeks (the hills, bushes, snakes, and women having become if not dear at least familiar) and will thus miss George and Clara's dinner. I sent regrets, of course, but since you and I had planned to comfort each other in this affliction, I thought you deserved a more elaborate excuse. Here it is: I am, despite the aforementioned physical symptoms (which have, by the way, considerably abated in the last few days), relaxed and happy. I get up cheerfully with the crew at five a.m. (and you know how I feel about

early rising) for morning prayers, mass, and breakfast (a good th..
weaned myself from croissants before I left; Louise's bran muffins are
hearty and tasty but not quite the same. And mostly we have hot,
multi-grain cereal, though I have been promised Kathleen's famous
scones), return to chapel several times a day, work in the garden, help
with the hens (they supply half the mountain with eggs), do errands for
Jan in the craft house (she's teaching me to make candles at the
moment but promises more sophisticated productions in the near
future), go out with Donna on her veterinary rounds, chat briefly with
Karen or Beatrice, help clean up after dinner. What I'm saying is that
I don't do anything keenly interesting, but I like the work (I have, however, volunteered to do house duty tomorrow, which means cooking
three meals on a wood stove—Louise has been giving me lessons—
laundry, floors scrubbing, and all those other domestic chores that I
loathe), and I'm growing more and more to like the company.

Louise has given me notice that another guest arrives on July 15,
so unless I want to pitch a tent (which, of course, I do not), I have to
leave before then, but everyone seems perfectly amenable to my two-
week extension. I need this time, my dear, away from Hemet, away
from students, away even from you. We are so used to our routines and
to each other that we carry on from year to year talking about the
financial problems of Hemet Hill, the personal problems of the students and faculty, the latest in counseling material, the politics of the
city and state, the newest sci-fi triumph—and the years go by. I'm not
averse to the casualness and the routine of our relationship; in fact, I
like them quite well. But I think, at this point, that we need to
acknowledge its limitations. It has been eight years since we first talked
about marriage, six since my divorce. But I'm forty and you're thirty-
eight; we're used to our separate single lives. It seems time we gave up
the pretense of an engagement—if that indeed is what we're pretend-
ing to. The times we've slept together have been among our unhappi-
est. It occurs to me—has often occurred to me—that given somewhat

...mstances we might both prefer sex with our own kind.
...s out. Please don't be angry or upset.

P.S. I know you're not keen on cooking, but Louise just gave me her recipe for the onion quiche. It's a bit time-consuming, but it's simple, and I'm sure you can cut half an hour from the onions without inflicting irreparable damage, and you can buy a ready-made crust from The Caged Squirrel (just don't put this lovely filling in one of those awful Safeway things). Gently cook two large thinly sliced onions in three tablespoons of olive oil (or a mixture of olive oil and butter) for an hour. Spread them on the crust and top with a cup of grated Emmenthaler (if you're feeling adventuresome, try using half fontina and half gorgonzola and let me know how it turns out). Blend together four eggs, two cups of milk (Kathleen admits to using top milk once in a while, so if you're feeling rich and thin, try half-and-half), 3/4 teaspoon salt, 1/8 teaspoon paprika, and a pinch of freshly grated nutmeg. Pour over the cheese. Bake in a pre-heated hot (425-450 degree) oven for fifteen minutes, reduce temperature to 350 and cook for another forty minutes or until firm. Cool for ten minutes before attempting to cut. You'll love it.

27 JUNE

Dear Clara,

My Sierra retreat is splendid. You won't recognize me—so healthy, relaxed, tan, and muscled will I be—when I return. Clara, I wish you could meet Beatrice, the abbess. She shares your flair for turning simple rooms into lovely and comfortable dwellings. My guest quarters, for example, located on the second floor of the building known as the common house, are furnished with obviously old but re-done pieces, including a beautiful oak chest rather like the one you worked on last summer for Barbara and Juliet's housewarming. The curtains are cheerful cotton prints, hand-made, lovingly lined. The patchwork quilt is a project Louise organized when she was laid up two years ago with a bad back; she got a nurse-turned-decorator friend (before Louise joined the community here, she was director of nursing at Mark Twain Hospital in San Andreas) to send her scraps. I inquired also about the origin of the four-poster bed, not an item you'd expect to find in a monastery. It seems that the bookstore owner in Angels Camp dabbles in antiques and passes on to the monastery (a connection made through Anne, who is a freelance writer and book reviewer) occasional pieces she can't sell, in return for Anne's review copies. And thus does every object have a story.

The nuns live in separate cabins scattered over their eighty or so acres. Each bears the mark of its inhabitant—or at least so I'm guessing. I've only been invited to visit three. Teresa's is wholly furnished (sparely furnished, I should add; she has only a bed, a dresser, a desk, a couple of chairs, and a bookshelf) in neighborhood pine. She works sometimes with a logger up the road and gets wood for both fuel and building in exchange for her labor; she made all her furniture herself. Anne brought her a stunning dhurrie mostly in reds—I've never seen one so brightly colored—from a thrift store in San Francisco. She claimed it cost five dollars. Teresa keeps wild flowers in a clay vase on her desk.

I write because I have extended my stay and so will be unable to attend your dinner on July 5. Please give my regards to George, Bill and Sarah, Jasmine, and Leo. Kurt has his own letter, of course, and will fill me in on the delicious dishes I missed. I'll be home mid-July and will call to arrange lunch at my house for a full report on both our summers. No slides, I promise.

Fondly,
Sharon

15 JULY

Dear Kurt,

I write from a tent. You think me mad, no doubt. No doubt, you're right. It's a rather large tent and, for such a crude and temporary dwelling, quite elegantly appointed. I did the decorating myself in a style I'm calling neo-Sierra to indicate the bold juxtaposition of rough-hewn mountain pine and stylish but deeply flawed pieces from the last century. That is, Teresa, who's a whiz with wood, made me a primitive desk/table, and I found a pockmarked, unsteady-on-its-legs Chippendale-style chair and beat-up but nicely carved dresser in the barn. To supplement my sleeping bag, Jan brought me one of the foam mattresses she uses for massage. I could, of course, spend my leisure, of which there is little at the moment, in the common house but this, in spite of its difference from my well-equipped and overly furnished Hemet house, feels more like home. Shortly after the first letter I wrote to you, the woman scheduled to appear on the 15th—a burnt-out drug counselor from Sacramento, I believe—informed us that a friend offered her a month's stay in a Hawaiian condo and she was taking him up on it. Karen looked at me with raised eyebrows as she finished reading the letter to the group—read in its entirety because it was amusing and witty (it seems that said counselor is also a published novelist, but I have never heard of her). I nodded, Yes, I'll stay.

Less than a week later, however, a young woman showed up at the common house door with a small suitcase which she carried in the hand that wasn't broken and a scarf cunningly draped to hide the bruises on her neck and the worst of the damage to her left eye. She had hiked the five miles from the bus stop in Arnold, though the emergency room nurse at Mark Twain had told her we would cheerfully pick her up, even if it meant driving into San Andreas. She didn't, she said, want to risk interrupting our prayers. She volunteered immediately for the tent, but I had had my luxurious weeks in the guest rooms and she looked like she needed comfort more than I. She's a relative newly-wed; Andy (the name has been changed to protect the guilty) runs a real estate office in San Andreas and got rough when he arrived home the night before to find Ellen playing the piano and the steak still only half thawed. He went for her throat but apparently thought better of killing the goose that lays the golden eggs and decided instead to break the hand that feeds him. It was, after all, playing the piano when it should have been defrosting the steaks. Bad hand.

Ellen's twenty-three and works part time in Andy's office. She used to be his secretary but now she just goes in mornings "to organize," she says. Strictly volunteer work. This is the second time he has hit her in the three months since the wedding, but the first time it was in the stomach so she didn't have to miss any work. And he was so sorry and tried really hard not to lose his temper, but, well, she's better with a typewriter than with a stove and he's particular about his meals. She says this sincerely, but she's scared. The bruises are starting to fade.

Teresa has been spending a lot of time with her and looking harassed. I gather the conversations are following the predictable pattern: Ellen thinks it's mostly her fault, and the less pain she's in, the more frequently she talks about going home. She's a sweet and intelligent young woman and has been working happily—and one-handed—around the house and in the garden. When no one's in the common house, I hear left-handed notes coming from the piano. My guess is that she's pretty good and mostly self-taught. She talks to me sometimes because I'm the only other outsider. Yesterday she wanted to know if I didn't think these women were living, well, a sad sort of life—not that they weren't good women and very kind to her—up here miles from nowhere with no one but themselves for company. No men, she meant.

This morning she said she went to a Catholic grammar school and the nuns there had always worn black skirts and veils and you would never guess that these women in their jeans and t-shirts (they wear white robes in chapel but never elsewhere) were nuns, would you? I think she was asking if I thought they really were nuns; that, at least, was the question I answered. She's becoming more critical. She now hates the spicy food, is awakened too early every morning by all that singing in the chapel, doesn't think it's fair that they won't let her call Andy from the abbey phone, can't bear the silence, doesn't understand why they have a stereo but no television set. At first, she said, you think they're holy but then you see that they really aren't. Her evidence: she heard Karen and Kathleen arguing yesterday about letting Kiera—the dog, named after some obscure saint—lick plates after dinner; and when she went by Anne's cabin last week she saw her light up a cigarette. I think she's getting herself ready, psychologically, to leave.

All this was supposed to lead up to an explanation of my pitching (actually Teresa and Jan pitched it for me) a tent among them. But frankly I don't myself know why I'm still here. I wish you'd write.

Love,

Sharon

3 AUGUST

Dear Barbara,

Yesterday I went to confession for the first time in five years. We didn't bother with the formula—Bless me, Father, for I have sinned—and it wouldn't have been appropriate anyway since my confessor was Karen, one of the nuns. She's almost six-feet tall, about our age, quiet (they're all quiet, of course, but the adjective here applies as much to her personality as to her behavior. When she sees me in the common room, for example, or the garden, she'll brush her hand across my shoulder rather than say hello, and will proceed, unspeaking, with her errand. The silence seems both effortless and perfectly companionable.) and does exquisite watercolors of herbs, vegetables, fruit, and flowers. She also tends the flowers in garden and greenhouse, her specialty being lavender roses that get ordered from as far away as Sacramento and, once last week, San Francisco. She laughed when I asked if she grew them for restaurants and upscale offices. "No," she said, "I grow them for myself, but three or four women's bookstores in the valley and the Bay Area recommend them to their customers, mostly lesbians who are courting or celebrating. That's nice, don't you think?" She sends them into San Andreas by way of the school van and splits the profits with the driver, a single mother of three, who is a near neighbor. I haven't yet figured out how they get from San Andreas to their destinations. Karen sells the flower paintings, too, but through the monastery catalogue, which Jan and Louise are getting ready for its fall mailing. I'm helping. Editing the copy is usually Anne's job—she's the resident writer—but she's working on a feature article ("Mountain Women") and is off most days doing interviews. She kissed me (these women kiss rather a lot. It can be disconcerting to someone like me, but I'm getting used to it) when I volunteered to take over.

Anyway, back to the confession I began with. Every detail demands, it seems, such extensive explanation that I'm unable to stay on track, and, again because this visit is so hard to explain, I haven't been writing many letters. I especially haven't been writing about Karen because I worry that exposing her priestly activities will cause trouble. I mean it would be just like Kurt to get so agitated at the thought of a woman saying mass and hearing confessions (of course, he believes passionately in the ordination of women but it must be done through official channels) that he'd feel morally obligated to do something about it. Beatrice (she's the abbess) laughed when I expressed this concern, thanked me for my consideration, and assured me that they have been dealing—persistently and successfully—with complaints for nearly ten years now, which is the length of time that Karen has been their priest.

I hesitated writing about this to you for different reasons. I know you've no patience with Catholicism—I doubt that Juliet does either— and I (worn down, no doubt, by all that annulment nonsense) have rather run out of such patience myself in recent years. But this, my friend, is another animal altogether.

Karen came to my tent for the occasion, bringing a bunch of wild flowers in a glass bubble. "To warm your house," she said, "as though anything needed warming at this time of year. You *are* watching out for snakes?" (Someone asks me that at least once a day, and I did find a rattler coiled not ten feet from my flap last week. I was terrified, but it soon took off for sunnier pastures.)

She sat cross-legged on my makeshift mattress which has, by the way, done wonders for my lower back aches, which is the main reason I didn't return to the guest quarters after Ellen left. To find out about Ellen you must ask Kurt because I can't bear to repeat the story (and I'm already plaguing you with entirely too many digressions) and because her leave taking occasioned such a crisis here, Teresa becoming a total hermit for almost a week, wondering, she said when she emerged from her cabin one night after dinner, her hair matted to her head, frighteningly large dark circles under her eyes, what they all thought they were doing here if they couldn't even help someone like Ellen. She looked better and calmer after she showered; she curled up on the floor next to Anne and fell asleep. She was still asleep when I went back to my tent and Anne was still there, her arm over Teresa's body. I think they're lovers.

Actually, I know they're lovers. The day before Ellen left was my day to be "house sister"—the person who cooks and cleans and does laundry and keeps, in cooler weather at least, the home fires burning, so I was up at 4:45 to start the coffee and breakfast before morning prayers. My tent is not far from Anne's cabin—actually three small rooms attached to an old barn—and I use her outhouse in the morning. When I walked by her bedroom I noticed flickering light. I looked in the window, since the curtains were open—they usually are—thinking to wave good-morning to Anne, whom I imagined at her desk writing. Instead I saw Anne and Teresa, legs entwined, asleep, naked and coverless (even mornings were unusually warm last week) in Anne's bed. I've often seen Teresa come out early from her own cabin and seen Anne quite late at night alone at her desk, so I don't imagine they often spend the night together, but they looked pretty together then. If I hadn't assumed that I was staying in a community of completely celibate women, I probably would have guessed much earlier from what seemed a rather lingering kiss one morning when Anne set off for an interview and another in full view of everyone before we dispersed for the night. So now I'm thinking that they all must know and wondering how long it has been going on and what the others think and if the relationship is another source of the "complaints" Beatrice mentioned and if any of the others....

So these days that I intended to spend in meditation and relaxation, I spend instead thinking thoughts of women in bed together, just like, I admit with embarrassment, the thoughts that pursued me when you and Juliet got together. Somewhat to my surprise, the dominant feeling in both cases has been not disapproval or disappointment but enormous fear that I am perhaps missing out on something wonderful and, I admit even less willingly, enormous sexual arousal.

Given what I've just written, the issue of my "confession" to Karen seems to have faded in significance. My love to Juliet. Please write and tell me all about your trip to France.

Your Friend,
Sharon

7 AUGUST

Dear Laura,

If you'll continue to water my plants and clear the answering machine of messages, you can have the house until September.

Sharon

10 AUGUST

Dear Kurt,

Louise, who has been doing substitute nursing this summer at Mark Twain Hospital, brought back news yesterday that Ellen had been in again, this time with a cracked rib. That's the bad news. The good news is that she said to Louise, "This is going to happen over and over, isn't it?" and agreed to press charges. There was an opening at the Angels Camp battered women's center (it was full last time and they have our name for emergency shelter) where, Louise says, they have an excellent counseling program, so we're hoping that she gets the help she needs. Teresa, who took her departure very hard, is looking more cheerful. (Teresa herself was battered in a long-ago marriage, I heard, and she seems still saddened by another departure, just before I came, of a young woman who had been a nun here for almost five years.)

I'm sorry that my letters disturbed you so much. I assure you that I didn't mean to "accuse" you of anything. Homosexuality is not something I would ever "accuse" anyone of, it being neither crime nor sickness, nor, as far as I can tell, a problem except insofar as people make it one. Frankly, I find it disturbing that you reacted so defensively, especially given that as dean of counseling you work so closely with students, some of whom are likely to be lesbian or gay. You said when Barbara was dealing with Alicia that you had never had a student admit to homosexuality. Now I see why. Why *would* they confide in anyone who, before the fact, radiated disapproval? Barbara and Juliet have felt rejected by you as well. I excused too much of your unwillingness to socialize with them by telling myself that you and Barbara had never been good friends, but now I think it was probably just plain old ugly bigotry.

No, there was no hidden agenda in my letter. I have not "decided" anything about my sexuality—or about yours. I only made what seemed a reasonable suggestion that economically explained the vagaries of our relationship. I repeat, though, that I'm surer than ever that we ought to drop the subject of marriage. I'm sorry, but frankly I can't believe that you want it anymore than I do.

See you in September.

Sharon

P.S. If you throw away the recipe just because you're angry with me, you'll be sorry. Crusts are not difficult to make, by the way. Just cut a stick of butter into small bits and work in (with your fingers) one and a quarter cups of flour. When the texture is uniform, pour the mixture into a pie plate and pat the dough into firmness. The result will be less

elegant than that achieved with a rolling pin, but it tastes jus~
and is a lot simpler. I gave up rolling pins years ago.

23 AUGUST

Dear Barbara,

Had you told me of your childhood fascination with the "trappings of
faith," I would not have "cheated" you out of the account of my
confession. Unfortunately for your prurient curiosity, however, *this* confession had little—at least at the end—of the furtive and sexually charged
anxiety of those of my adolescence and young adulthood. If I seem to
dismiss such anxiety from my more mature years, don't be fooled. I actually rehearsed for days a confession I made after the first time Kurt and I
spent the night together. There I was, almost thirty-five years old, needing forgiveness for some small physical pleasure in a li confession had little—at least at the end—of the furtive and sexually charged anxiety of
those of my adolescence and young adulthood. If I seem to dismiss such
anxiety from my more mature years, don't be fooled. I actually rehearsed
for days a confession I made after the first time Kurt and I spent the night
together. There I was, almost thirty-five years old, needing forgiveness
for some small physical pleasure in a life singularly devoid of such. And
that particular pleasure was so very small that I fiercely resented the guilt.
In fact, that confession was my last, so silly did it seem and so humiliat-
ed did I feel, apologizing for sex at my age and in my circumstances.
Adultery has always seemed to me a more dignified and interesting sin
than fornication, but the annulment robbed me of even that distinction.

"I haven't been to confession for six years," I said to Karen, not without some defiance.

"The Pap smear syndrome?" she asked. I had no idea what she was
talking about. "You know," she explained, "an embarrassing ritual, easy
to put off, especially when you're not sexually active."

"And what," I said, "makes you think I'm not sexually active?"

She laughed. "I deduced it from six confessionless years. To most inds sin without sex is about as likely as cervical cancer

know it happens, but the risk seems minimal."

about ten times in the last six years."

larly."

"Well," she said, "this is beginning to sound serious. Sex without pleasure ten times. What other horrors have you perpetrated?"

I was angry. She wasn't taking me or my sins or my confession seriously, reducing it all to sex, which had nothing whatever to do with it, well, almost nothing. It had taken me two weeks to work up to asking her to hear my confession and it was just a joke to her, perhaps to all of them. Maybe Ellen had been right, I thought, they're not really nuns at all. I could feel my face flushing and my temperature rising, a situation that you should appreciate, since my quick temper has so often been a source of amusement to you (which amusement, you must know, only infuriates me further).

Before I had a chance to speak my fuming mind ("Fuck you," was the phrase in readiness), she put her hands on my shoulders. "Sharon," she said, "Sharon. Why are you fighting me? If you want to talk, I'm here. If you want forgiveness for whatever you've done, I offer it, from me and from all of us. Peace, my sister."

First, I rolled my eyes, but when I started to tell her she sounded like refugee from Haight-Ashbury, suddenly everything was gone, my anger, my resentments, my guilt. I don't mean permanently, of course, but, for then, completely—like the moment aspirin kicks in and the pounding pain that seemed as if it would hammer at you for the rest of your life just stops. That was it. We sat for some minutes, maybe fifteen, in weightless silence, and then she rose without making a sound, kissed me on the lips and backed out of the tent flap. Though I wondered briefly if I had undergone a profound spiritual experience or if the woman was some sort of psychic healer or hypnotist or if the high altitude had finally unhinged me, the questions soon seemed irrelevant, the possibilities indistinguishable. I sat there, unmoving, suffused with the pleasure of the painless.

You see, perhaps, why I avoided this narrative, at once so charged and so plotless–and why I can't seem to tear myself away from Julian Pines.

Love,
Sharon

P.S. Remember that potato curry recipe we tried last spring? This one— it's Anne's—is much better and just as easy, except that you need a few more spices. Peel and dice about two pounds of potatoes. Heat three tablespoons of oil and gently brown a large onion and a clove of garlic (both chopped, of course). Add 1 teaspoon salt, 2 teaspoons cumin seeds, 2 teaspoons mustard seeds, 2 teaspoons ground coriander, 11/2 teaspoons turmeric, 1/2 teaspoon cayenne and stir for a couple minutes more. Put in potatoes, stir until evenly coated and lightly browned. Add two cups of water, preferably vegetable water and simmer slowly until potatoes are soft (about half an hour). Add a cup of yogurt and a cup of any cooked vegetable or vegetables (Anne used left-over peas and red peppers) and cook for ten more minutes.

1 SEPTEMBER
Dear Laura,

If you'll continue to water my plants, you can put your own message on the answering machine. My house and my job are yours (I've already talked to George, who has by now doubtless talked to you. He seemed perfectly willing to have you "on board"–that nice degree from Bryn Mawr covers a multitude of high school scandals.) until further notice.

Gratefully,
Sharon

1 SEPTEMBER
Dear Barbara,

This is all your fault. When you wrote that Laura was thinking seriously of deferring grad school for a year and trying to get a teaching job, I ran all the way to Beatrice's cabin and practically fell in the door. It had never before occurred to me that Hemet Hill could function without its star English teacher (I can say that, now that the English faculty has lost you to the vice-principalship—congratulations), and, of course, I've never done anything like this before (I don't mean stay in a monastery, though I've never done that either, but make such a last minute decision). "Can I stay?"

Beatrice looked at me for a long time, then explained their policy of asking aspirants to return home for several months after their first visit. What about going back for first semester then returning in January?

"No, no," I said, horrified at this misunderstanding. "I'm not asking to join the community, just to stay for the school year."

She looked at me again and suddenly I saw that she was quite right, that given my record so far, asking to stay for a year was tantamount to asking to join them, perhaps permanently. I said as much. Beatrice laughed. "My dear, you sound horrified at the prospect."

"No, no, it's not that," I lied, "it's just that I can't believe what I just said. I mean, I haven't thought about becoming a nun since I was a teenager. It's unreal and crazy."

"Yes," she said, "it is that."

"But maybe it's what I really want."

"Maybe it is."

"But maybe it's not."

"Maybe it's not."

"Beatrice," I said, "why are you being so damned echoic?"

"That's my job."

She sent me around to talk to the others, all of them, which is what I've been doing for the past two days. Tomorrow night they've scheduled a meeting to discuss my proposal. I may attend or not, as

I please, but the outcome seems, on the basis of my private poll, fairly straightforward: I can stay. The conversations were amazing and ranged from ten minutes with Donna (who said basically that the animals trust me—meaning Kiera, the hens, and Donna's patients, several creatures, mostly domesticated, who live in these parts–as though that were the deciding factor for her. Maybe it is. She's the strangest and most laconic woman I've ever met.) to a three-hour session with Anne.

"I'd like to stay," I started, without preliminary, since I had used up all my easy openers on Donna, Jan, and Kathleen. She motioned me to the little couch in her sitting room, then went to her desk for a cigarette.

"I smoke," she said, "when I'm agitated."

"Does the thought of my staying agitate you?"

"Of course," she said. "The thought of anyone staying agitates me, agitates all of us. Only slightly less than the thought of anyone leaving. We are creatures of habit."

I laughed. "Teresa says you have punning ways."

"Hardly an original pun around here," she said. "But it's true that, unlike my sisters, I'm promiscuous with words. Words are the breath of my body, the food of my soul, the sex toys of my crotch."

I try for cool, but I must admit she disconcerts me. She didn't stop for air. "Beatrice has probably told you that when someone starts talking seriously about staying, we usually send her home for a while, away from the seductions of these holy hills, so she can decide whether she really wants to do something so rash and irrational as plant herself in a nunnery. And to make sure that she's not running away. As I was, when I came. Thirteen years ago."

"Yes," I said. "Beatrice told me."

"But usually is usually, and not always. You're smart enough and, at forty, certainly old enough to know what you're doing."

"Frankly," I said, "I haven't the faintest idea what I'm doing."

She laughed. "Just as frankly—'frankly,' you use that word a lot—I don't think many of us did. My theory is that we all came here for bad reasons and sometime in the course of life in this crazy place stumbled upon good ones. Or ones that sound better, at any rate. You will, too, if you stay."

"Do *you* think I should? I'm here for advice. Or something."

"Something," she said. "Something sounds more promising than advice. Here's "something." For the last two weeks, you've avoided me and twice when I have touched your arm, you've pulled away."

"I have?" I was genuinely surprised to hear it.

"You have. Let me guess. It suddenly dawned on you that Teresa and I sleep together sometimes and you've been worried about it ever since. You've been wondering whether you should bring up the subject. You've been wondering if everyone knows—they do—and if so, you are mildly shocked that such behavior is tolerated. On the other hand, well, it doesn't seem all that shocking. Am I right?"

You can imagine how thoroughly embarrassed I was at her almost perfect reconstruction of my state of mind. That and the thought that I was going to have to deal with the issue right there and then and the prospect of having afterwards to face Teresa as well made me moan aloud.

"Sharon, I'm sorry," she said. "I didn't mean to be unkind, but we have to talk about this, don't we? And I think we have to talk about it now." I longed for Karen's simple, undemanding, no-details-no explanations-necessary absolution, and it occurred to me that she could give it so easily because the hard stuff got hammered out elsewhere. Like here. Like now.

I took a deep breath.

When it was finally over we both had hair stuck to our foreheads and huge patches of sweat on the underarms of our t-shirts. It was wrenching, but I wish that you and I had done it, because I see that I pulled away from you, too. I'm sorry. This realization comes after I wrote a nasty letter to Kurt accusing him of that very thing. Anne laughed when I told her that my best friend is a lesbian. I stumbled over the word. I also admitted that I've been afraid since Judith (this of course entailed telling her that whole story) to get close to another woman—or to anyone. She said that life in a monastery—or at least in this monastery—is intense and intimate, much more so than it probably seems to me now. "The routine," she said, "and the silence mitigate both intensity and intimacy, but fearing either will make your life here hell." She's an extremely intelligent woman and I saw for the first time how compelling she can be. It scared me. I mean, what would happen if I fell in love with her? Or with one of the others for that matter? Hard as it is to imagine now, away from the momentum of the conversation, I actually asked her that.

"I don't know," she said. "That's just a chance you have to take. Love's risky—and unpredictable. We do the best we can and we try not to be afraid—or at least not to let fear paralyze us or turn us to stone."

"Anne," I said, "I want to know what the good reasons are. The ones you stumble upon if you stay."

"I'll make you a list."

Love,

Sharon

25 NOVEMBER

Dear Judith,

"Listen," you said, "listen to my heartbeat." You held my head against your chest until I stopped shaking, until, lulled by that rhythmic throbbing, I fell asleep. Like a child on her mother's breast, though not the child Sharon and not the breast of the mother of the child Sharon. That breast was untouchable and untouched. (My mother said she cried when my father told her she couldn't nurse me. He said nursing was a Mexican thing. She said she was a Mexican. He said, "Not anymore.")

And I was not a child and you were not a mother. We were grown women, young women, living on dreams. Not of prince charming, the dream of choice among my college chums, but of washing down the streets of the city of angels, turning the poor black and Chicano teens into nice, educated middle-class Americans—as you were, as I had become. I don't mean to make fun of us; it was the sixties and filled with dreams like those. Besides, we would have been good at such dreams—good with the kids, good with their folks, good with the neighborhood. You were, after all, a nun, and I was, or had been, prac- tically a street kid myself. I can picture us, as I always pictured us, you in that blue denim skirt you wore every day like a habit and me in my jeans, standing in the doorway of the green stucco house we picked out on one of our forays to Olvera Street to get those tortilla-wrapped hot dogs—what were they called?—deep fried and juicy. We were going to let the kids paint murals on the walls, remember? On the walls of Casa Teresa, Teresa-the-tireless-reformer being, at the time, our favorite saint. And turn the empty lot next door into an open-air teen hang- out. One day you drew it—with complicated gym bars, a gigantic tree house, and tables, benches, and barbecue pits. Later, with an old set of water colors and a shedding brush, I painted the grass green, the sky blue, and the round-faced children, racing for the tree house ladder, all shades of brown. I was going to suggest that you show the picture to your mother superior, a visual aid to persuade her to let you take this venture on.

The finished masterpiece was on my desk, waiting for you, the day you held me and then—when I woke up and told you about Bill— walked away. It has been close to twenty years and I have never, though I've gone over that scene hundreds of times, figured out why you walked away. But then, I have other questions, too, about that time, about us—like why I hadn't told you before then about my marriage. I wanted, I guess, to erase it altogether, and it was so short-lived and so strange that it seemed to involve a different Sharon altogether from the one who afterwards went to college, got a teaching job at St. Catherine's, met you. Bill was the only boy who had ever looked at me, and at seventeen I thought I'd lose him—he said as much—if I took his hands out of my pants one more time. I was, after all, a good Catholic girl; I was "saving myself" for marriage. On the wedding night I cried—and wondered how I'd ever get the sheets clean. No one told me sex would be so messy. My other memories of those few months are of bed, bowling, scrambled eggs, and chicken backs, the only food and recreation we had money for. He had a job, I stayed home, but I honestly can't remember what I did all day. Maybe I washed sheets.

I got pregnant, he left me, I miscarried. And that was the sad-ever-after story of Mr. and Mrs. William Hodges. Such a short story, Judith, but it turned you to stone. Was it the words—marriage, sex, pregnancy, miscarriage—that petrified you? Words of betrayal to a young nun who had given them all up? Or was it more that I had kept them from you, until the day he came back, crazy, accusing me of killing his kid? Or, my most recent theory, did it have nothing to do with my story and everything to do with the position from which I told it, my head on your breast, your arms around me? Did you want me, Jude, and did that scare you as badly as it scared me, later, on the rare occasions I let myself remember it?

Do you know what I did then, after you rebuffed my attempts to talk to you, returned unopened my anguished letters, abandoned me to my fear of Bill and my rage that he had found me and my bewilderment that I had lost you? I ate. And after I'd gained fifty pounds, I slit my wrists. A melodramatic gesture to end the melodrama that was writing my life. At least it seemed a *clean* ending. I let the fear and the pain and the memories bleed out of me. Before everything else bled out of me along with them, Mama found me. I knew she would. I loved you, Judith.

"Write to her," Beatrice said.

"I wrote to her, " I said. "Several times."

"That was then," she said. "This is now."

Yesterday I walked into the chapel at Julian Pines Abbey to eight voices singing, "How good it is, how good it is, when sisters dwell in peace." Karen wrote the music herself, I didn't even know she wrote music, so much to find out about them all. Kathleen, Teresa, Donna, sopranos; Karen, Anne, Jan, altos; Beatrice and Louise, tenors. Beatrice unfolded a white wool robe, just like the one she was wearing, just like the ones they wear, every day, to sing the hours, put it over my head, and kissed me. They all kissed me. I am one of them. I don't think I can tell you why; Anne says I'll stumble upon good reasons eventually. I'd like them now.

I think sometimes of your anguish over your "vocation"—we used that word a lot; I don't think I've heard it once in the five months I've been here. Remember when you thought you might be in love with that long-jawed biology teacher? What was his name? "But Jude," I kept saying, "what about your vocation?" Maybe what I meant was "our" vocation. I envied your life, a life I couldn't have or even think about, because I had married (a fact that seems to bother no one here. Teresa was married, maybe others), but I thought I could share in it. I thought we were friends, partners, blood sisters without even having to prick our fingers. Do you remember the bright orange mums you brought me? You put them on the desk, next to the drawing of Casa Teresa. I'm surprised you didn't take them back. I threw them at the door when you closed it (no, you didn't slam it; your years of convent training made such a gesture impossible) behind you.

Karen gave me roses yesterday, at the celebration, before we danced. Three white and three lavender.

Kathleen baked me a chocolate cake filled with apples, pecans, and chocolate chips.

Anne gave me something she wrote. "Don't open it," she said, "until next week."

Donna gave me an animal that she carved out of manzanita. Manzanita is hard to carve, Jude. I think it's a mountain lion.

Jan gave me some special clay, almost blue, because she's teaching me to make candlesticks now that I'm so expert at candles.

Teresa gave me one of her paintings, a very small one, of a woman's face, not mine, not hers, not anyone's I know. Maybe yours, Sister Judith McPherson. You could look like that now if you have worked hard these many years and loved someone very much.

Louise gave me dove gray stationery. It says, in black, Sharon Ortiz Hendrikson, Julian Pines Abbey. If you answer my letter, I'll reply on a sheet of it. Today it seems too precious for this paper airplane flight into the once known, too good for you.

Beatrice gave me a book called *Loving in the War Years.*

Your Friend,

Sharon

Chapter 3
Anne's List of Sixty-five Good Reasons for Being a Nun at Julian Pines Abbey
and One Bad One

THAT you love the women here, that you like birthday parties, that baking potatoes in the solar oven makes you feel ahead of your time, that the manzanita is as tough, stubborn, and bent on survival as you are, that you can swim naked in the pond, that Donna has decided you're an antelope, that you don't mind making coffee once a week for your sisters in return for the freshly brewed cup that miraculously appears at your place on the other six mornings, that you like the muscles you get in your legs from walking these hills, that the smell of pine reminds you of childhood Christmases you remember nostalgically but that, in fact, never lived up to your expectations, that if everybody lived like this there would be no more war, only short tempers during pre-menstrual season, that we don't have a television, that you think Beatrice can read your mind, that one morning you looked across the meadow and saw a deer watching you, that after the first two years you never gain weight, that the rhythm of the abbey days matches your heartbeat, that you like zucchini sauteed, pureed, boiled, broiled, roasted, grilled, fried, grated, mashed, baked, and raw, that when you see Teresa lift the axe to chop firewood, you think, what a beautiful woman, that you don't have to talk to anyone before breakfast, that when you go home to visit, you can tell nobody thinks you're a real nun and you never know whether they're right or not, that you never have to iron, that at an impressionable age you saw Rosalind Russell in *The Trouble With Angels,* that you think motherhood is overrated, that if you need to die no one will hook you up to a respirator, that your favorite desserts are bread pudding and apple crisp, that Louise clucks over you when you're sick, that when you were a kid you liked tree houses, that you find silence seductive, that you never have to wear high heels or panty hose, that singing Matins and Lauds at five-thirty in the morning feels almost as good as coffee, that you like to play Scrabble, that you always have someone to talk to about the book you're reading, that Karen's lavender roses stun you every time you go to the greenhouse, that you love some of the women here, that after the revolution there will be people with experience, that Jan's massages make you feel the way you always thought sex should make you feel but never did (or did only when you were fucking someone seriously unsuitable), that you're not afraid of snakes anymore, that all your birthday presents come wrapped in the *San Francisco Chronicle,* that you have a built-in audience when the urge to melodrama overcomes you, that no matter what the pope says, you know that Karen is a better priest than Father O'Malley, that fresh-baked bread makes you feel loved, that you've always wanted to build your own house, that if everybody ate this low on the food chain, fasting would—given equitable food distribution—always be voluntary, that nobody minds if you throw a temper tantrum once in a while, that just when life is finally settling into a routine, someone comes or someone leaves, that peeing in the woods makes you feel like a child of nature, that you know that some-day Teresa will be a famous artist and you will have known her when, that there's only one phone, that Kathleen's wild berry jam and Sunday scones are better than Fortnum and Mason's, that no one ever comes to your room without knocking, that if everyone lived like this the ozone layer would repair itself, that you love to dance but were never good at following, that if you hang a "hermitage" sign on your door you can lie low for days and someone will leave bread and coffee on your doorstep, that you think men are overrated, that your favorite Aunt Mary became a nun and she was the only female in the family who got a college degree, that the white robes cover everything except your work boots, that you can see the stars and Donna can name them for you, that mostly you believe in sisterhood, that you have constructed a fantasy mother and Beatrice looks a lot like her only younger, that Jan has plans for a solar-powered jacuzzi, that the library has at least one issue of every left-wing magazine published in the last twenty-five years, that you've never seen the point of lawns, that for the first year your friends think it's fun to visit, that bleeding in the woods makes you feel like an earth goddess, that someday Teresa will be a saint and you will have known her when.

That God has chosen you to be his bride.

Chapter 4
A Portrait of the
Abbess as a Young Nun

(Teresa: 1985)

PART I

I was not happy to discover that the short story—the one that kept Anne at her desk every day last month from ten a.m. until noon—started with my name and with something that happened to me. Sort of. I mean, that's the trouble with fiction. Someone you love is writing it and you look at it and there you are, only it's not you at all, it's this woman named Teresa which is just what you are named, and she meets a snake in a pond, which is something that happened to you a few weeks ago, too, and so

naturally you're interested but then all of a sudden, before you've even got past the adverbs—I don't like them and I told Anne right away she shouldn't have put them in, but I'll tell you about *that* conversation a little later—it's a different Teresa and a different snake altogether. And that's fine if you don't know the person who's writing the story, I mean if the name and the snake are just coincidences, but if you know her then you know that she's really not writing fiction at all but she's writing you, and I'm not sure that's fair. She could at least have called her Barbara and made it a bear on a mountain and then everyone else wouldn't read it and think it was about you and the snake when really it wasn't. Anyway before I get too far into this literary discussion, I should give you the story so you'll see what I mean. Anne refers to it as her first foray into fiction. She's like that. My personal opinion is that she's better at book reviews but you can judge for yourself:

Teresa dove deeply, absently, nakedly into the half-shaded pond and surfaced in a stretch of sunlight head to head with a rattlesnake, diamond-backed. She registered the pupils, black, and the irises, grey with flecks of yellow, and then she grabbed it firmly half an inch behind the head with her left hand and reached for the tail with her right. Six segments on the rattle. It opened its jaws, threatening. Sister Snake, she said, you do not belong in the pond. Sister Snake, she said, if I could get both of us safely out of here, I would have to take you to my cabin and kill you with the hoe, but I cannot, so I am going to throw you into those bushes where you must stay. Now shut your mouth. An open jaw does not become you.

Teresa threw the snake into a low manzanita and swam under water, without coming up for a breath, back to the deck, makeshift, well-worn and warped, too many inches between the wooden planks. She dressed slowly, thoughtfully, the way she did everything, but in her still-shaking hands the buttons of her shirt resisted the buttonholes, the zipper of her jeans stuck on her cotton underpants, and the laces of her left work boot formed a loop on only one side and came untied as she walked back to the common house. No one was there. It was 10:15 a.m., already hot in the foothills. She took a cold shower, to wash off the snake, she told Anne after dinner. And then she sat, still, silent, even when Karen came back from the garden with a basketful of greens for lunch. Karen lightly touched Teresa's shoulder in greeting and walked without a word into the kitchen.

Wait, Teresa told herself, don't tell until the story slides away from that second of not knowing if you grabbed its neck in the right place and that second second of wondering what would happen when you tried to throw it. Wait. You can tell them all at lunch. All except Anne who is in town. And by then the story will cohere and we will all laugh and it will become another abbey anecdote like Anne and the Deer, Jan and the Solar Oven, Karen and the Thirteen Lavender Roses, Kathleen and the Great Zucchini Canning Project.

But how did you know, Sharon asked at lunch, that the snake was female? Sister Snake, you called it. Teresa looked at her and said slowly, seriously—such a serious answer, Sharon thought, she told Teresa afterwards, months afterwards when she knew her better, knew, that is, that Teresa had not, after all, been serious)—it didn't bite me. Beatrice watched and listened. Teresa could feel her. Be careful, Teresa, Beatrice was saying, saying in that way Beatrice has of saying without speaking, be careful. Teresa laughed then and laid her palm on Beatrice's arm. O Mother Beatrice, I will. I am. I do.

Anne came home in the middle of dinner with a stack of mail and a package for Sharon. Brownies (chocolate chip), cookies (hazelnut), tea bags (Earl Grey, decaffeinated), a box (dusty rose) of ten new feather-soft, no fuss tampons, and a mug filled with chocolate-covered espresso beans, fast melting. Sharon passed the treats, Teresa first, she said, because of the rattler. Jan said to Sharon, Let me guess. You got it from the English teacher and the chemist woman, the ones who came to see you last month. They think you must be starving for decadence, missing the perks of small town Southern California, languishing without your adoring students and that guy you were going to marry. You older women have such sordid pasts. I used to get boxes.

What rattler? Anne said.

The rattler, Louise said, that the madwoman met in the pond this morning, don't ask why she was swimming in the pond at ten in the morning when it doesn't warm up until late afternoon and then she picked the thing up and threw it. If you folks had to treat rattlesnake victims every summer like I used to you wouldn't swim in that pond at all. You swell. You turn black. You vomit. You thrash in pain, you think you're going to die. One of my patients did, she was only three. It was pretty horrible.

The mad snakewoman looked up from her fork-full of chard and said, It didn't bite me.

Karen and Teresa washed the dishes and Anne paced the kitchen. There was a mix-up at the library, Anne said, they were supposed to hold a book for me and the new librarian lent it to someone else and I'm supposed to review it. That was the first thing. Then I went to Jenna's shop and she was behind so I had to wait around smelling oil for nearly an hour before she could get to the car. It needs new brakes. Not urgent urgent but sort of urgent. Her exact words. Deirdre had an emergency and had forgotten to leave Louise's prescription, so I had to wait there too. She saw Patricia at some gynecology conference last week and I am supposed to convey greetings to everyone, but I got a little distracted at dinner. By a rattlesnake.

Anne put her head into the common room where Sharon was playing the piano and Jan and Donna were sitting on the floor, a Scrabble game between their legs. Beatrice, Kathleen, and Louise were still on the porch, not talking, Anne reported, just watching the faded day cooling. I'll tell them all later, she said. Teresa, how could you?

It's still light, Teresa said. Let's go for a walk before Compline. Barely light, Karen said. She raised her hand in blessing over the two travelers. That might keep you safe, she said, but take the snakebite kit anyway.

Come with us, Teresa said.

No, Karen said loud enough for even the porch sitters to hear, I might want to play Scrabble with the younger set or maybe I'll meditate with the senior citizens.

Anne and Teresa walked silently up the hill toward the end of the abbey's eighty acres. Slowly because it was still hot though cooler than the kitchen. I think it's time, Anne said at the top of the hill, to haul out the solar oven. She took Teresa's face in her hands and kissed her, then held her hard at the shoulders. Teresa laughed. Here, she said, feel my arms and my legs, too, if you want. No swelling, no bruising, no tell-tale fang marks. I'm young, I'm strong, I'm whole, and I love you.

You love us all, Anne said.

Yes, Teresa said, I love you all.

Protect us, O god, while we are awake and guard us while we sleep that we may keep watch this night and rest in peace. It was hot in the chapel, hot under the long white robes, not heavy robes but wool—pleasantly, comfortingly warm in Sierra winters, but hot over jeans and shirt on intemperate days in June of which there are many some years. Teresa repeated the invocation in silent fugue. Protect us, keep us safe, keep me safe. I was awake. I was keeping watch. It was a big snake. O keep us safe from rattlesnakes. Keep her safe. Give us rest, O mothergod, rest and comfort in our beds. Keep us cool and send us sleep and peace, in your arms, O god, in her arms. She named the beneficiaries of her prayers. First in order of age. Kathleen, Louise, Beatrice, Sharon, Karen, Anne, Donna, me, Jan, but she never could remember if Louise was older than Beatrice, and then in order of years at Julian Pines, Beatrice and Kathleen, Louise, Karen and Anne, Donna, me, Jan, Sharon and then in order of appearance, left to right, on the wall of the art gallery in Sacramento which was, at that very moment, exhibiting the series she had painted. Donna (engrossed in a birthing sow), Kathleen (radiant in the garden), Karen (wry and shy in the greenhouse), Anne (at her desk, defiantly sane), Louise (managerial in the kitchen), Jan (mischievous with her arms in the solar oven, which she made herself), Beatrice (omniscient, omnipotent, and omnipresent). And then in order of affection, which, Teresa thought to herself, I should not do, but she did. Anne, Beatrice, Karen, Kathleen, Jan, Donna, Louise, Sharon, and she added, myself somewhere, first on, say, Saturdays and fourth on Tuesdays and last when I remember Jason, once my husband, and forget that I have forgiven him. Then she began the silent chant of the others. First the ones who had gone, in order of their departure. Patricia, grey-haired pioneer, a doctor in San Francisco, a visitor, occasional; Helen, truculent, Teresa pictured her (Helen had left many years before Teresa had come, gone back to the Midwest and Mt. Carmel); the legendary Lisa, flamboyant and scheming, a photographer, now married, twice; Jesse (the first of the ones-who-had-gone whom Teresa had known), young Jesse, too young, too earnest, too mad. And Lynn, whining, Teresa remembered her on bad nights, whining and pious. On good nights, on this night, she remembered her broken, clinging all night long to her, Teresa, who had been, Anne and Beatrice said, kind. Lynn now lost. Then friends and family, living (keep them safe) and dead (may they rest in peace), Mama, the three Marias, Aunt Elizabeth, Papa, David, Abuela, Carolyn, Jason (it never came easy, eight years it had been since his blows, heavy, and her body, first astonished, then dark, swollen, vomiting, mortal. And it still wasn't easy to add his name, though she had long ago forgiven him, hadn't she). Then heroes, in thanksgiving for, in no particular order, the litany that varied most from night to night, Suzanne Valadon, Lena Wertmuller, Lee Krastner, Margaret Cameron, Georgia O'Keefe, Louise Nevelson, Camille Claudel, Louise Dahl-Wolfe, Jennifer Bartlett, Susan Seidelman, Kathe Kollwitz; shapes, films, canvasses, photographs passed slowly, one by one, under her painter's eye. And she saw, for a moment, there behind the frames, a woman in a white robe, translucent, her foot on a long, thick snake. She heard a voice, a deep voice but clearly the woman's voice, say Teresa, Teresa. She watched, she listened. When she opened her eyes, the chapel was empty except for Beatrice on one end of the polished redwood bench and herself on the other. Beatrice stood up and walked quietly out.

Teresa stood up, too, left her robe, in turn, on a hook in the coat-room, took her flashlight from its appointed place, and into the cooling night followed several yards behind Beatrice until the silent abbess turned off the road and onto the path that led to her two-room house, across the garden now big with zucchini leaves and tomato vines and artichoke stalks, no fruit as yet, across the meadow, up a small hill covered with manzanita and low pines. Teresa followed the whole route in her mind but stayed herself on the dirt road past the chicken house, newly cleaned (she had gone to the pond after that job, so dirty, but she had promised Donna), down to the barn or, more precisely, the end of the barn which had, many years before her arrival there, been turned into a two and a half room apartment. She knocked gently on the door and waited calmly, patiently, for almost a minute, waited, even though she knew the door was not locked, for Anne to answer.

Finally she did. Teresa? she asked to the now dark night.

Yes, Teresa said.

Come in, Anne said. I was just airing out. So hot in here.

Too hot for me to stay, Teresa said. She meant it as a question, teasing, but—since her voice didn't rise at the end of her questions, a trait which Anne had once found confusing, irritating even, and now, she often told Teresa, found only endearing—it sounded more like a statement.

It's never *that* hot, Anne said, pulling Teresa through the dark, shallow entry into a long, narrow bedroom, lit by a candle in a tin, rose-scented. Lie down, she said, my lovely young nun (though Teresa was thirty and when Beatrice was thirty she had been a nun for a dozen years) and let me undo your buttons. You'll be cooler then.

They spoke quietly, almost in whispers, not because there was anyone to hear but because Julian Pines is a place of great silence, and nighttime, after prayer time, is a time of great silence. They had learned to take their solace slow and silent in the spirit of this place and this time.

When Teresa went up to the common house at 4:30 to start breakfast—the morning was cool, even cold but she didn't go back to her cabin for a jacket or even back to Anne's closet for another shirt, let her sleep, she thought, we were late last night—there was a note from Beatrice, Teresa didn't know how it had gotten there: I am feeling ill. Will stay in my house today. Karen had ground grains for cereal the night before; Teresa decided to use the propane burner rather than to heat up the wood stove, too much effort, too much heat when it would be 90 by eleven even if it was cold at five, so she had time to take a cup of coffee and some slices of bread across the meadow to Beatrice before Matins.

Nothing serious, she said when Teresa came in. Just a summer cold. But I'm stuffed and sneezing and don't want to spread it around. It was good of you to come. Not necessary.

I have been here for three years, Teresa said, and this is the first time you haven't come to morning prayers. I was worried.

In that case, Beatrice said, perhaps I should absent myself more frequently. Someday, you know, you'll have to do without me altogether.

Of course, Teresa said, but by that time I'll be eighty years old and quite used to doing without.

Abbess yourself perhaps, Beatrice said. She stifled a sneeze. You would make such an interesting abbess, Teresa. Beatrice raised her hand in blessing. I like this vision, she said, Abbess Teresa Natalie, so walk carefully. I saw a rattler in the meadow when I brought the note. It was biting its tail.

Teresa walked slowly back to the common house, slowly even though she knew she would be late for morning prayer. She shivered. Not so much from cold as from the far-away look on Beatrice's face when she said, Abbess Teresa Natalie. It was a silly thought, unworthy of Beatrice who was not a silly woman. Beatrice saw things that others did not. Beatrice was often right about people and events and she had that look when she said Abbess Teresa Natalie.

On the other hand, Teresa reassured herself, Beatrice has a cold.

PART II

"Anne," I said, "before I even finished reading the first sentence it was all wrong. For one thing—and this is not the main thing, Anne, but it bothers me—you don't write like this. Those three adverbs all in a row. Not like you at all. You are lean. Lean and spare."

"But this is a story," Anne said. "For once. Not an article, not a book review, not an interview, a story. And I can use whatever words I want. Adverbs, adjectives, fibetoes, agrotolites, gorfossils. Even verbs. All for you. All for love. All for Gnat."

When she's in one of those moods—affectionate, manic, and mildly mad—she calls me Gnat, though this time she pronounced it with a British "a," so that it might have been knot or naught. She amuses herself in that way. When she's less manic but just as affectionate she calls me Teresa Natalie. I was surprised the first time she called me Gnat because I had known her a long time and she had never done it before. Actually I thought it was Nat for Natalie and I thought it was odd but better than Terry which is what Jason used to call me not out of affection but because he didn't like Teresa, until one day I found a note from her on my door and it said, Dear Gnat. But she usually calls me Teresa.

"And it's not very funny," I said. "I always laugh when I read what you write, even the book reviews, and that's the best part."

"It's funny," she said, "if you know you."

I decided to get on with the main point, which is the one I was trying to explain before. "I know it's a story," I said, "but when you use my name and my cabin and the common house and all of us, well then you can't just go and make things up like this.

"Like what?" she said.

"Like what," I said, "like the whole damn thing. First of all there are no diamond-backed rattlers in this part of the Sierras and you know that. You may even be the one who told me. Those were not diamonds on her back. They were splotches. Dark splotches, and it was a Northern Pacific."

"Mea culpa," she said.

"And then you made me sound cool and courageous and confident. Grabbing that snake and hurling it into the bush. I think it was a pine actually but that doesn't matter. I mean I'm not being unreasonable here, I don't care about minor details, it might well have been a manzanita, you can do whatever you want with the details, but the spirit, Anne.

"You make it sound like when you meet a rattlesnake in the water the heroic thing is to pick it up and toss it casually into the nearest bush.

What if some kid reads this and then meets a rattler in the water and tries to grab it and gets bitten and can't make it out of the pond?"

"Kids don't read *The New Yorker*."

"*The New Yorker*. Anne, be real. They don't print stories like this in *The New Yorker*. Too many adverbs."

I wasn't getting my point across. What I was trying to say is that the shaking hands, afterwards, didn't paint the right picture. I panicked. Period. I did just the wrong thing—which was not quite the way Anne wrote it actually. I mean, you couldn't throw a snake if you were in deep water, could you, which it sounds in the story like I was but I wasn't—and I was lucky that it worked out. I should have ducked as soon as I saw the snake and paddled calmly back to the deck. Up and out. That's what the books say. That's what Donna told us all to do. Just the week before. She made us all listen to a little lesson on meeting rattlers, in the water and out of the water. But mostly in the water because she had just seen one and because snakes out of the water are common enough, especially around the garden, and we are used to them, and I think we have all killed one or helped kill one except for Jan who has decided that you can't kill an animal even in self-defense, if you can ever rely on what Jan says she thinks, and Sharon who has only been here since last year. Donna can be pedantic, but I should have followed her instructions, I would have followed her instructions, but I just sort of automatically reached for the neck. And then that open mouth, those fangs. First you're scared and then you start to imagine things. The bite, painful, the trip to the hospital, endless, and Donna, the obvious person to drive you, a veterinarian, lots of experience with snake-bitten mammals, or Louise, an ex-nurse, either of them, both of them, patient and worried.

"And how could I count the segments of the rattle," I said. "I was too scared."

"You should have," she said. "Then we would have known her age."

I didn't know what that had to do with anything but it's hard to argue with Anne because she's good at words, writing them and talking them, I admire that about her, though she's bad at looking. I mean, she doesn't see what I see when she looks at a painting or a movie—not that we see movies all that often, only three times since I've been here and that's over three years—or the garden. She might not even have seen the snake. Who knows.

"And that bit about Sister Snake. I did not say that. Or even think that. You make the whole thing into something it wasn't. A moment of mystical encounter. Pond of Eden. Woman and the Snake."

"I just write what I know," she said.

"You can't know what isn't true," I said. "I learned that in Philosophy I. There would have been no way to tell on such short acquaintance that the snake was female."

"It didn't bite you," she said.

I bit her. Not hard of course. She has smooth, cool skin. "If I had called it Sister Snake, which I didn't, I would not have announced it at lunch. You made up that whole conversation. You weren't even there."

"That's why I had to make it up," she said. You see what I mean about Anne being hard to argue with. I usually just change the subject.

"And about our solace," I said. "*We* didn't learn to take it slow and silent—in the spirit of this place and this time. Nice line, but you are the one who learned. With Karen."

"And then," she said, because she knew I didn't mind, because it was so many years ago, twelve maybe, because I love Karen almost as much as I love Anne, because the Lisa-legend too is old, eight years old at least, "I practiced it and perfected it with Lisa and you, O lucky one, are the beneficiary of all those nights and days of seeking solace in my sisters' arms."

"Put that in," I said.

"No."

"You left out Kiera," I said.

"She's a dog," she said. "There are already too many female names in this story. Another would have been confusing. I know my limits."

What I'm trying to explain here is that she does not know her limits.

And the main one is that she shouldn't be writing stories at all. At least not stories this confusing. And certainly not stories about me.

"Besides," she said, "now you're complaining about my sins of omission. A writer has to be able to leave out whatever she wants. Otherwise, we'd still be stuck on our morning pee."

I thought maybe I could disarm her. "I must admit," I said, "I didn't mind the scene in the chapel. It wasn't like that, not that night, that night mostly it was the rattlesnake over and over but it might have been. I felt strange reading it, it was as though you had gotten into my head because it is like that sometimes. I have those litanies. Or ones like them. And you put in the woman in white. I haven't seen her for over a year but she fit there somehow. I liked that scene Anne. I really did. Except for the bit about the snake."

"I thought you would," she said, "I worked hard on it. But," she said.

"But what?" I said.

"But now you're going to tell me what's been bothering you all along, that when you went to Beatrice's house it wasn't like that at all."

"It wasn't," I said. "You know it wasn't. She said what you said she said. I mean I did repeat the whole conversation for you, you even quoted pretty accurately, but she didn't say it the way you said she said it. She was laughing when she said, Abbess Teresa Natalie. I told you that too. And I did not, *did not,* think about it all the way back, I did not walk slowly, I was not late for prayers. The thought of being abbess has never, ever crossed my mind."

"Until you read my story," she said. "And now it has."

"It's absurd," I said, "pure fiction."

"Of course," she said. "Fiction. Though possibly not pure."

"And the title, Anne. You can't use that title."

"You knew the snake wouldn't bite you, Teresa Natalie," she said.

I mean at this point I was sinking pretty badly, don't you think. Even if she's not great at writing stories, she does know me well enough to know when I'm sort of hiding something, even if it's only a small thing and not at all that relevant to the conversation.

"All right," I said, conceding defeat, "seven. There were seven segments in her tail."

"I rest my case, " she said, not even trying not to sound smug. "The title stays."

She has started another story. A detective story, she says, with Beatrice as the detective, herself as the sidekick, and Sojourner Truth Johnson—a musician who stayed here once a couple of years ago—as the wrongly accused murderer of an opera singer. She invented the opera singer. And everything else, I guess. I hope. But maybe not. Maybe she's mixing things up again, true, false, fact, fiction. I did extract a half-hearted promise that she'd use quotation marks, edit out adverbs, and change the names and identifying details before it left the property.

A Novel by Susan J. Leonardi

Chapter 5

The Downhill Path

I BEGAN my career in crime—at the age of fifty-one a late bloomer—with a murder, and said career followed approximately the downhill path described so stylishly and succinctly by Thomas DeQuincy: "For, if once a man indulges himself in murder, very soon he comes to think little of robbing, and from robbing he comes next to drinking and Sabbath-breaking, and from that to incivility and procrastination." I attribute my continued observance of the Sabbath to maturity, sex, and residence. A woman in her prime,

that is, might well deviate from the inevitable progression of DeQuincy's young man, and life in a monastery presents certain obstacles to Sabbath-breaking, makes it, in fact, a great deal of unnecessary trouble.

I had just returned to my little house from one of our several Sunday chapel sessions when I unfolded the *Examiner/Chronicle*—heroically delivered to this isolated Sierra spot by an industrious twelve-year-old girl who braves rain, sleet, hail, and darkness on a surprisingly regular basis—and saw the headline, a typically sensationalized *Examiner/Chronicle* headline, such and various other minor shortcomings being the reason that I am the only one of the nine of us besides Anne who includes the paper in her Sabbath ritual. Anne's excuse, besides repeated refusals on the parts of both the *Los Angeles* and *New York Times* to seek us out, is that as a former *Chronicle* employee she is naturally interested in the deterioration of its journalism; mine is that someone around here needs to stay in touch with west-coast happenings, all four of the news weeklies we subscribe to being east-coast productions. I read the paper before Anne does because I am abbess, and first crack at the morning paper is the position's one perquisite. Anne, however, has been known to abscond with the editorial page and the book review before Lauds.

"Rock Star Arrested in Rival's Death." The forced resignation of yet another cabinet member relegated the crime to the bottom half of the front page, and I might easily have overlooked it entirely but for the fact that I caught the dead rival's name, Ariana Hart, whose recording of early opera arias was a foolproof restorative to my occasional low spirits and whose recent Cherubino in the San Francisco Opera production of *The Marriage of Figaro* had been a thunderous success. She was, in fact, a quiet, almost hidden treasure of the company, and although I had never met her or even seen her perform, I had come, I suppose, to feel that she belonged to us because her voice often rang out of the silence of our lives and pervaded our common space with the rich and mellow mezzo tones for which critics invariably praised her, when they acknowledged her existence at all. She was, after all, local. Besides that, she was small and she was black. Now she was dead. Poisoned, the piece vaguely implied. The case was, of course, under investigation, and the San Francisco music community was shocked, and any careful reader could have predicted the subsequent details but one: the arrested rock star was Sojourner Truth Johnson.

Had I been given the phrase "rock star" and asked to list individuals or groups who belonged in the category I'm sure I could have come up with a dozen names whose ceaseless repetition in the pink pages of the *Chronicle's* entertainment section made them familiar to me and several hundred thousand other readers. It would never have occurred to me, however, to include Sojourner Truth, with or without the Black Widows, whose music might with some small justice be labeled rock but whose star status was non-existent. Then, at least. The notoriety of the murder case has already begun to fulfill the headline's prophecy, Sojourner tells us.

But it wasn't, of course, the unwarranted epithet which so surprised me. Sojourner's voice was indeed considerably less familiar to me than Ariana Hart's. We do have a copy of the Black Widows' single album, but after an initial burst of enthusiasm for it, mostly Anne and Jan's, it had taken a neglected place with many of the other musical gifts we receive, most notably endless recordings of *The Sound of Music* and used copies of *The Singing Nun.* (We are assumed—wrongly I must add—to revel in their conventual motifs). The Black Widows, however, were shelved not for their insipid lyrics or repetitive melodies but because their raucous rhythms and relentless lyrics crashed too obviously into our silence. Though we had not, as a consequence, heard much of Sojourner's voice, her presence among us had been eloquent.

Three years ago she arrived, announced only by a note from Patricia, a friend of thirty-odd years, one of the original members of the Julian Pines community, now part of a group practice of women gynecologists in San Francisco. Sojourner Truth was her patient, she said, and because of scar tissue on her larynx caused by several bouts of laryngitis and no corresponding diminution of vocal activity, she was not to utter a word for fifteen days. She came for healing in our silent company. I liked having her here, her serious, large brown eyes watching us carefully but not, I thought, resentfully or critically. And then there was her music. She brought both guitar and violin, but it was the violin—baroque pieces mostly, ones I had never heard before, Marines, de la Guerre, Sirmen, she wrote on her notepad when I inquired—that carried from the small guest quarters to the common room and kitchen below. Both lush and orderly,

Sojourner's chosen pieces pierced our silent space at breakfast, which she seldom shared, and, the sister on kitchen duty would often remark, at sundry and uncannily appropriate times during the day when said sister, alone with the endless household tasks, was feeling more than usually weary, when a spot of self-pity surfaced from a remembrance of past wrong or present slight, when a surge of sorrow overcame her, when an attempt at quiet prayer turned angry and reproachful. Karen seemed to love the floating sounds most or at least to articulate most frequently, most precisely, their effect. She took to trading kitchen for other, less exhausting tasks just to hear the daily practices, and I, convinced that the music came not in intuitive, sympathetic response to the moods and thoughts of the day's house sister but at predictable intervals, put off on occasion at those very intervals my own chores to keep Karen company.

Anne cast Sojourner as the brooding spirit of the abbey and liked to share a wordless cup of coffee with her before the rest of us appeared for breakfast. Lynn and Louise were the only ones who found Sojourner's presence intrusive, but both of them were going through the kinds of hard times—emotional for Lynn, physical for Louise—that are inevitable when nearly a dozen people live together. Lynn left. Not, of course, because of Sojourner Truth, but perhaps partly because of what Sojourner represented—political punk, racial consciousness, something alien in our midst, something almost as alien as the anger-and-desire-filled Lynn who wouldn't leave the peaceful, the good, the holy Lynn alone. She would, I fear, have felt more triumph than compassion when she read—if she did read: Lynn was opposed in principle not only to the *Chronicle* but to all our news sources—that Sojourner Truth was in jail for poisoning a long-time friend. Louise, on the other hand, stable, managerial Louise, found Sojourner so irritating—I am guessing—not on grounds of race, politics, appearance, or religious belief, but for the same reason that she sometimes snaps at Teresa and Jan, what I have heard Louise herself describe as the inefficiency of youth, an interesting phrase, I think, suggesting not just a fault shared by persons of a certain age but a fault of the age itself, its inability to effect the maturation of which it is itself a promise. Teresa is thirty.

But Louise, unlike Lynn, would respond—did, in fact, respond—to the news with instant pity, with instant explanations, even empathy, like George Eliot's singer who, hearing news of a murderess, cries, "Poor wretch! The world is cruel and she could not sing." Only Louise's version is "and she could not pray" or "she had no community." The Eliot version would of course, in this case, have been singularly inappropriate anyway, because Sojourner Truth can sing very well indeed, at least if her performance on *Black Widows Waltz* is representative.

I have always thought that Eliot's singer had a good point, however, and it was that as much as the conversation I had with Sojourner the day she left which provoked my own initial response, so far from either triumph or pity, of unadorned incredulity. I knew as calmly and clearly as I have ever known anything that Sojourner Truth was innocent.

I re-read the article. Loveday Brooke, Lady Detective, I seem to recall, once solved an entire case with clever deductions from attentive perusal of a newspaper murder account. Either Miss Brooke's mind was far, far sharper than my own, or the art of journalism has deteriorated substantially since the 1890's. I could hardly even figure out the sequence of events, much less understand the grounds on which Sojourner was being held. First frustration, then a kind of rage, followed the incredulity. I tossed the entire newspaper to the floor and sought the increasingly indispensable comfort of my Victorian brocade chair, which suits its location in a forest cabin in the Sierra foothills not at all, but which suits me very well indeed. The chair is an inheritance of sorts from Faye, who lived up the hill on the piece of land that borders our eighty-plus acres and was a good and kind if eminently predictable neighbor, from the founding of the monastery twenty years ago (or at least from the month after; we had first to allay her suspicions that we were going to preach to her or pray for her conversion from the Presbyterian church which had claimed her family for generations) until she died last fall. "Give Beatrice my chair," she told her daughter. "She sat in it once and it looked good on her. Rose is her color. I just don't know what makes those women tick and some of them as pretty as can be and you'd never guess that Anne was a day over twenty-five." Such was her final judgment on Julian Pines. Anne is almost forty.

During that half hour, in an exercise which seems to me a fruitful amalgam of contemplation and self-hypnosis, I simply sat and stared. Despite the biblical injunction to ask, I regard intercessory prayer with some suspicion as a greedy gesture for a person like me who is healthy, strong, and never wants for food, clothes, respect, love, gentle care, and regular amusement. I have, in fact, grown so out of the habit that even then, when a "Please take Sojourner Truth under your wing" would have been a piece of harmless altruism, I chose instead merely to sit in that Presence and wait. At the end I slowly and systematically remembered— though "reconstructed" might be a more accurate word—Sojourner Truth sitting on my couch the morning of her departure, the occasion on which I heard her speaking voice for the first and only time. Her small feet looked childlike in the thick wool socks and hiking boots that made seem even slighter her already slight legs, legs which ended abruptly in deep purple suede shorts, multi-pocketed, belted with wide, soft leather. Her olive green turtleneck shirt looked new; the "B" of "Black Widows" followed closely on a large spider just above her right breast, high, compact, and braless. Although it was a cool morning, cool and misty, she wore no jacket and turned down my offer of something hot to drink. Like the rest of her, her face was dark, thin, and long—though assembled she was not over 5'4"—a thoughtful face if not at all striking or conventionally beautiful. The lines around her eyes, across her forehead and down from nose to chin were many and deep but did not make her look any older than her thirty or so years. Most surprising was her voice, not, as I had expected from Patricia's diagnosis and stern regimen, husky and uncertain, but so rich and clear that the mid-range pitch seemed low until I countered it with my own almost tenor tones.

"I came to thank you," she said. "I have enjoyed being with all of you. And my voice, as you can hear, has mended."

"I'm glad you came," I said. "It has been good for us to hear your music and your silence. Visit us again, bring your band."

"Maybe," she said, "but you are very white, all of you, and it's a long drive from San Francisco."

I didn't answer; no answer seemed required. Her point was well-taken, though Teresa is somewhat Chicana and Sharon half Mexican, and Donna a quarter Mi-Wok and a quarter Chumash. She rose and went to the door. "That was ungracious," she said, "what I just said. I have felt close to you and it has frightened me because my friends are black and my music is black and my goddesses are black, if I have any. And that's how I like it. But I have the sense that if I stayed you would make a place for me. I have the sense that I could belong if I wanted to, and I have never felt that way with whites, except maybe Patricia. She is like you. You are like her." Before I could respond, she grinned and added, "On the other hand maybe it's just that my defenses are down."

"Come back," I said, "any time. It would be good for us to hear your voice. I like your voice." We walked in silence to her car, a silver coupe, newish, and after she got in and closed the door, she rolled down the window and said, "Do you know who Ariana Hart is?"

"Yes," I said. "She has a lovely voice, too."

"She's a lovely person. I'll bring her."

Conjuring up that odd exchange, trying to recall it word by word, tone by tone, nuance by nuance, I knew that Sojourner Truth could not have killed her lovely friend. Certainly I recalled as well a thousand articles about suspects whose neighbors and family members proclaim said suspects nice quiet sorts who wouldn't hurt a fly and it turned out that, whatever their behavior toward winged insects, they had indeed stabbed, raped, shot, and mutilated fellow humans. But no evidence offered in this private court had any effect on my conviction that that forthright, thoughtful, watchful woman had not poisoned someone she loved. Oh yes, friendships wane, but the voice was sure and loyal, Ariana Hart was black, and Sojourner Truth could sing.

I pulled on my work boots. Hot and unpleasant as they looked and felt, the rattlesnakes were more plentiful and the various burrs and dried pine needles more prickly than usual, thanks to a dry spell exceptional even for these dry parts. And in this time of worry about the water supply, boots kept our feet clean. At least that was Kathleen's theory and she, even more than I, hated work boots, so much less refined than the blue and white saddle shoes she wore until she entered Mt. Carmel, less refined even than the black wedged Oxfords and seasonal sandals she wore for the twenty-odd years of her monastic existence (St. Teresa's *barefoot* Carmelites being less a possibility in Wisconsin than in sunny Spain) before coming with me, Patricia, and Helen—now back at Mt. Carmel, my cabin her legacy—to start Julian Pines. That was in the mid-sixties, and both of us are still wearing the boots we bought that winter at the Army Surplus store in Angels Camp. That I contemplated the nature, the function, the necessity, and the longevity of work boots during the five minute walk to Anne's rooms indicated to me that I was already seeking distraction from the brown eyes and interesting voice of Sojourner Truth Johnson.

Anne was as amazed and concerned as I but a bit more willing to entertain the possibility that Sojourner Truth had, a result perhaps of some deep and horrible rift between her and Ariana, in a moment of passion, killed. Poison, I reminded her, is not the preferred method of the frenzied, raging, passionate assassin. A kitchen knife maybe, a heavy vase or marble statue, a long-unused gun purchased for protection, but not poison.

"Feeling motherly today, O holy one?" she said, reaching into her desk drawer for the cigarette that I knew meant tense and focused thinking. "Let me guess. You are thinking that I haven't been to San Francisco for several months and that one of the corporal works of mercy is 'Visit the imprisoned' and that my connections at the *Chronicle* can't hurt any and that Patricia would be happy to put me up and that if you had a coherent account of the incident you might be able to help, even to search out with those all-seeing eyes the proper culprit. My connections are now almost non-existent, you haven't been to San Francisco for years, why don't you go?"

Why indeed. Except that the city is not my territory the way it is, or was, Anne's. I had, in fact, only been there on half a dozen occasions since coming here, to attend a meeting, to spend some time with Patricia when her schedule didn't permit even a short visit to Julian Pines. During my years at Mt. Carmel I only left the property twice, both times because of illness. We went and we stayed or we went and we left—but only once. I suppose I have retained that habit, a habit become perhaps both need and desire, of staying put. I didn't try to explain all this to Anne; she knew; she was only teasing. She was, in fact, packing a bag.

Anne's first trip to Julian Pines Abbey was made in a nearly new VW, in the days when you could, Anne informed us, purchase a lightly-used bug for less than $3000. Thanks to an incredibly resourceful mechanic in San Andreas—she has replaced the engine four times—the machine still functions. While it is not our primary car, we continue to shelter and feed it; it has been a faithful if not always reliable friend. Since Anne drives it most and since she brought it to us, we older members of the community still refer to it as "Anne's car," but Teresa, Jan, Donna, and Sharon call it "The Slug." It is, they claim, maddeningly slow on these mountain roads, but in that regard, Anne assures them, it wasn't much more energetic when it was new. It breaks down with alarming frequency but seldom when Anne is the driver; she volunteered, therefore, to take it to San Francisco, just in case anyone needed the real car while she was gone. "For the night," I said, knowing and being unhappy in the knowing that she could accomplish nothing in only one day. "See you tomorrow," Kathleen said. "Give Patricia my love." Kathleen was making lunch when Anne and I went up to the common house in search of Teresa, but Teresa was neither there nor was she in her cabin. We finally found her reading by the pond, stretched out on the hammock that Sharon's friends gave us last Christmas. Sharon is the newest, though not the youngest, member of our community, from Southern California where lying on hammocks seems to be a year-round activity and where friends think it small inconvenience to drive for eight hours to visit.

Teresa looked lazily up from *Housekeeping* and said to Anne, "I was hoping you'd find me," and to me, "Great Book. Thanks for the recommendation." She motioned for us to join her on the hammock. Anne looked as though the temptation was severe, but I reminded her that it takes four hours to reach San Francisco in the Toyota; in the VW it could take five. Teresa's response to the news was sober and definite. "No," she said. "She didn't do it. She couldn't have."

"You're as bad as Beatrice," Anne said. "Why couldn't she have?"

"Anne," Teresa said, "you're shocking. You know as well as I do, as well as Beatrice does, that black widows never kill fellow females."

"I know no such thing. Since when are you such an expert on arachnid habits?"

"Kiss me good-bye," she said, "and get her out. I'll miss you."

"I'll be back tomorrow," Anne said.

Teresa looked skeptical. "That's what you think. Tell Sojourner this never would have happened if she'd stayed here. No don't. She's in mourning. Teasing won't cheer her."

It didn't seem, Anne reported that night—reported in such loving detail that when I look back on it, I am half convinced I was there myself—that anything could cheer the despondent woman she visited in jail. "What are you doing here?" she asked Anne, as though, Anne said, questioning a foggy figure, a long-dead grandmother maybe, in a dream.

"I'm here to see you. Beatrice sent me. And the others, too."

"To convert the criminal?" Sojourner asked. The sharp question, Anne said, contrasted so unexpectedly with the vague greeting that she was momentarily irritated. "Besides," she added by way of excuse, though none was needed, "the drive through the valley was long and hot, and I had to change a tire just outside of Fairfield." She reminded herself, however, that it had been three years since Sojourner's brief visit to Julian Pines and that the wordless kinship she felt with her then may have been solely one-sided and largely a product of her overactive imagination during a particularly vulnerable time. "Why should she have welcomed me?"

"No," she said in answer to Sojourner's accusing question. "We know you didn't do it."

I interrupted Anne's narrative. "*Do* you know?"

"Yes," she said. "Seeing her again brought her back and I am as sure as you and Teresa that she's innocent. I don't think I ever thought otherwise actually. But someone had to counter your infuriating certainty."

Sojourner nodded at Anne's declaration, "No, I didn't do it. Sit down."

"I can't tell you exactly why I'm here," Anne said. "I wondered all the way down what I could possibly do for you, and the only thing I can come up with is helping you figure out who did do it."

"I have a lawyer," Sojourner said. "A good one." Anne thought at first that the statement was a dismissal, but after a few seconds, Sojourner looked up, squinting, and said, "I think she believes me. But she's busy. Yes. It would make things a lot easier if we had another name. Actually I have several. And it could have been a freak accident, I suppose, not a murder at all."

"Suicide?"

"No. I'm not saying she would never have taken her life but she wouldn't have done it in my presence, in my house. Never."

"Tell me what happened."

"Ariana was a friend, a *good* friend. I can't believe she's dead except that I watched her die. It was horrible. Helplessness has always been my worst nightmare. Watching while other people suffer. Wanting to do something. It's what makes me so angry when I see the homeless curled up on doorsteps—there are more and more of them, Anne. It's not their presence, you know, that makes me mad but that they make me want to do something and I can't. Write a song maybe. Play the violin for a while. Great. Just what they need. But with Ariana, God, I've known her for a million years. We went to high school together. Whittier for the Arts. We sang in the madrigal group. We took voice lessons together. There weren't many blacks at Whittier then. In most of my classes I was the only one. Either that or it was me and Ariana. Only at first her name was Linda. Linda Hartman. She hated it. So common, she said. And then one day—I think we were sophomores—she read a story and the girl's name was Ariana and she said, that's it, that's what I want to be called. Ariana. And since we all wanted to be singers or dancers or concert pianists or actors, name changes were pretty much an every day occurrence. Not that I ever changed mine. When your mother gives you a name like Sojourner Truth, you don't want to be messing with it. Anyway even the teachers at Whittier were very obliging about calling you whatever you wanted. So she became Ariana. She didn't drop the "man" until she started singing professionally.

"So, where was I? We've stayed friends all these years. Sometimes we saw a lot of each other. Sometimes not so much. She went on tour. I went on tour. Months went by. We don't write. Didn't write. I hadn't seen her for a while. Not since my housewarming party in March. And then she called last week, opera season over, wanting to see me. I invited her for lunch. We had bread and butter, a green salad, and a Spanish omelette, which we shared. I made it. It had three eggs, salt, chives, cream cheese, green olives, and salsa, which came out of a just-opened jar. The salad dressing was olive oil, wine vinegar, salt, pepper, garlic, and tarragon. Nothing else. We had a whole bottle of wine. She picked it out of my rack. Eden Valley Chardonnay. The cops took the empty bottle. There was no shrimp. No crab. No lobster. Not a speck. Not in anything."

Anne had no idea what she was talking about. "You've lost me, Sojourner, shrimp? crab? lobster?"

"Oh, sorry, I thought you'd know. She was allergic. Very, very allergic. That's how she died. Anaphylactic shock."

"You knew she was allergic?"

"Yes, of course. Everyone did. Spreading the word was her lifeline. There's always a chance, you know, that someone will use fish stock or shrimp flakes in a harmless looking meal. After the last attack she stopped going to certain restaurants—seafood, Chinese, Japanese, Thai, Vietnamese—just in case. In fact, she had been a little reluctant to go out to eat at all. That's one reason I suggested my place instead of Molly's, you know that cafe on Clement. For years it was our favorite hangout."

"When was the last attack?"

"About ten months ago. In a Chinese restaurant. I was there. With the Black Widows and a friend of Ariana's from the opera. We ordered chicken and cashews or something like that and she took one bite and started to swell. I'd never seen anything so scary. Five minutes later her eyes were swollen shut. But by that time Sarah had called an ambulance and I had given her a shot of epinephrine. She carried it in her purse, always, and she told all her friends how to use it. It started to work right away and on the way to the hospital she relaxed a little and the swelling started to go down. But by the time we got her to the emergency room, it got worse again and they gave her another shot. After a couple of hours and a third shot she was fine. But they kept her overnight, just in case. That was her third attack but the first one I had seen."

"But she had told you about the others?"

"Sure. The first one seemed such a fluke that I don't think she really believed in the allergy. She ordered shrimp at a Thai restaurant, and a few minutes later she started to swell. It was only when her eyes got puffy that she panicked and had Neil—that's the guy she married but they weren't married at the time—take her to the hospital. He thought she was just being a 'prima donna,' but they were still in the courting stage so he indulged her whim. The swelling was as far as it got that time. A few weeks later she had an allergy test and she reacted so strongly on the first dose—the one that the allergist said would be too minute a quantity to cause a problem—that she had to have an epinephrine injection.

"Then several months ago she ran into an acquaintance in Safeway and *touched* a package of thawed shrimp. She said to the woman—I think it was someone from the opera—"That little sucker is death," and within seconds her hand and arm broke out in welts. I saw them the next day. Big, ugly things and by then they were fading. So after that she wouldn't even go near a shellfish. And that's pretty much when she started to balk whenever anyone suggested going out to eat."

By this time, Anne said, she could feel her own arms breaking out and her own throat constrict—that's how you die, Sojourner had explained to her, asphyxiation or heart failure. Since she had become more animated and coherent in the course of the narrative, Anne was a little reluctant to press her for more painful details, but she, too, was beginning to be oppressed by the surroundings and it was getting late. "And at your house?" she asked. "What happened then?"

"Suddenly about halfway through lunch she started to swell. I got the syringe out of her purse and injected the stuff, then called an ambulance. But she kept on swelling and swelling and then she couldn't breathe and I tried mouth-to-mouth and everything else I could think of and nothing worked. She just died. Right there in my arms. In less than fifteen minutes. Just as the ambulance driver knocked. They tried, too, on the way and at the hospital, of course, but she was pretty dead." She closed her eyes, thinking, Anne opined, to block the vision of her dying friend and the panic of utter helplessness. She cried. Anne thought it best to let her.

"But," she went on when Sojourner stopped sobbing, "I still don't understand why they arrested you. You did everything you could."

"The first thing they tested was the syringe. Not a trace of epinephrine. It was just plain water clinging to the sides. Just plain water. They think it's a little unlikely that she should get shellfish in the lunch—it had to have been there somewhere—and water in the syringe by accident. And I can see their point."

"But," Anne objected, "anyone could have tampered with the syringe and then it would have been just a matter of time."

"No," Sojourner said, "she was careful, especially after that incident in Safeway. Most people with these allergies, Ariana's doctor assured her, manage to avoid dying and even manage to avoid having to use the epinephrine. I keep thinking 'accident,' but it does seem almost impossible that shellfish could have found its way into that lunch accidentally."

"And why did you supposedly do it?"

"I'm not sure they care about the why. I was there. But the press cares. Don't you remember the headline? We were rivals. And besides, this is a devilishly clever plot if it is one, and I'm a devilishly clever woman. A Black Widow. A rock singer. Undoubtedly into drugs and debauchery. Can murder be far behind?"

Anne reported all this, after dinner, from Patricia's flat in the city. Since I was there once, I could picture her clearly, sitting at the little pickled pine phone table near the big bay window surrounded by huge plants, some of which Patricia has been cultivating since she left Julian Pines almost fifteen years ago, the first and hardest leaving. She had come with me to California to start a new life in the wild west. We used the phrase jokingly among ourselves, but we did feel like pioneers, like Teresa of Avila, like all the rebel founders of communities held up to us during our novitiate as heroes but considered more critically when invoked as precedents. Patricia, in my band of postulants and just my age—seventeen-and-a-half when we entered—had been my best friend at Mt. Carmel, insofar as any nun in those days had a best friend, and then became a tireless builder, both literally and metaphorically, of this monastery. Besides her work here, she spent two days a week with Louise at Mark Twain Hospital in San Andreas. By the time we had planted ourselves firmly in the mountain soil, she had fallen in love, just as firmly, with the hospital. The decision to go to medical school necessitated, she thought at first, only a temporary break from her twenty years of religious life, five of them at Julian Pines, but the more deeply involved she became with a San

Francisco obstetric and gynecology clinic—not to mention the soup kitchen, battered women's center, and science summer school for working women—the less personally compelling and socially relevant the routinized, contemplative existence of Julian Pines seemed. I miss her still and tried to hold fast during the conversation with Anne the words Patricia breathed hurriedly into the phone as she rushed off to a birthing patient. "Beatrice, my dear, when are you going to give up that sedentary life and come help me deliver babies from mothers and women from men? I love you."

"Patricia is fine," Anne began. "As funny, beautiful, busy, and energetic as ever. Sojourner Truth is less fine; here's what happened."

In spite of occasional volatility and minor lapses into unsuitable behavior, Anne is a most reliable and observant woman; her account contained enough details to stimulate the detecting cells which, I knew from many years of accurately predicting villains in even the most cunningly crafted murder mysteries, lurked among the more normal cells in my brain. By the time she called, Anne had a piece of information additional to Sojourner's account: the just-returned lab report on the wine showed a small quantity of shellfish antigens. One more nail in Sojourner Truth's coffin, Anne observed.

"Nonsense, my love," I said. "An egregious cliche as well as a gratuitous piece of morbidity. You've done a good day's work; do stay over if you don't mind and ask Sojourner tomorrow where the wine came from and find out the full name, address, and phone number of this Neil person who is, I presume, now the ex-husband. Oh, and ask the police if you can see the cork. Look for any sign of a needle hole. Look hard. And Anne, I know you've given up the prying life, but find out please the precise nature of the relationship between Sojourner Truth and Ariana Hart."

Sojourner's eyes were swollen and red-rimmed, Anne reported, when she went to her apartment the next day. "Jail," she said, "made it all seem unreal and unfamiliar. Now, here, I keep remembering. And I know more certainly that she's dead. I loved her."

A sobbing jag, Anne knew from her reporter days, was a perfect opportunity for prying into strangers' lives, but since Sojourner was neither a stranger nor the subject of an article, Anne held her and cried, too. The admission surprised and pained me—Anne hardly ever cries. "But," Anne said, "old instincts die hard and I did, after all, have an assignment."

"Were you lovers?" she asked. Sojourner pulled away from her and Anne thought she had ripped the fragile web so recently and tenuously woven between them. Suddenly, though, as if remembering something amusing, Sojourner smiled. "Like you and Teresa?"

Anne smiled back. "Like me and Teresa."

"Ariana was my first lover. Senior year of high school we thought we were very sophisticated. We were also very scared. When she went off to Bloomington on a big music scholarship, she got involved with a guy, and then another. I tried, too, but I couldn't do it. It just didn't seem right."

"And then she got married."

"No. Then she came to San Francisco. I had moved up here to go to San Francisco State, which I did, on and off while I worked odd jobs and sang odd jobs, and I didn't get my degree until a couple of years ago. Anyway, Ariana and I lived together for two years. The first one we were lovers, the second one we weren't."

"Men?"

"Just one. That's when she met Neil."

"Were you upset?"

"What kind of a half-assed question is that, Sister Anne? Of course I was upset. He was male, he was white, he was a jerk, and I loved her. But that was over two years ago, just after I got back from Julian Pines, actually, and I didn't kill her."

Anne had been so absorbed in the story line, she said, that she had forgotten the subject at hand. She realized as soon as Sojourner spoke how the question must have sounded. She was mortified and decided to give me my share of the blame. "Sojourner, I'm sorry. That *was* a half-assed question. I know you didn't kill her. We've just got to find out who did, and Beatrice said to make you talk. She wants to know everything. What happened to Ariana and Neil-the-jerk?"

"Maybe he's not a jerk. I don't know. You should probably talk to him and make up your own mind. She told him about me right after they got married, and he freaked. Spent a whole year ragging her every time she called me. When we had lunch he'd want to know if we slept together. The answer was no, in case you're wondering. I honored her commitment even if I didn't like it."

Anne took the bitterness only half personally and relegated the other half to Neil. She waited silently—we're all good at silence—for Sojourner to resume the narrative.

"If she didn't have dramatic enough orgasms, he'd want to know if she liked women better. By women he meant me, of course. I guess he stopped doing that sort of stuff. At least Ariana stopped telling me. Actually she pretty much stopped calling me. They had moved to Calistoga by that time and I was basking in the minor success of *Black Widows Waltz,* doing some touring, and being in love with the new drummer, so I didn't call her either."

"And then?"

"And then we sent each other Christmas cards and three yellow roses on our respective birthdays—long story, not relevant—and that was it until the divorce."

"Which was when?"

"Listen, do you think Neil did it? I mean, he was the first person I thought of, but then I would, wouldn't I? And why didn't he kill me instead of her?"

"Maybe with her allergy she was an easier target. And besides, whoever set this up knew he or she would be hurting you in the process. When was the divorce?"

"Last year sometime. She called me, I think it was at the beginning of the summer. Apologized for keeping away, for letting Neil decide who her friends would be, said she'd had it, they were separated, she was moving back to the city. I think he may have hit her, but she never told me that. I heard rumors. She was a mess for a while, though she kept performing, wonderfully in fact, through it all. She saw a shrink for a few months. You know, the usual."

"Did you get involved again when she moved back?"

"No. No. For one thing she didn't move back. Neil did. And then I had just broken up with Lora, she was the drummer. And Ariana was pretty clear that even though Neil hadn't worked out, she wasn't giving up on men altogether, and I wasn't willing to take a chance on an off-again, on-again het. So we decided no sex. She helped me move last February and that night I admit that I wanted to ask her to stay, and I think she wanted me to ask her to stay, but I didn't. The same thing happened the night of the housewarming party, and then I went on tour and the opera season was in full swing and we only talked on the phone a few times until last week."

"Did she say anything about Neil when she called or when she was here for lunch?"

"Only that they were being very mature and civilized about the divorce and still saw each other socially. He dropped in the night of my party, by the way. In my part of town, heard I was having people, just wanted to say hi, see my new place, great neighborhood, no hard feelings. He stayed maybe half an hour. I noticed that Ariana avoided him. Maybe that was before they were being mature and civilized."

"Did he bring you a housewarming present?"

"Yeah," she said, startled out of the listless tone with which she had been answering Anne's relentless questions. "Yeah, a bottle of wine."

Anne spent the rest of the afternoon, she reported, taking Sojourner Truth through every exercise either of them could devise for retrieving the memory of Neil MacKenzie walking in her door the evening of the housewarming party and handing her a bottle of wine. Finally Sojourner announced that she couldn't remember because, in fact, it hadn't happened that way at all. She had never seen the bottle in his hand, hadn't actually seen him come in, but *had* heard him say as he left, Enjoy the wine. At the end of the evening, the exercises further unearthed, there were eight bottles on the kitchen counter, three of them open, and several long thin bags—brown paper, gold and silver foil, museum prints—only the Gauguin with a name and that wasn't Neil's. Sojourner was, however, quite sure that the Eden Valley Chardonnay had appeared that night because she is not herself a great fan of chardonnay, thinking it less likely in the under ten dollar a bottle range to be as interesting as a nice grapefruit-y sauvignon blanc. Anne concurred, though she is not a white wine lover at all, much preferring what she refers to as the Big Reds.

Anne's quick call to The Wine Barrel put Eden Valley Chardonnay well out of the ten dollar range anyway, and Sojourner assured her that she never spends that much on wine. Never ever.

Anne called out for Szechuan Bean Curd and Eggplant in Garlic Sauce from a local restaurant ("I was in the mood for Kung Pao Shrimp," she said, "but it seemed inappropriate under the circumstances.") and started the memory games again, this time to recreate—a difficult task since Sojourner was in the kitchen when it happened—Ariana's choosing of the Eden Valley from the twenty or so bottles in Sojourner's wine rack, a lovely wine rack, Anne added, wrought iron and sort of Art Deco-ish. "And you'd like her apartment, Beatrice, white walls, molded ceilings, lots of antiques and only about half a mile and somewhat upscale from Patricia's," which meant, I gathered, that the roofs were not collapsing. Anne and Sojourner went to the wine rack and pulled out bottles. "First of all," said Sojourner, "she would have eliminated the ten reds; Ariana never drank reds, said they made her sneeze." Two of the whites were German, one French, one Washington State. Ariana was a Californian, born and bred; one of her neighborhood chums was now a winemaker; she was loyal to the industry. That left eight California whites: a dry chenin blanc, three sauvignon/fume blancs, four chardonnays. Sojourner thought Ariana, faced with "blancs" versus chardonnays would have gone to the chardonnays as the more expensive, the more elegant. Lunch looked elegant, Sojourner said. "I had flowers on the table, wine glasses, new cloth napkins. I was, I admit, trying to impress—and maybe trying to seduce." She would have eliminated the Glen Ellen. Too common. Left would have been a Schafer, a Kendall-Jackson, and the Eden Valley.

Sojourner sat with her head in her hands for a long time, Anne said— I could tell from the number of details in the narrative that Anne was building up to something dramatic: she's an accomplished storyteller— and suddenly jumped up. "Ariana did say something. She said, 'I've been there.'"

No, Ariana did not again refer to the winery or the wine except for an appreciative "ummm" after her first sip. It was, Sojourner said, a good wine. "You mean," I said to Anne, "'complex and buttery with a hint of vanilla and just the right amount of toasty oak?'" Anne laughed for the first time in the conversation. "Beatrice, you're a marvel. How did you guess?"

The cork had been ripped apart by a failing corkscrew. Anne preached a short sermon on the advantages of a cork-pull as she examined what pieces they could unearth in Sojourner's waste can. The police hadn't bothered and Anne couldn't find any evidence of a needle hole, which, she said, proved nothing since there was more hole than cork. By the time Anne had finished her report of the day's activity, I had formed what seemed a logical and reasonable plan of action. I outlined it to Anne.

"First, ask Sojourner for a list of names of any party-goers who had possibly brought wine. Call them and see if they remember what they brought or what anyone else brought. Don't mention the Eden Valley until the end of the conversation. If no one claims the bottle, and I don't think anyone will, ask Sojourner for a picture of Ariana and Neil together." But Anne had already asked and she didn't have one. "Try Ariana's, then," I said. "It's a small theft, Anne, in a good cause.

"Take it to Eden Valley winery; see if anyone recognizes them. They would, after all, have stood out from the mass of wine-tasters. Yes, of course, she could have gone there with someone else, but Neil was at the party, he did bring wine, he mentioned it leaving, he has motive to harm both women. If he and Ariana had visited Eden Valley together and liked the wine, he would have known she would drink it again, given the chance. And I suspect that if she had gone there with anyone else, she would have told Sojourner the story when she picked out the wine. The laconicness of 'I've been there' suggests to me that she didn't want to talk about it. And that suggests Neil. Indulge me."

Anne's one-day trip promised indefinite expansion, an expansion that seemed to make her anxious. "San Francisco," she said, "is a beautiful city, I admit, and I like to visit, it belongs more to my urban past than to my rural present." She looked out Sojourner's window at the thick fog rolling in and missed, she told me after she returned, the sunny Sierra foothills, missed even more the soft and quiet routine of Julian Pines, the five times a day we gather for prayer, the three times we sit down together for meals, the morning hours at her desk, the silent nights in her cabin, mostly alone but sometimes with Teresa, whom she loves. "And most of all, I guess, I missed, I always miss, even when I'm away for a day, the comings and goings, quiet and competent, of my sisters." I admit with some embarrassment and with full knowledge of its probable effect on my reputation that I waited—and wanted fiercely—for her to say that she missed *me*. She did not say it.

Sojourner's hand on her shoulder interrupted these sentimental—for Anne, who pretends even to herself to hardheadedness—musings. "I have a package of squid ink fettucine," Sojourner said, "that I can toss with garlic and olive oil if you'll stay for dinner." They talked so obsessively—about Ariana, allergies, Neil, wineries, monasteries, Lora, rock bands, Patricia, gynecologists—that Anne forgot to notice how squid ink fettucine tastes, "especially disappointing," she said, "since I'm not likely to be eating much of it at Julian Pines." I was pleased that Sojourner seemed to be holding up well. She even laughed aloud, Anne said, at Anne's re-creation of her days at Julian Pines, her impression of Sojourner as intense, unsmiling, vigilant.

"I was scared," Sojourner said. "For three weeks every time I rehearsed, my voice cracked. Some nights it took two hours to start cracking, some nights only one, but the night it happened after fifteen minutes I called Patricia in a panic. And talk about intense, unsmiling, and vigilant. She lectured me for twenty minutes about the chances I was taking with my voice and shipped me off to the abbey within forty-eight hours. 'Not a word,' she said, 'you must not say a word. And don't whisper either. That's worse than talking. Bandage your mouth if you have to, but maybe you won't have to. Julian Pines is the quietest place I know. Too quiet.'"

"I liked you there," Anne said. "though you disconcerted me at first. You seemed to be a presence calling us to account, always watching."

"Oh yes, I watched. But I wasn't sure what I was seeing."

"The usual, I imagine. Tension, irritation, affection, exhaustion, boredom, self-scrutiny, doubt, satisfaction, rage, pleasure, pain, lust, love. The usual."

"And which of those were you, Anne" she asked, "then, when I was there?"

"You were the watcher." Anne said, "What did you see?"

"Oh, tension, irritation, affection, exhaustion, boredom, self-scrutiny, doubt, satisfaction, rage, pleasure, pain, lust, love." They laughed.

"But," Anne persisted, "if you had to pick one or two?"

"Lust and love."

"Good eyes. I was, at the time, trying to deal with my passion for Teresa. Teresa the beautiful, the exotic, the vague, the holy."

"And now?"

"Now she is less vague, not at all exotic, still beautiful, terminally holy. I love her. We are occasional lovers. She keeps me honest—and mostly chaste." Anne said this firmly because, she admitted later, she was finding Sojourner a very attractive woman, especially after they finished off a bottle of wine. Three years of loving Teresa and what Anne only half-jokingly referred to as the onset of middle-age had lulled her into a certain complacency about lust and love, the waters of which were being unexpectedly and disturbingly stirred. She asked herself sternly if she had reached for Sojourner's hands *only* because she looked sad again.

"Anne," Sojourner asked, "are you going back to Patricia's?"

"Yes. Soon."

"You can stay here."

"Thanks, but Patricia's expecting me."

"What I mean is that I'd like it if you stayed here. I'd like it if you held me. Just that."

"I'm not sure I can," Anne said.

"Hold me?"

"*Just* hold you."

Sojourner laughed. "That's the nicest thing anyone's said to me in a long time. But holding is all I want and all I can handle right now." She kissed Anne on the lips as she handed her the phone. They spent the night, Anne assured me (quite unnecessarily), modestly clad in twin red silk nightshirts (Macy's clearance, Sojourner announced), Anne's arms around her curled up body. At first, Anne said, she was embarrassed by her fast-beating heart and what seemed to her to be transparent desire— though Anne is never transparent—but when Sojourner started to sing, something she wrote called "Seven Sorrows," Anne's mounting passion quieted into contentment at the warmth of the body next to her and into firm commitment to keeping Sojourner free and safe.

"Teresa," Anne said, after she returned, "I held her. I wanted her."

"She needed you," Teresa said.

"That's all," Anne said to me later. "She said it simply, straightforwardly, lovingly. You know Teresa. Saint Teresa."

I was right, Anne reported. Thirty phone calls over the next two days yielded nine people, Neil among them, who couldn't remember what wine they brought to Sojourner's party, if indeed they brought wine, one man who couldn't even remember the party, and one woman who claimed the Schafer: "A houseguest gave me three bottles for Christmas. The only problem is that I don't drink."

Anne left her name and Patricia's number in case anyone's memory returned, and one person actually called back, Black Widow's bass guitarist, who said that the more she thought about it, the surer she was that she had brought a red, poured herself a glass, and put it out for general consumption. "I remember," she said, "because I usually prefer white, but it was a cold night and the red seemed warmer." The message ended with, "Please remind Sojourner that we have a rehearsal tonight and if she doesn't show, we'll come and get her." Anne liked both her voice and her message.

While Patricia's answering machine was waiting for calls, Anne spent the whole day gaining access to Ariana's apartment and absconding with a picture of her and Neil. Because the story is long, and because she had to resort, at my behest, to both prevarication and theft, I won't dwell on the details. I take full blame. Before she left Sojourner's that morning, though, she called Eden Valley winery for directions and discovered it to be one of those small, tasting-and-touring-by-appointment-only places, a circumstance that seemed to augur well for our little project. She made an appointment for the next day.

Sojourner went along—Anne didn't want a solo tour—and diplomatically ordered a case of wine—six fume blanc and six zinfandel, their specialty, Anne said, big, oaky, and assertive, which she loved immediately, even though it was not yet noon when they tasted it. Her enthusiasm and Sojourner's largesse ("Nothing like the prospect of life in prison to stimulate spending," Sojourner said later) must have disarmed the proprietor who said they must call her Eve and who nodded without hesitation or suspicion at the photograph. "Yes," she said. "Ariana Hart. She was here with that young man last winter. Christmas time it was because my daughter was home from college, helping out with holiday orders and crowds. She's the one who recognized Hart, she's an opera fan. She went on and on about her after they left. Smart girl, my daughter I mean. I just wish she was more interested in wine. Claims she likes beer better. But I guess that's adolescent rebellion for you."

Eve had clearly not heard about the death. The wine country weeklies had probably relegated it to the back page if they had mentioned it at all, and Sojourner and Anne didn't tell her either. They stopped at the Domaine Chandon champagnery—"if that's what one calls a place that makes champagne"—on the way back from the winery, sat out on their patio overlooking the valley, sipped their driest offering, and lunched on their bread and pate. Anne was beginning, she complained to Sojourner and later to me, to feel entirely too comfortable with the decadent life. Sojourner assured her that tasting expensive wine and sipping Domaine Chandon was not how she usually spent her weekdays. When they got back to Sojourner's it was almost three and there was a message from Patricia that there was a message from a Neil MacKenzie: "I just remembered. I brought a Stag's Leap Cab and the bottle was empty when I left." Right, Anne thought, right.

By evening she was ready to call Neil back and cross-examine him, but I, having been in touch with Sojourner's lawyer, advised against it. ("The same lawyer," Anne asked, "who claimed she couldn't possibly see Sojourner again until next week?" The very same.)

"Neil would only deny knowing anything about anything, and we have no evidence except that he once visited Eden Valley Winery. No, my dear, what we need now is an allergist."

"A little late for that, Beatrice."

"Not just any allergist. Neil's allergist."

"How do you know he had one?"

"Trust me. I've been thinking about this for three days. First of all, you've got to find this doctor. He or she may well be local, so just start calling. Claim to be Neil's secretary making an appointment or something. What we want to know is if, several months ago, he requested an allergy test for shellfish."

"Beatrice, no doctor is going to give out that kind of information. And I'm not going to break into a doctor's office."

"You don't have to break in, Anne. You can walk in. Haven't you been breaking out in hives every time you eat in a Chinese restaurant?"

Which is how, two days later, Anne found herself with an allergist's appointment. Sojourner cleverly saved her the trouble of twenty phone calls as an insistent secretary by calling Neil, thanking him sweetly for the wine information and asking him, in view of her recent hour-long sneezing fits, for the name of Ariana's allergist. As she predicted, he made a disparaging comment about that dumb broad of a doctor and suggested someone he had seen, a Dr. Krozier in St. Helena. Neil, Sojourner remarked after she convincingly sneezed her good-bye, always knew best—one of his more endearing qualities—and would not, she had guessed, have been able to resist the temptation to assert the superiority of his own find. And kind. And, Sojourner reported to Anne, he assured her that he and all his friends figured Ariana's death was a freak accident and no hard feelings.

Dr. Krozier was blond, tan, and under thirty. The diploma said UCSF and was disturbingly recent, Anne said, or would have been if she had really needed an allergist. Coached beforehand by Sojourner, she described her symptoms. Severe hives, minor swelling. "The only meal I had was chicken breast, asparagus—isn't the crop just wonderful this year—and salad. Watching my weight, you know. Left hungry. I did have just a tiny mixed seafood cocktail at Fisherman's Wharf after dinner. But that surely isn't important. I mean, I've been eating crab and shrimp all my life and I always go to the same vendor for the cocktails."

"How soon after you ate the cocktail did the hives begin to appear?"

"Oh, right away, so it couldn't be that, of course. I hadn't even had time to digest it."

He explained patiently to the poor misguided and probably not too smart middle-aged woman—he called her Mrs. Stratford—that these sorts of allergies have nothing to do with digestion and that they can develop suddenly and severely.

"But I've never heard of such a thing," she said, and I can imagine the shocked expression she must have feigned.

"Oh, you'd be surprised at the number of patients I get with this problem."

"How can I find out for sure that it's the shellfish?"

He told her that there's a simple test, a small amount of shrimp extract slipped painlessly under the skin. Now with a reaction like hers the test probably involves very little risk, but there is risk—of something called anaphylactic shock. If her reaction had involved more swelling he would definitely recommend a RAST test, a little more complicated and expensive but risk-free. It was her choice.

"Do you give this test, the less expensive one, often, Doctor?"

"Oh yes. Quite routine."

"Oh, maybe you gave it to my friend, the one who recommended you, Neil MacKenzie, I think he mentioned it."

"Yes, yes, in fact, he did have the test, let's see, last winter sometime or maybe early spring, but I believe it came out negative and we never did find the culprit. He hasn't had any more allergic reactions, has he?"

"Oh, no, I don't think so."

"Now, let me ask you just one more little question, Dr. Krozier. How do you get this, this whatdoyoucallit? Do you take a tiny piece of shrimp and just inject it?"

"Antigen. And no. We use this. He took a tiny bottle from his refrigerator to illustrate. Shortly after the demonstration, he took a phone call, leaving Anne there with easy access to the refrigerator and knowing just what to abscond with, if such had been her intention. He meant her to set up another appointment for the test and make her way out of the examining room, but she waited instead outside of his inner sanctum until she heard him hang up the phone.

"Dr. Krozier, one last question." She unthinkingly abandoned her dumb blond routine, relatively easy to do, I would imagine, since she has never believed in the syndrome anyway and since there is really very little blond left—a situation that surprises me on occasion just as my own grey hair can still startle me when I catch my reflection in the rare mirror I come across.

"Were you missing a bottle of this extract sometime late last winter, say February or early March?" Anne asked.

The good doctor looked startled, whether at the question or at Anne's suddenly assertive manner she didn't know, but he hesitated a second before he denied any such absence.

"I don't know. What difference it would make anyway?" he said. "It's not like it's poisonous or anything."

"Unless, of course, you're prone to anaphylactic shock reaction to shellfish antigens," Anne said, as sweetly as she could manage in the heaviness of her disappointment, "and someone has replaced your epinephrine with water."

She emerged from the office sober, feeling that she had thoroughly failed Sojourner, whom she found in the waiting room in animated conversation with the receptionist. "You won't believe this," Sojourner said to Anne, "but this good woman actually owns *Black Widows Waltz*."

When Anne gave her the mixed results of her appointment, Sojourner refused to be discouraged by the doctor's denial, pulled off the road at the next phone booth, and called her admirer in Dr. Krozier's office. She came back to the car, Anne said, waving her arms in the air and shouting, "He lied. He lied." Anne still isn't sure whether she was referring to the allergist or the assasin, but since it seemed to be true of both, she didn't ask. The receptionist willingly acknowledged the missing vial, remembered when she first noticed it, and confirmed that Neil's visit had occurred the previous day. Contacted later by Alison Sargenti,

Sojourner's lawyer, she expressed such gleeful willingness to testify that Alison pursued the issue and found herself embroiled in an hour-long monologue about patronizing doctors, rude patients, and brilliant musicians.

Meanwhile, although the late spring heat wave had abated, I spent a restless day alternately pacing my cell—I use "cell" to remind me of my calling but the lovely two room cabin complete with kitchen and bath hardly qualifies as such—and drinking tea in my rose brocade chair. It seemed to me that everything hinged on Anne's visit to the allergist— everything, I fear, including not only Sojourner's future but my own reputation as Beatrice the wise, the competent, the solver of problems.

I envisioned Anne in the doctor's office, assumed she would, as I suggested, affect innocence and naivete—an easy enough pose for a small woman—to elicit confidence and conversation. Her husky voice and glasses would, I thought, somewhat mitigate the illusion, but her reporter's instincts, though long unused, would, I reassured myself, revive and assert themselves under these circumstances. Almost clever, this plan. Neil's, that is. Ariana-the-much-envied who—so he would have interpreted her involvement with Sojourner Truth and her desire to persist in the friendship—preferred a woman to him, especially unbearable in that he had probably cast himself in the role of the generous and enlightened lover, overlooking her race and her not entirely respectable profession. If her death, I imagined him reasoning, is seen as anything but accidental, the blame will fall on the offending female, or if she somehow manages to prove innocence, on jealous opera colleagues (everyone knows the unpredictable and sinister power of the prima donna, aspiring and arrived). He, on the other hand, has not even seen her for months. But did he think they wouldn't notice the drops of water clinging to the epinephrine injector? Did he think the bit of wine left in the bottle couldn't be tested for shellfish antigen or did he just assume that whatever else Sojourner served her would be judged contaminated somehow, poison being, after all, a woman's weapon? Was he surprised, given what he knew about their former relationship that the lunch or dinner was so long delayed? Did he worry that the wine would be drunk by someone else meanwhile and that he'd have to sacrifice another bottle of Eden Valley Chardonnay?

Such were the thoughts and queries that fueled my pacing and tea consumption. Such, and wonder that Anne's absence of only a few days put the whole community slightly off balance. Or, I probed and poked, was it only I who found her absence so disequalibriating and disquieting? Every day for almost fifteen years (and I can cite the exceptions—a weekend workshop on book reviewing in 1979, two days in 1981 with her sister when her niece Erin was in an automobile accident, three days last year with her mother, who was recuperating from a hysterectomy, and the occasional illness or personal crisis common to us all), I have at five a.m. cherished her small stern face, explored at other times—prayer times, meal times, celebrations—small changes in her, signs of age, signs of distress, signs of joy, signs even of uneasiness. I have agonized over the passion which I knew from her first visit here would plague her in this life lived intimately among women. I have listened to her fears and doubts and extravagant unhappinesses, like that occasioned nine years ago by Lisa's leaving, Lisa whose twenty-minute attention span—though I grant that the twenty minutes could be intense and brilliant—would in any case have precluded steadfast affection. (I offer in evidence two wedding announcements and the sporadic postcards, extolling the current attachment, by which she keeps us abreast of her breathless existence.)

When Sharon knocked at the door, I hoped that Anne's call had come early, but she reported instead the good news from the county inspector that the suspected contamination of our main well was a false alarm. No sooner had I snapped that I, like everyone else, could have waited until dinner for such an announcement than I regretted my incivility to this newest of our sisters, who, it turned out, had used the exonerated well as a prelude to a reluctant and anxious confession of the obvious—that she had gained twenty-five pounds since her arrival last year. She was bewildered by it; a diet of vegetables, fruits, and grains was, according to all the experts, supposed to keep you thin as well as healthy. Did I think that the weight gain was sign of some repressed emotional distress beneath surface contentment? That is, did I think she had made the wrong decision in coming here and did I recommend a therapist to sort this out?

I reminded her that she's a large-framed woman with a history of erratic weight and that she had lost thirty-five pounds on a crash diet just before she left Southern California. She didn't, she had explained to me during our first conference, want us to think she was undisciplined.

"Sharon, you look ten years younger and ten times healthier than you did seven months ago. You are strong, energetic, and sensible about everything except your weight. Make whatever arrangements you want—get a physical in San Andreas, see a therapist, reassess your commitment to Julian Pines, talk to Karen, but my opinion is that you're lovely and fine. And I'm very sorry I snapped at you when you came in. It's this murder business."

"I wish I could believe that I'm lovely and fine," she said. "I feel ugly and fat. Maybe I'll talk to Karen. Who *is* this Sojourner Truth person anyway?"

My anxiety and subsequent incivility were, in the end, needless. Armed with the information from Anne and Sojourner's various investigative activities, Sojourner's lawyer persuaded the prosecutor to drop charges and arrest Neil, who, during his arraignment alternately denied calmly any knowledge of the crime and denounced hysterically the "black butch bitch" who started all this in the first place and whose "fucking black ass" he's going to get at the first available opportunity. He's being held without bail and Sojourner's off on a Northwest tour with the Black Widows. That's the good news. The bad news is that Anne's non-existent *Chronicle* contacts assured her that he will, if convicted, be out in a few years, unbloody crimes against black-bisexual-female-singer-ex-wives not likely to rouse the sleepy ire of justice.

Anne, of course, is home. She arrived in the middle of dinner to cheers and hugs and kisses; she arrived with ten bottles of Eden Valley wine, six fume blanc and four zinfandel. She and Sojourner Truth had toasted the tour with one of the other two zins, and as the bottle emptied speculated on a cyanide-laced Eden Valley Zin for Neil's coming-out-of-prison present. Anne persuaded her to keep a bottle just in case. By the time we had drunk carelessly from the unwonted store, we all thought it a splendid idea. The festivities were marred only by a long-distance call from Sister Joanne, head of the Association of American Superiors of Religious Orders, wondering why she hadn't received from me the Contemplative Caucus report. "Because," I said, no doubt too cheerfully, no doubt a bit drunkenly, "I have not yet written it."

"Not like you, Sister Beatrice, to be remiss." And how could I respond to this deserved scolding but with good will and polite, procrastinating promise?

Chapter 6

Bernie Becomes a Nun

SHE knew as soon as she saw the book that the Hound of Heaven was barking at her heels. And she didn't like dogs. Bernadette Frances Palermo, aged eleven and a half, was appointed by Sister Mary Ascension, aged somewhere between twenty-five and forty, to organize the sixth grade library. It consisted of 154 books. That left a lot of space on the two shelves that ran the length of the cloakroom opposite the shelves for lunch pails and, below them, the hooks for sweaters and coats. The forty hooks were mostly empty; it was mid-September in the Southern California valley and hot, even early in the morning. Bernadette Frances Palermo pulled at the bib on her uniform jumper. So hot, she thought, so stuffy in here. There was a dim light in the cloakroom, a naked bulb that you turned on by pulling a dirty string. The light made the room even hotter, but without it you couldn't see the book titles. The cloakroom smelled like sweat, overripe bananas, and warm peanut butter and jelly sandwiches.

She looked at our records,

Bernadette thought, and that's why she picked me. Bernadette's record was filled with A's, straight A's, in fact, from first grade through fifth. Her mother said she spent all her time with her nose in a book and should be helping out more around the house. But what could you do around the house when there was so little of it and so many of them? Bernadette was the oldest. Her father didn't say anything at all. He went to work in the morning and came back just before dinner. He had a beer while he waited for his meal. He watched TV. Mr. Palermo bought the TV when Bernadette was in second grade. Before that he sometimes sat her on his lap while he drank the beer and let her put her fingers in the foam. It tasted nasty but she liked the soft wet bubbles on her fingertips. Then her mother would say, Bernie, set the table.

Now they had a chart and Bernie only had to set the table on Mondays and Thursdays. On Tuesdays and Fridays she washed dishes; on Wednesdays she made dinner; on Saturdays she cleared the table and swept the scratched wood floor. Sundays, Mrs. Palermo said, were days off, so she did the chores herself. But Bernadette always helped. She was the oldest. These, of course, were only the dinnertime chores. Bernadette's main job was taking care of the baby, Jimmy, born in May. It was now September and Mrs. Palermo still looked pregnant. Bernadette was afraid she was. Not still, but again. Bernadette wasn't sure how it kept happening. Her sister Mary Angela saw a movie during science period about a cow giving birth, but Bernadette didn't want the details. It sounded nasty. Jimmy filled his pants twice every day and Bernadette had to change the diapers. She was glad to be back in school and hoped that he would do it at least once while she was gone.

The cloakroom didn't smell good, but it didn't smell like dirty diapers either, and there were a lot of books she hadn't read. Like *Bernie Becomes a Nun*.

The best thing about the cloakroom library besides the books was the little table. On it were a file box filled with lined 3x5 cards and a date stamp, just like the one at the public library. You could move the month roll and the day roll and after the first couple of times, you could even do it without getting ink on your fingers. Bernadette supposed that "organizing" meant making a card for every book and putting the books in some kind of order. Alphabetical seemed simplest, even though the books at the public library had letters and numbers which Bernadette knew belonged to the Dewey decimal system, and she could probably do it that way because there was a chart at the public library. But it seemed like a lot of trouble for 154 books.

At the public library you could check out books for two weeks, but Bernadette figured out—quite rapidly, being very good at math—that if each of the forty students in the class took out six books for the fortnight ("fortnight" was a word she picked up from *Little Women* and introduced into the family chore chart) there wouldn't even be enough to go around. Bernadette was not, of course, so naive as to think that everyone read three books a week as she did. Her mother pointed out on an almost daily basis this discrepancy between Bernadette's reading habits and those of other children her age. You never saw Cousin Nancy, for example, with her nose buried in a book. She played outside like normal children and helped Aunt Rosa around the house. The example of Cousin Nancy particularly enraged Bernadette because although it was quite true that Nancy never read any books, Aunt Rosa was always screaming about her messy bedroom. And Nancy only had one brother and one sister to clean up after, not two brothers and three sisters and who knows what growing where.

Maureen, on the other hand, read just as much as Bernadette and had even more brothers and sisters—though some of them were older—but Mrs. Palermo didn't want to hear about Maureen because those kind of people were different and lived in a different neighborhood and Maureen's father drank too much. Everybody knew that. Mrs. Palermo was not prejudiced against the Irish, she was not prejudiced against anyone, how could Bernadette say such a thing, Father Callaghan himself being from Ireland and as good a priest as you could find in any parish even if he did sometimes give a whole rosary for penance.

So Bernadette decided to suggest a one-week loan period, renewable. She would have to change the rubber stamp every day.

There were two advantages, Bernadette saw right away, to being librarian. First of all, you could go work in the library when everyone else had to practice penmanship (Bernadette herself wrote in perfectly formed letters even at the age of eleven and a half. Mrs. Palermo sometimes asked her to address envelopes) or start their homework. Homework, Bernadette always thought, was work for home and that's where she liked to do it even if she had to use the flashlight under her covers after Mary Angela and Jenny and Clara were asleep. She didn't mind that actually. It was so quiet then. And if she had to get up and give Jimmy his bottle it was better if she was already awake. Then she wasn't so mad at him because he was only a baby after all and couldn't help waking up in the middle of the night. It would only be for another month or two anyway because her mother said just for a little while, I'm so tired, and besides Clara started sleeping through the night when she was six months old, so maybe Jimmy would, too.

Maureen's mother always got up with the O'Connor baby, but she was breast feeding. Mrs. Palermo said that the LaRosas and the Palermos didn't come all the way to America so they could breast feed their babies and that was another reason she didn't like Maureen around the house unless they were having spaghetti for dinner because she felt a little sorry for Maureen, she told Bernadette after Bernadette reported that Mrs. O'Connor put hamburger in her sauce and broke up the spaghetti into small pieces before she cooked it. After the first time, Bernadette made excuses when Maureen asked her to stay for dinner on Tuesday nights, which was the night, the only night, the O'Connors had spaghetti.

The second advantage was that the librarian had first dibs on the books. And Bernadette didn't see why she couldn't just keep renewing something, like *Bernie Becomes a Nun* for instance, and pretty much leave it at home all year if she liked. It wasn't that Bernadette *wanted* the book, she didn't, but she had to take it because if she didn't someone else would and then there would be no end to the teasing. It was every bit as bad as she expected, too. The very first page informed her that Bernie's real name was Bernadette. Bernadette had a hard enough time getting people to call her Bernadette without this stupid book giving them all ammunition. Bernie was a baby name, her mother called her Bernie and so did Mary Angela and Jenny and Clara and Joe. And she supposed Jimmy would too when he was old enough to talk. Mr. Palermo used to call her Bernie, but now mostly he didn't call her anything. Aunt Rosa called her Bernadette but Nancy wouldn't and neither would Uncle Joe. He said it was a French name and what did he care about St. Bernadette, she probably made up the whole story about seeing the Virgin and those cures were just psychological or maybe the water at Lourdes had some drug in it. Aunt Rosa screamed when he said that and after she calmed down she always said, Bernadette is a beautiful name, honey. Your grandmother thinks it's a beautiful name, too. But at the end of Grandmother LaRosa's letters, when she seemed to be listing all the grandchildren for her blessing, there was no "Bernadette," only "Benedetta," which was not the same name at all. Mrs. Palermo said that it was because Grandmother LaRosa couldn't write and it was really Uncle Francesco who wrote what Grandmother told him and he was a little deaf on account of measles.

The name, of course, was only part of the problem. If they saw the book they would probably call her Sister Bernie or something stupid like that. So it seemed better that she just check the book out—and out and out. If Sister Mary Ascension wanted the book for some reason, she could bring it back, but who knows, maybe Sister Mary Ascension didn't even know the book was there. After all, this was her first year teaching sixth grade and only her second year at Holy Angels.

When Bernadette Frances Palermo fell in love for the first time, she discovered the third advantage to being sixth grade librarian and having access to that dark, private cloakroom, but that's another story altogether.

The book Bernie became a Maryknoll nun, they were missionaries in Africa and India and South America, which is where Bernadette wanted to go if she ever became a missionary which she didn't think she would. They spoke Spanish in South America and Spanish was a lot like Italian. Bernadette didn't speak Italian because in the Palermo house it was only used when Mr. and Mrs. Palermo fought or when Mrs. Palermo talked to Aunt Rosa on the telephone. But Bernadette could sometimes understand parts of the conversation and she thought she might be able to learn Spanish, but you couldn't learn another language until high school and then you might want to learn French instead. Or Latin, which would be good if you ever wanted to become a doctor, which Bernadette did, but she kept it secret because the girl in *Hitch Your Wagon to a Star* wanted to become a doctor and everyone laughed at her, which is just what would happen to Bernadette. The girl did, though, become a doctor. Lots of Maryknolls were doctors, too, but in the book Bernie was going to be a nurse.

There were photographs in the book. Bernie as a senior in high school, on the volleyball team, in the debate club. Bernie had a cute flip hair-do and she was a very pretty girl who was normal in every way including liking boys and going to parties every weekend, though she was always home on time. Bernadette hated her and loved her and wanted to be just like her and thought she was a drip. Bernadette wondered if the Maryknolls picked out the cutest girls to join their order. The Sisters of St. Clare certainly didn't, though Sister Mary Ascension might not be too bad if she had a flip. She had a nice figure. Mrs. Palermo said that in Italian to Aunt Rosa after last year's open house. Easy enough, Aunt Rosa said, also in Italian, if you don't have a houseful of kids. Mrs. Palermo didn't know that Bernadette could understand sometimes. She saw right away what her mother meant about Sister Mary Ascension's figure. She tried not to look too hard at her chest but you could imagine her in a bathing suit. Bernadette didn't think it was a sin to imagine Sister Mary Ascension in a bathing suit as long as the bathing suit wasn't two-piece. Maureen's sister Patty was at St. Clare's High School, just across the street from Holy Angels Elementary, and her homeroom nun told the girls that two-piece bathing suits were a mortal sin because of tempting boys, but Patty didn't believe her and showed Maureen and Bernadette pictures from a magazine to illustrate her point. There were two kinds of two-piece suits, Patty said, the kind that probably were a sin like the bikini and the other kind which covered you up pretty well and was more comfortable than a one-piece suit and look at the cute material you could get them in. Some girls practically *had* to wear them because it was the only way you could get big tops and small bottoms. Bernadette thought that Sister Mary Ascension might be one of those girls. Except, of course, that being a nun she didn't have to worry. There were a lot of things nuns didn't have to worry about.

When Bernie became a nun she changed her name. Sister Joseph Marie wasn't as bad as Sister Mary Ascension, but Bernadette thought that the cute, popular, drippy, flippy girl could have shown a little more imagination.

The year that Bernie was a junior in high school (by this time the battle to be Bernadette had been lost to the pressure of the pack), Mrs. Palermo decided that since Nonna Palermo was not up to cooking big holiday meals anymore, she would do the St. Joseph's Day celebration herself with help from Bernie and Mary Angela and Jenny and Clara. Even five-year-old Gina could knead dough for the St. Joseph's bread and form the small round loaves. In the dusty throes of the spring housecleaning mandated by the affair, Bernie whispered to the toddling Rose that she should enjoy her youth. Were she slightly steadier on her feet, she, too, would be recruited for polishing tables or sponging off the plastic-wrapped pink brocade sofa. Bernie finally suggested removing the plastic, so yellowed and cracked from three years' use as to be impervious to her best efforts, and, to Bernie's surprise, Mrs. Palermo agreed but voiced her anxiety about a hundred small sticky fingers unable to resist the temptation of the virginal surface. Bernie thought but did not say, having been severely scolded for similar remarks in the past, that the deflowering would more likely take place at the hands of her beer-spilling uncles. Uncle Pete's left hand, on the nearest female ass if it wasn't on a beer can, was her private candidate. She shuddered.

Bernie appreciated her mother's urging her to invite as many friends as she wanted, but Bernie found the spectacle of the altar, which Nonna would cover with every saints' statue she could garner from her well-stocked house and enough flowers for a mafia funeral (not that Bernie had ever been to one, but that was a phrase Uncle Joe used), embarrassing. Maureen's family weren't so ostentatious in their piety and they were more faithful Catholics, Bernie thought, than her relatives. Besides, two years ago Bernie had dragged Maureen to Nonna's in return for Bernie's having worn green—a color which Bernie had never liked—on St. Patrick's day to please Mr. O'Connor (who was sure that a nice girl like Bernie must have *some* Irish blood) and Uncle Pete had pawed her. Maureen hadn't spoken to Bernie for days.

Worst of all, Father Callaghan would be invited to bless the altar and the St. Joseph's bread and Uncle Pete would offer him a beer—or worse, some of Nonna's homemade wine—and eventually Nonna's goddaughter Antonia, whom everyone called Aunt Tony, would sing. She had been a singer, right after she came to America, in a nightclub where Nonna's brother worked, but of course after she got married she only sang for friends and then only when her husband, whom everyone called Uncle Tony even though his name was Carmine, had had a few beers. Bernie cringed at the thought of Aunt Tony, who always changed for the performance into a red net skirt with black stockings, seams as thick as pencils. She painted her face, too, with thick black around her eyes, dark red lipstick, and bright pink rouge. She said they taught her to do that when she worked in the nightclub. Bernie thought it looked cheap. And Aunt Tony was almost ten years older than her mother. Worse than cheap. All this, though, Bernie could tolerate because really Aunt Tony had a good heart, as Mrs. Palermo periodically reminded her judgmental daughters, and had been a loyal friend to the Palermo family and hadn't balked when

Mr. Palermo married a Napolitano. What made Bernie cringe was the point at which Aunt Tony would sidle up to Father Callaghan and put her hand on his knee as she sang "That's Amore," and what made Bernie crazy was the inevitable conclusion, billed as everybody's favorite, dedicated tonight to the first Palermo girl, who had grown up into such a beautiful young lady. Standing right in front of the beautiful young lady, hips wiggling, arms reaching, Aunt Tony would belt out—If you knew Bernie/ Like I know Bernie/Oh,Oh,Oh what a gal.

All this came to pass much as Bernie had feared, and while Aunt Tony was changing back into her flowered dress, Bernie climbed to the attic room she shared with her sisters and moaned in relative peace. Within ten minutes, however, Jimmy burst in, whispering that he needed a place to hide: they were after him. He dived under Bernie's bed and Bernie pretended to be reading a magazine when Gina, Tommy, and Cousin Johnny came stalking their prey. Tommy, who at the age of four knew every hiding place in the house, headed straight for the fugitive, who emerged cheerfully with a book in hand. He had learned to read. He laughed. He took the book downstairs to share the joke. *Bernie Becomes a Nun.*

Bernie's going-away party had much the same cast of characters as the St. Joseph's Day celebration except that Nonna had died and Uncle Pete was in the hospital with some mysterious kind of cancer that no one wanted to talk about but that Bernie, in the process of writing her senior research report on common cancers, had concluded was prostate. On good days she prayed sincerely for his recovery; on bad days she thought it served him right. The one addition was baby Natalie, after whose birth the Palermo brood was stabilized by a hysterectomy. Bernie secretly suspected that the "uterine cysts" which necessitated it represented a silent collusion between her mother and Dr. Sargento to halt the pregnancies while adhering to the tenets of the Church. Bernie applauded the move, though she knew that a tubal ligation would have sufficed and been a much less debilitating procedure. But it was a forbidden one. Half the hours Bernie spent in the library working on the cancer project she had Natalie along in the stroller. She was tired of raising children and figured that her mother must be too. Besides, Natalie seemed a little slow and Bernie had visions of slower and slower babies weighing down the rest of her mother's life.

The Palermo family had moved into Nonna's house, which wasn't any bigger than their old house had been but had the advantage of a converted garage so that Bernie, Mary Angela, Jenny, and Clara no longer had to share a room with Gina, Rose, and Natalie. Joey and Jimmy complained that they still had Tommy but Bernie spoke to them so sharply about all the years that the six—now seven—girls had stuffed themselves into the hot, low-ceilinged attic that they stopped grousing and built themselves a tree house. Bernie wondered why she and Mary Angela had never thought of that, though she had a few ideas.

Mrs. Palermo was cheerful when she wasn't asleep, and quite insistent on the party. We're all so proud of you, Bernie: the oldest child is going to God. Bernie herself agonized daily over her motives. She loved God and she needed to get out of the house. Unlike the book Bernie, who gave up a proposal of marriage and her parents' offer of a college education in order to become a Maryknoll, the real Bernie's other prospects didn't seem good. Aunt Tony's beautiful young lady found herself distinctly unattractive, for one thing. She had darker than acceptable skin, a big nose (it's nicer than my freckled button, Maureen always said when Bernie complained), and twelve pounds more than the chart recommended. She spent her weekends reading novels or going over to Maureen's house and for lack of anyone else had asked Maureen's brother Patrick to the senior prom. He went grudgingly and didn't speak to her for days afterward. Sister Mary Augustine said that she could get a scholarship to Immaculate Heart, but Mr. Palermo refused to fill out the financial aid application. He wouldn't say why. He didn't seem to like the convent idea either, but Mrs. Palermo insisted that if God wanted Bernie, *she* at least was happy to make the sacrifice. Had Bernie's heart burned with missionary fervor, she would have gone to the Maryknolls who might have sent her to medical school. But the fire wasn't there and they might have decided that she wasn't smart enough to be a doctor anyway. Thus feared Bernie who graduated high school with only two exceptions to the ubiquitous A's: P.E. and Latin IV (Natalie and Mrs. Palermo had come home from the hospital the night before that Latin exam, and Bernie never was much good at volleyball). Bernie who could have gone to Smith or Radcliffe or Barnard if she'd known they existed. Bernie who might have gone to UCLA or UC Berkeley if Sister Anthony Mary hadn't harped all junior year on dens of iniquity. But Bernie only thought these bitter thoughts many years later and had to remind herself that even his much-admired Notre Dame (had they then deigned to admit a mere female) could not have moved her father to reveal his financial insecurity to strangers, which was the excuse she made for him the year he died but which seemed less convincing the year afterwards.

Maureen came to the party but by this time Maureen and Bernie had had their first real falling out. Maureen was going to become a nun, too, but in the spring when she and Bernie had driven the O'Connor car to the beach for the first—and only—time, two boys who, it turned out, had gone to grade school with Maureen before she transferred to Holy Angels, asked if they could join the girls' card game. One thing led to another and by the end of the week Maureen had been kissed and had questions about her vocation. Bernie felt abandoned and accused Maureen of preferring sex to God and Maureen yelled back that Bernie was jealous and would question *her* vocation if Ronnie had kissed *her,* which Bernie said was the most asinine thing Maureen had ever said and if that's what kissing did to a good brain, she was glad she'd never have to do it. Kissing Maureen didn't count, of course. Nor did kissing Pat in the sixth grade cloakroom.

Bernie and Maureen only stopped speaking for two weeks but Maureen was spending more time with Ronnie and his friends than with Bernie, and by the night of the party Bernie didn't care if Maureen came or not. Bernie didn't care if she became a nun or not. Bernie didn't even care that Aunt Tony cried when she sang If you knew Bernie/ Like I know Bernie/Oh,Oh,Oh, what a gal. Mary Angela, Jenny, and Clara gave Bernie a guitar because it said on the list of things to bring that you could bring a musical instrument and Mary Angela had a friend who was selling his old one for only ten dollars and Mrs. Palermo lent them the money and served a cheaper cut of beef for Sunday dinner. Bernie did cry when she opened the guitar, not so much because she couldn't play it as because she knew that Mary Angela and Jenny and Clara had already made plans to re-organize the garage. They asked her to move her stuff out and there was no place to put it, not that she'd ever need it.

If it hadn't been mid-August, Bernie would have burned the box of ratty underwear, old school papers, and the other possessions that her sisters didn't claim, including a teddy bear that was torn and dirty and that Natalie wanted but that Gina shamed her out of. Between the papers and the underwear she slid the copy of *Bernie Becomes a Nun,* its photo cover still intact, and left instructions that the box was to be sent out with the next trash pick-up. Those were her last coherent words, in fact, to her brood of siblings. The rest were hugs and kisses and tears and babbled promises. The Sisters of St. Clare's mother house and novitiate were in Mt. Clemens, Michigan, so good-bye was good-bye. She practiced guitar chords on the plane.

Bernie's quarrel with the convent, at least during the first six months, when she was a postulant, was that the dormitory was not much different from the garage or the attic. Like them it was filled from one end to the other with narrow beds, each with a girl in it from nine o'clock in the evening until five the next morning. Granted, the beds had curtains around them like hospitals so you could, at least, undress in peace. Most of the girls were drips, just as she feared. And she got a letter every week from Maureen, now miserable because Ronnie had dumped her. Sometimes there were words or sentences or even whole paragraphs blacked out of Maureen's letters. Knowing that someone read and censored her mail made Bernie angry, but she didn't complain, except to Peggy O'Toole, who *did* complain. Bernie got A's in all her classes and sighed audibly whenever the mistress of postulants initiated them into some new phase of religious life. Like the little ritual of kneeling in front of her when you needed a new tube of toothpaste or box of sanitary napkins. Or the announcement three months later that there would be no more razor blades. That is, no more shaving your legs or under your arms. Three girls left that week.

Rumor was that Bernie herself would not make it to the novitiate. She had a questionable and questioning attitude. But for some reason which Bernie does not, even now, understand, they let her stay. She didn't much care one way or the other, but she attended prayers faithfully and darned stockings nicely and kept her drawers neater than most and made sharp square corners on her bed and during recreation entertained the Band of the Holy Spirit—the name given to her class of postulants—with simple folk songs accompanied by seven guitar chords. She answered Mother Mary Agatha's interview questions quietly and simply. Yes, she wanted to stay. Yes, she thought she had a vocation. Yes, she would work hard in the novitiate. Yes, she missed her family but no, she didn't want to go back home. Perhaps Mother mistook her lethargy for quiet fervor and her terseness for simplicity of heart. Perhaps Mother was just nervous that seventeen of the thirty-six postulants had already left.

So Bernie became a nun. During the ceremony they draped her with a long brown habit and a white veil which would eventually, if she made it through the novitiate, be replaced with a brown one. They asked her what name she wanted (subject, of course, to Mother's approval), and she chose, in a moment of inspired cynicism, Sister Joseph Marie. The habit, she soon noticed, made her look taller; the white around her face made her brown skin look acceptably tan; the veil covered her always nondescript hair, and Sister Mary Henrietta's lousy cooking took twenty pounds off her frame. Besides that, she and her sixteen cohorts—two more left before clothing—moved to the novitiate where for the first time in her life

Bernie had a room to herself. She spent several months discovering the advantages of being a novice and having a room of your own. You could study after nine o'clock, you could cry, you could keep a diary, you could sleep for eight hours straight without listening for a waking babe or hearing a sister toss and turn. You could admire your now slender—if hairy—legs.

When Bernie fell in love for the second time she discovered a sixth advantage, but that's another story altogether.

"Bernie," Mrs. Palermo said, "you left several pairs of perfectly good underpants and a book that still had its cover. I saved it. We're putting you in the garage, bambina, just like in the old days. But you can have it all to yourself. Mary Angela has the boys' room and when Tommy comes home he has Gina and Rose and Natalie's old room. You know, Tommy has a hard life in that business, sometimes there's work, sometimes there's not. Bernie you're like a bean pole, *mangia,* eat."

Bernie was trying. She had in fact a fork full of fettucine in her mouth when she remembered what book it was that she had thrown away with its cover still on. She wanted to laugh, she really did, but she was too tired. Instead tears came rolling down her cheeks. "It's all right, Ma," she said. "It's nothing. I'm just tired and it's been so long since I've been here. Do you still have the pink couch?"

"It's in the garage, honey, we fixed it up for you. Tommy helped us move it, he's a nice boy even if he does drink too much. You won't be hard on him will you, Bernie? He's got a good heart."

"No, Ma, I won't be hard on him."

"Bernie, you're so skinny."

"It's all right, Ma, I'm just tired. A week of your cooking and I'll be fine. Fat and fine."

"Bernie, honey, why are you here? You're not leaving are you? Nuns leave all the time now. There are only three at St. Clare's and four at Holy Angels, Gina says. She loves teaching there but she has no respect for the nuns. You talk to her, Bernie, while you're here. She has no respect for anybody. She says here she is teaching in their school, making $12,000 a year—which is more than your father ever made, may he rest in peace—hardly enough money to pay the rent, and they eat steak every night. You don't look like you eat steak every night. You talk to your sister. I don't know why she doesn't live here. We've got all this room now."

"I'll talk to her, Ma. But let's go out to the garage. I've spent the day in airports and I'm exhausted."

"You're leaving the convent, aren't you?"

"No, Ma, I'm not leaving. Just taking a little rest. A week here and then a month in Northern California with some other nuns. I'm not leaving."

"Only a week, Bernie, after twenty-five years, you're only here for a week and you don't even know your nieces and nephews, wait till you see them, Bernie, and Jenny's house. You just won't believe the beautiful house that girl has and they're sending little Bernadette, we call her little Bernadette but she's taller than you, Bernie, they're sending her to Immaculate Heart College. You wanted to go there. I remember. But it was just as well that you didn't get in because God wanted you, just like in the book. And you got to be a doctor after all, that was a real surprise. You know, you never even told me you wanted to be a doctor. You know how I know? Maureen told me. I won't even tell you what I heard about Maureen but she lives in San Francisco so what can you expect? A grown woman with a daughter. It's that family. Mr. O'Connor died of drink and now the boys are at it except for Patrick. I think he lives in San Francisco, too. Mrs. O'Connor told me she was there and it was foggy the whole time and Patrick's wife cooks tofu and sprouts. Can you imagine living in a place like that?

"Bernie, you miss having a husband and children. Is that it? I can't blame you for that, honey. Nobody would blame you for that."

"No, Ma, the very thought of either husband or children sounds exhausting. I don't know how you did it."

"What a thing to say. Exhausting. What's life for anyway?"

"O Ma, I'm forty-two. Besides I've changed enough diapers to last anyone a lifetime."

"But, baby, it's different when they're your own."

"No, Ma. The diapers still stink." Mrs. Palermo, a woman not without a sense of humor, tapped Bernadette's cheek with the back of her hand and laughed. "O Bernie, you always did have a mouth.

"What do you want, honey? Do you know?"

"Yes, Ma, I know. I want a night of uninterrupted sleep."

"Now, Bernie, be serious. I want you to look at Mary Angela while you're here. She's got a lump in her breast the size of a walnut and she won't go to the doctor. So, I say, we'll bring the doctor to you. Bernie's coming home."

"Ma, I'm a psychiatrist. But Mary Angela should see somebody right away. How long has she had the cyst?"

"Four, five years. I don't want her to die on me, Bernie. It was bad enough with Natalie, I can't lose Mary Angela, too."

"I'll talk to her."

Sister Bernadette Frances Palermo—she had, of course, gone back to her birth name in 1977 with all the other Sisters of St. Clare, or at least the ones who hadn't been Daisy or Dolly—laughed and cried in alarming, to her, succession when she recounted the visit home to the nine nuns who were putting her up in the guestroom of their monastery. Beatrice, Kathleen, Louise, Anne, Karen, Teresa, Donna, Jan, and Sharon let her talk and didn't seem to mind the mood swings. Bernie liked them right away. (Except for Kiera, the dog, who followed her around. Bernie didn't like dogs very much, never had.) She liked them so much that she requested another month's leave and then another. Mother Agnes Donnelly didn't seem surprised nor did she seem overly concerned about the young nuns who were used to frequenting Sister Bernadette's office. There hadn't been any of this therapy nonsense when she was a novice and there had been a lot more novices then, too. Only seven in the new band

and half of them in their thirties and entirely too much coming and going for her tastes. But who was she? Only the mother superior and no one took her opinions very seriously. She supposed she should resign. Bernadette laughed. Mother, she said, just pray for me, would you?

Beatrice laughed too. She laughed at all of Bernadette's stories, but she stopped laughing when Bernadette cried and sometimes she held her. Bernadette loved Beatrice.

She's probably only eight years younger than Ma, Bernadette thought one day. She's probably in her mid-fifties and she looks my age; Ma's sixty-one and she looks seventy-five. Bernadette tried to make the thought go away.

Bernadette liked the food. There was no meat, but she didn't miss it. There were curried potatoes and cheese enchiladas and stir-fried vegetables from the garden, and onions and zucchini sauteed in olive oil over spaghetti and eggplant cous-cous, and broccoli quiche and stuffed red peppers and lemon parmesan rice. Bernadette made polenta with red sauce. She picked the tomatoes, the fresh garlic, and the basil from the garden. She made a lot, much too much, she thought as she watched the cornmeal swell in the huge pot. But they ate it all. The person on house duty cleaned up as well as cooked but Anne said no, you've done enough and took her instead on a long walk over the eighty-odd acres of hilly, bushy Sierra land, took her then to her own rooms and poured her a glass of red wine, a gift, she said, from a good friend, and told her stories. Bernadette liked Anne.

Jan gave Bernadette a massage, quiet and slow. Bernadette said no, at first, when Jan offered, but Jan offered again and seemed eager to give her something so Bernadette said yes. She was afraid, though. She tried to remember the last time anyone had seen her unclothed. It must have been Maureen, it must have been twenty-five years ago. Jan didn't watch while she undressed and stretched out, face down, on the foam mat and covered herself with a sheet. Jan said, turn over and we'll start with your face. That's all Jan said for over an hour as she touched, oiled, and pressed her strong fingers into every muscle of Bernadette's body. She moved from her head to her arms and hands, gently stretching even the skin between her fingers. By the time Jan started working on her feet, Bernadette had given herself over altogether. She didn't even care that her crotch began to moisten when Jan kneaded her inner thighs. She hadn't felt that since she and Peggy O'Toole took to whispered confidences and passionate kisses after lights out in the novitiate. But Peggy had disappeared one day (Bernadette remembered this every time she heard about "the disappeared" in Argentina, though she knew that it wasn't the same sort of thing at all) and the mistress of novices patiently refused to answer any of Bernadette's questions, would say only that she and Sister Margaret Ann had together decided that Sister Margaret Ann was not, in the end, suited to the religious life. Bernadette felt angry, abandoned, betrayed, bereft, inconsolable. She later, in the course of her psychiatric training, admitted to her shrink that she missed most, or at least longest, the heavy, pleasurable throbbing between her legs. Bernadette tried twice in the last five years to find Peggy O'Toole, but the mother house had no record and who knows where she lived now or what name she had taken.

Bernadette liked Jan.

Sometimes Bernadette talked to Karen who was about her age and very tall and thoughtful. Karen said their mass, Karen heard confessions, Karen laid hands on the sick, Karen said things like, Go in peace, my sister, and next time bring your own Kleenex. "No and yes," Karen said when Bernadette wanted to know if the bishop knew about her priestly activities. "I think he's afraid of us, especially of Beatrice." Bernadette couldn't imagine being afraid of Beatrice. But then she wasn't a bishop. Bernadette liked Karen.

But it was Beatrice whom she loved. It was the prospect of talking to Beatrice that made Bernadette smile when she got out of bed in the morning and hungry when she smelled the day's house sister grind the coffee beans, cut for economy and health with chicory. The coffee tasted good.

Beatrice's house was beyond the garden and across the meadow.

Bernadette liked the walk though it frightened her a little because they had all warned her about rattlesnakes. They hadn't yet seen the first of the season, but it was April and one would eventually rear its head and rattle its tail. Donna warned her often, urged her to take Kiera along on her walks, but Bernadette didn't like dogs.

She talked to Beatrice almost every day. She made Beatrice laugh, sometimes for extended periods, like when she told her about Aunt Tony's song. Bernadette did a good imitation of Aunt Tony. Even Mrs. Palermo recognized that and smiled when she said, "But she's got a good heart, Bernie."

"I brought the book," Bernie said one day when she arrived wet and breathless at Beatrice's little house. "I just wanted you to see it." Beatrice took the book and opened it slowly. She was sitting in her rose brocade chair. She started to read. "It's awful, isn't it?" Bernie said, as she pulled the chair from Beatrice's desk and sat down next to her. "Pure propaganda. And of the worst sort. White, thin, Anglo-Saxon, pretty, popular Bernie—the kind of girl God likes best. That's the message, isn't it?" Beatrice didn't answer the question; it was, after all, a rhetorical question, so Bernie kept on talking.

"That's always been the message. And I was brown and fat and poor and ugly and there didn't seem to be many alternatives. I've been a nun for twenty-four years because I found that fucking book in the sixth grade library." The adjective wasn't one usually in Bernadette's vocabulary though God knows she heard it often enough from her clients. She had heard Anne use it the other day, too.

"I went through four years of college and six years of medical training while my mother and father tried to keep pasta on the table. Gina's the only other one who made it to college and she teaches in a Catholic grammar school and barely manages to survive. Mary Angela works at Bullocks and takes care of Ma and the house and goes for five years without seeing a doctor. The cyst is benign, by the way, but the next one won't be. Jenny's got a big house and a husband about as communicative as Pa was and four kids. Clara has three and she's sick all the time. Rose lives in a tiny apartment down the street from Ma and is afraid to come out. She wouldn't even talk to me. Natalie's dead. And Ma with her swollen ankles and painful joints thinks it's a good life and everybody should love God and pray to St. Joseph and be grateful." Bernadette cried but she kept talking.

"And then you should hear the stories my young nuns tell and the students at the University of Detroit. I listen to them from eight in the morning until eight at night every day and they call me in the middle of the night. Every night, Beatrice, at least one call. I have sixty-two clients. They are raped and molested and jailed and shot at and their parents over-dose and stab each other and they drop out of school every other semester because their funds run out and they hang themselves and jump off buildings and people spit on them for being black or Jewish or Italian or gay or fat or one-armed. And they have ulcers and cancer and AIDS and weird diseases that eat away at their vision or their hearing or their nerve endings. All this and I don't even take the drug addicts.

"And Mother Agnes sits around worrying that if the novices work at the soup kitchen downtown they'll bring back roaches and lice. Roaches. My God." Bernie started to cry and then she took the book from Beatrice's lap and threw it to the floor, hard, then leaned close to Beatrice's face, which she loved. Not the way she loved Peggy O'Toole but the way she wished she had loved Mary Angela and Jenny and her mother. The way, she thought angrily, that Mother Agnes wanted her to love God and she could not. But that wasn't it either, because mixed in with pure and passionate affection was wild desire and fury. Bernie wondered briefly, fleetingly, where it was coming from and if she could survive it. She saw herself in the rose brocade chair, listening with calm concern to her raging clients, all of them at once. She hated the woman sitting there.

"And you, Beatrice. You sit up here on your mountain and do what? Pick vegetables and pray and not much else as far as I can tell. Even I do more than that. I listen and I nod and I dispense anti-depressants because everyone knows now that depression is biological and has nothing to do, really, with watching your father kill your mother or being sodomized or going blind. I go home at night and one of my sisters has dinner ready and I soak in the tub and I read a book. While the city burns. And Ma doesn't understand why Gina has no respect for nuns. Gina at least brings kids back to her apartment when they show up with mysterious bruises and weirdly broken arms.

"What do you do, Beatrice? You eat curried potatoes and mushroom quiche and spinach terrine. You're surrounded with women who would wash your wounds with their tears or throw themselves in the path of a snake to save you. You are healthy and strong and look ten years younger than you must be. You're just like her." Bernie kicked the book across the room.

"Beatrice, are you listening to me?"

"I'm listening."

"What are you going to do?"

"I'm going to hold you."

"While the city burns?"

"Yes, Bernadette, while the city burns. Or for an hour or two or five. All night if you want. I don't have anything else to do," she said with a funny smile, because she was a woman not without a sense of humor, "but pick vegetables and pray."

And because Bernie, too, was a woman not without a sense of humor, she took a deep breath and stopped crying or screaming or whatever it was she was doing while those words, words she hadn't recognized as her own, had come uncontrollably out of her mouth.

"I'm sick, Beatrice, and I'm tired."

"I know."

"What's my name, Beatrice? Tell me my name."

"Bernadette. Bernadette. Bernadette."

Chapter 7

Run, Karen, Run

(Karen: 1987)

KAREN started to run on the day after the end of the world. She ran even though less than a year ago she had been very ill, with a mysterious liver ailment, and almost died. She ran even though she hadn't run since her last high school track meet a decade before. She ran even though the mountain roads knocked the breath out of her before she had gone a quarter of a mile. She ran for four years, though not with the determination or desperation of the first day, the first week, the first month. She ran in the early seventies, before runners became (even in the mountains where you'd think just living would be exercise enough) familiar figures and before the books appeared telling you how to maximize your endorphin high and minimize the damage to your limbs. She ran until her right knee gave out, whether from the running itself or from what she heard as she ran by Lisa's open window, she didn't know.

What she did know was that half a mile into her run that day, her knee buckled and she fell. She limped home and cried—whether from the pain in her knee or from the pain of hearing what she heard as she ran by Lisa's open window, she wasn't sure, though she had a pretty good idea and she didn't like it—until her eyes were swollen shut. She was afraid to cry anymore, so she lay on her bed and willed away the pain so successfully that by morning she could walk without limping. The areas around the knee and around the heart, however, felt tenuous and sore, and her eyes were still swollen. The swelling was ugly and uncomfortable but hid the angry, disgusted, pleading looks she directed, against her will and better judgment, at Anne all through Matins and Lauds. She spent the afternoon alone, tending the flowers in the green house, taking special care of the lavender roses, whose skins she touched, whose outer petals she blew gently, whose inner petals, though she could not see them, she sang to in a low quiet voice. Eventually she sang their favorites, "Lavender's Blue, Dilly, Dilly" and "Purple People Eater" in reparation for the folksy laments she sang at first, laments that suited her mood but might, she feared, make the roses droop.

She skipped Vespers and dinner again, telling herself aloud that she should lay off her knee as much as possible, not telling herself but knowing that she did not want to see Anne or Lisa. She wrapped the knee thickly in winter wools and wished she had hot water to soak it in. As she feared or as she hoped, Anne came knocking on her cabin door about seven. Karen didn't answer the first knock or the second. She knew Anne was there, of course; she knew Anne wouldn't come in unasked; she knew from the absence of footsteps that Anne was waiting and from the absence of any sound at all that Anne was waiting patiently, humbly, apologetically, wearily, and defiantly outside her door. She didn't get up from her reading chair ("I must stay off my knee," she said to herself by way of excuse), but called out, "Come in."

She hardened her heart when Anne hugged and held her. She said, "What do you want?" When Anne didn't answer, she said, "Why, Anne, why?" and looked out the window so that she wouldn't cry again.

"Because I love her."

"You're infatuated with her."

"How do you know that?" Anne asked.

"Because she's not your type," was the first thing that Karen said, and then she said a lot of other things about Lisa—how loud she was, how obnoxious, how disruptive, how careless, how intrusive, how self-centered, how lacking in self-control, how immature, how ill-suited to life at Julian Pines—before she repeated the observation, "She's not your type." Karen said all these things in a measured, calm voice, all the time looking out the window. She waited for Anne's explosion, hoped for it, longed for it in some part of herself (probably in the fat that lay around her left ventricle) she thought she had melted off running.

Anne reached her neck around Karen's face so that Karen had to look at her, but she didn't yell that it was none of her goddamn business and she didn't kick the desk and she didn't pound her fists on the wall, any or all of which Karen waited for, hoped for, longed for, expected. Instead she brushed her cheek against Karen's and so forced her to pull away for the second time. She said, "Who is my type, Karen? You?"

"Of course, me. I love you. I've loved you for five years. I go out every day and run you off and just when I think I might be getting somewhere, you pull this. My God, Anne, look what you've done to my knee."

They talked late into the night, in and out of a circle the circumference of which was Anne's contention that they would be lovers still and always if Karen hadn't decided that their attachment was somehow inimical to the community life they were trying to lead and Karen's conviction that in spite of her unspeakable sorrow—"It felt like the end of the world, Anne"—she was, after all, right. Inside the circle was this new relationship which, Karen said, was equally inimical, which, Karen thought several times but only said once, was really much more inimical because Lisa was herself inimical to the whole spirit of Julian Pines Abbey, a place of silence, order, peace, prayer, and simple pleasures. Inside the circle, too, was Anne's desire for sex, which Anne wanted (but Karen didn't) to include among the simple pleasures, to make a congenial companion to or (when her argument became most intense and emphatic) a necessary component of silence, order, peace, and prayer. At that Karen snorted, but the conversation proceeded amicably and, it must be admitted, predictably, given the other conversations, theological, philosophical, literary, political, and psychological that Anne and Karen had had, usually late into the night, during those years of daily runs. Conversations that were as often as not about lust, love, and community life.

Somewhere around two a.m. Anne advanced the theory (and Karen expressed skepticism of it, though later she began to think it had some merit) that the essence of life at Julian Pines, what made it different from other monasteries, what made it a place where women like she and Karen (and, yes, Lisa) could survive and flourish, was the blank pageness of it, the way you had to invent life every day and eschew the hierarchical assumption that peace is a higher good than passion or the clichéd assumption that peace and passion were mutually exclusive. Karen's refutation descended from these lofty heights to a more personal level at which point Anne accused her of seriously undervaluing Lisa, a brilliant and beautiful woman, and Karen charged Anne with so blatantly overvaluing brilliance and beauty (Anne insisting here that "beautiful" referred not to any physical traits but to a wide spectrum of virtues) that they blinded her to the presence of serious defects.

Somewhere in the midst of all this heady (though Karen could feel it in her throbbing limb) talk, somewhere, that is, around three, came frantic knocking at the door, and, without waiting for Karen's response, Lisa threw the door open and stumbled in, face dirty and tearful, long hair wildly knotted, shoulders defeated, voice distraught. "O my God, Anne, where have you been? I'm a mess. I've looked everywhere. Do you have any idea what time it is? I was afraid you were lost in these fucking mountains." She took Anne in her arms. "O how could you do this to me? Anne, darling, what are you doing here in the middle of the night?" Karen, wondering at the extravagance of the drama, cynically admiring

Lisa's convincing performance, and trying to figure out if Anne were so deeply deluded that she didn't detect the artifice, forbore turning Lisa's last question back on her, and said, quietly, calmly, as though soothing an overwrought child, "We were talking, Lisa, but we're finished now."

Anne looked a bit bewildered, from one woman to the other, then kissed Lisa on the cheek and said, "Go back home, dear one. I'm fine. Karen and I are talking and we're *not* finished." This firmness reassured Karen that Anne smitten was still Anne, but she noted unhappily the longing in Anne's fingers as Lisa let go of them and left. "Quite a scene," Karen said.

"Did she ever tell you," Anne asked, "that her mother worked for the American Theatre Company?"

"No," Karen said, "she told me her mother was a gypsy."

Although they talked until dawn, Karen didn't manage to convince Anne that Lisa's flamboyant immaturity was, in fact, flamboyant immaturity and hardly conducive to a decent much less elevating relationship. Nor did Anne manage to convince Karen that licking Lisa's labia did, in fact, contribute to her own growth, to the mission of the abbey community, to the spiritual renewal of the universe. Lisa left Julian Pines a month later (as Karen knew she would), wanting loudly and melodramatically to take Anne with her, but Anne, in spite of an anguish which she, too, expressed rather too vociferously for Karen's taste, stayed and Karen's knee healed, slowly, over the years. Although the conversations changed somewhat—Anne's rhetoric, for example, became a bit less grandiose and Karen's dismissal of Anne's defense of lust and love a bit less adamant—they continued dense, long, loving, and repetitive. Karen had hopes, unspoken even to herself, that Anne would settle down, embrace celibacy, and cease in general to agitate quite so severely her, Karen's, life. Endorphin highs were nice but running was dangerous.

The hopes persisted for years, seemed, in fact, fulfilled, until Teresa came. And then Karen let them go, because you couldn't make the same objections to Teresa that you made to Lisa. It was actually hard to make any objection at all except that she was sometimes vague and never raised her voice at the end of a question. She loved Teresa. Everyone loved Teresa. And Teresa's sexual relationship with Anne seemed so quiet, simple, and joyful that you almost, sometimes, might think that Anne was, at least partly, right about lust and love. You might even romanticize the relationship, you might say to yourself, well Anne *has* settled down, to monogamy if not celibacy. Karen did all these things, and thought that she had finally come to terms with both the issues and personalities involved when, engaged one night with Anne in late talk and mutual comforting, she felt desire, and Anne, too, wanted more than holding. And suddenly, though she walked away still longing, the hard edges of Karen's hard won clarity blurred, and when that night she ran her hands down the inside of her thighs to stop the longing, she felt a certain blurriness there, too, and thought, for the first time in many years, of running again.

By then, though, Karen was the priest at Julian Pines (Beatrice had argued against using that word, so concretely did it conjure up a male human being, a hierarchy, a corrupt church, in the imaginations of all who heard it, but Anne had countered, cogently, most of them thought, and voted accordingly, that the very contrast between those expectations and the reality of *their* priest—a woman who conceived her priest part as just that, a part, no more or less important than other part she could play in the group—was itself salutary both for themselves and for their many visitors and correspondents) and spent the hours she wasn't painting and tending roses talking through troubles, fitting words to music and music to words, laying on hands. And in this way three more years passed without Karen taking up again her weird and long-winded sport.

Late October in the Sierras can be starkly dry with pine needles and cones crunching underfoot, giving off the scent of mountain forest and holiday greens. Halloween day reached eighty-six degrees at three o'clock, was seventy at five, and plunged to forty by nine. As soon as it began to get dark, mountain friends brought children, theirs and neighbors', to the common house for tricks and treats. For treats, Jan made hot chocolate, Kathleen baked black-bottomed cupcakes, and Karen caramelized small apples from the orchard. For tricks there were witches' incantations. *Good* witches, the nuns carefully, superfluously, explained to the children (and naively hoped that the parents, some of them, they knew, born-again Christians, would absorb, too), as most witches were, they urged, and are.

Anne, Jan, Karen, Teresa, Sharon, and Beatrice dressed the parts in costumes culled from years of rummaging through used clothes sent, unsolicited, by supporters of the contemplative life. "Pray for me," said the letters accompanying the clothes, and so the community did, in their fashion, even as they pulled ruffled polyester blouses, barely wrinkled, out of bottomless boxes. Those they sent on, along with most of the skirts, coats, nightgowns, belts, dresses, and handbags, to local thrift stores and shelters. What they kept were an occasional pair of jeans, wool and flannel shirts, fabric remnants, and, more rarely, attire suitable for dressing up, down, or different. Donna had in a recent box discovered a grey bodysuit that she wore this hallowed eve with oddly shaped corduroy ears. "Coyote," she whispered in response to a young questioner. Louise and Kathleen, having declared themselves weary of witches, wore, respectively, a dramatically colored and designed Renaissance gown, somewhat too large and badly stained, and a huge brown paper garment stuffed with cereal boxes collected from a neighbor's trash. "A bag of groceries, of course."

The children laughed gratifyingly at the cackling but not particularly scary women and at the overexcited dog, Kiera, who ran in circles and licked their sticky faces. They shifted in their seats in the middle of Jan's ghost story, a sign not so much, Karen thought, of boredom as of longing for more conventionally sweet pastures of miniature Hershey bars and full-sized Snickers. After they left, Karen sighed at the mess made in less than an hour and took the largest broom to the common room floor while Louise and Beatrice shook crumbs out of the rugs and wiped up the brownish stains. Donna reported a puddle of pee in one corner and Kathleen seemed to remember a small boy huddled there. "I'll bet his mother told him not to ask to use the toilet," she said, "either because she thinks we don't have one or because it seemed to her unseemly to mention such an object in a house of prayer."

Jan drew the curtains, dimmed the lights and chose carefully from her collection of tapes. Before her arrival at Julian Pines, the good nuns, under Louise's tutelage, did contra and Irish folk dancing on Halloween and other celebratory occasions. But Jan had brought rock music and amazing dance skills that she insisted could be easily learned and soon she had all but Louise convinced of their cathartic capabilities. Louise she won over by incorporating lower back exercises and by learning with great enthusiasm the folk steps for less raucous entertainment. Karen was not, on either contra or rock nights, a very enthusiastic dancer, but some times, Halloween usually one of them, she let herself be pulled, always by Anne, to the middle of the floor, where she abandoned herself to the pounding rhythms and lost for an hour or two that persistent sense of herself (though it was, of course, less acute now, less pervasive than it had been at seventeen) as too tall for grace.

She had used that phrase once, "too tall for grace"—it had been her Aunt Pearl's pronouncement on Karen-at-fourteen-years-and-almost-six-feet—when she and Anne were first experimenting with sex. She had felt so, well, limby and jerky next to Anne, who moved smoothly over Karen's stretched-out body and who, Karen had thought with awe and unstinting tenderness, moved like a dancer even when she came. "You may be," Anne had said, "too tall for Grace, but you're not too tall for me." In that sweet and silly pun (word play being one of Anne's many addictions and attractions), was, Karen recognized, the beginning of her long, slow, and sometimes painful process of standing up straight.

The witches left their costumes on and were the first to dance; Karen

liked the long skirt at her calves and found softly erotic her circle of five—
Beatrice seemed to have disappeared—women shaking, stretching,
rolling, waving, and bending their black-outfitted bodies. "We look like
nuns," Teresa shouted above the music, and they all laughed. Beatrice
reappeared and joined the circle, which after a few minutes broke into a
circle of four and a pair, Anne and Teresa. Damn them, Karen thought,
oh damn them both.

On another night she might have scolded the voice, called up her less
belligerent spirits, repeated, incantation-like, the numerous virtues of the
two witches dancing alone. But it was Halloween, there was mischief in
the air, and she let the curse stand without censure, without comment,
without even wondering what she meant by it. She just kept dancing.
The large circle widened again, by the addition of the now uncostumed
Kathleen and Louise. Donna, coyote ears still attached, joined the duo.
A weird woman, Karen thought, not for the first time, even weirder than
the rest of us.

When she set out for her cabin, it was almost eleven, a late night for
the good sisters. She flashed her light only when she needed it. Unlike
Anne, who was night-blind, she saw well in the dark and didn't like to
obscure the stars. She walked alone (having taken time to remove her
witch's garb), fifty feet behind Anne and Teresa, engaged in some intense
exchange that ended with a brief embrace when they reached Anne's
rooms. A strange sight, Karen thought, two witches embracing in the
dark, a small pool of light at their feet. She watched them. Teresa pulled
away first and continued at a measured pace down toward her own cabin.
The path to Karen's place diverged to the right from the road, about thirty feet before Anne's. As she turned off, the remaining witch walked
toward her. She wasn't crying—Anne almost never cried—but the veins
stood out at her temples and her eyelids were red-rimmed, signs, Karen
knew from many years' experience, of trouble.

"Turn off that flashlight," Karen said, in an effort to ignore what
brewed. "Witches are supposed to be able to see in the dark." Anne

looked down at her black clothes as though she had forgotten them and pressed the button. The two women stood there for a moment, in silence, under a moon that was not quite full and partly obscured by a small cloud. "I can't see your face," Anne said, gesturing toward her door. "Can we talk inside?" She fumbled for a match to light the propane lamp in her entry way and let the lamp provide the light for the bedroom as well. Dim but sufficient. Karen sat cross-legged, as was her wont, on the bed and waited without speaking for Anne to initiate the inevitable ritual of sitting backwards astride her desk chair as though she were going to plunge into conversation, then, before saying anything at all, turning back to the desk, opening the top drawer, taking out a cigarette, getting up and searching for matches, which were never in the porcelain ashtray where Karen would have kept them, were never, in fact, in any predictable place. She ended up going back to the box in the entry way. After she lit the cigarette, she abandoned the chair and joined Karen on the bed, an action that would within a minute or two, Karen knew, necessitate getting up for the ashtray, now out of reach. Karen liked knowing the moves ahead of time, liked knowing, for example, that there would be only one cigarette, to get them started, and that, once started, Anne would get right to the point.

"I'm a sex fiend."

Karen laughed. "You look like some sort of fiend in that outfit, but sex fiend wouldn't be my first guess."

"I'm not trying to be funny, Karen."

"Yes, you are, or you wouldn't have said that."

"I was trying to express, in a pithy but admittedly exaggerated way, a serious problem. I mean, when I assess the situation rationally, I decide I'm just a normal woman with a normal sex drive. But here, among the saints, I feel like a nymphomaniac."

"Translation: Teresa doesn't want sex with you as often as you want sex with Teresa."

"Your translation," Anne said, "like most translations, is literally accurate but misses the subtle nuances."

"Like?"

"Like the fact that Teresa likes sex but doesn't seem to need it, like the fact that you liked sex once upon a time but seem to have transcended it, like the fact that Donna and Sharon and Louise and Jan and Kathleen and Beatrice do without it and never complain and never seem to fill the common space with erotic tension and never seem about to explode. What's wrong with *me?*"

Karen decided to be fair. "Maybe the question is what's wrong with the rest of us."

"I tell myself that sometimes," Anne said, "but it won't wash. You are all fine. You are affectionate and more or less sane and intelligent and fun and well, fine—not twisted by frustration, not anguished by erotic energy, not driven by the need to channel your sex drives into creative endeavors."

"You are affectionate and sane and intelligent and fun and fine, too, Anne, maybe even more so than the rest of us. Besides Beatrice."

"Then why do I feel like this? I love Teresa, I want her, I want her desperately, I want her to want me. She says yes, okay, fine, anytime, thanks, but she never wants me, and so mostly I've just stopped asking, and we haven't slept together in weeks."

"I'm sorry." Karen did feel sorry, rather to her surprise.

"Why should you be? You haven't slept with anyone for fifteen years and you never moan and groan about it."

"Never to you. I could hardly moan and groan about it to you, friend, when your answer would be—and it would be a fair answer—'You're the one who walked away.'"

"To whom then?"

"Oh, to Beatrice."

"I bet you did it once, Karen, maybe a dozen years ago. Am I right?"

Karen laughed. "I think it was more like ten years ago. But..."

"But you still have desires. You just breathe them into your roses, sing them into vespers, paint them into flowers, send sweet loving messages with them to us all and maybe you even masturbate once in a while. Don't worry. I'm not asking. Damn it, Karen. I like my work, too, and I love vespers, and I feel close to my sisters, and I masturbate. But I want *sex,* with another living, breathing, panting human being. Who doesn't even have to be Teresa. Who could be Sojourner, who could be Jan, who could be that journalist who came, what was her name, Marta, who could be you. Sometimes I even think about sex with Beatrice. I'm promiscuous as well as desperate.

"Do you understand what I'm saying, Karen? I live surrounded by women I love and I want them and I don't understand why they don't all want each other."

Karen took a deep breath. She didn't know where to start. She lacked Anne's eloquence and perhaps her passion, but she, Karen, had things to say to this woman who mistook control for calm, who discarded effort, who, like the fisherman's wife, wanted castle for cottage and even then wasn't satisfied. She wanted to start five minutes back and say that if Teresa said yes, it was enough, take it, love her. It was greedy to want more than Teresa's yes. She wanted to say that Donna, good, kind, dependable Donna, preferred animals to humans and had who knows what kind of secret desires or secret holiness wrapped up in her silent ways. She wanted to say that Louise was single and celibate when she arrived at the monastery, in her thirties. What, if any, repressions had brought her to them virginal were as incomprehensible to her, Karen, as to Anne. She wanted to say that Sharon hadn't been there very long but was, Karen strongly suspected, going to have a lot of trouble with this very desire and that Jan, Karen knew for a fact, though she wasn't at liberty to say so, had as much trouble with it as Anne; that Jan had actually, since she'd arrived, had an enormous crush on Anne, which she worked with touching diligence and ingenuousness to overcome. She wanted to say that Kathleen and Beatrice had desire beaten out of them at Mt. Carmel and that Beatrice sometimes seemed to beat back desire still. Once, at least, Karen thought she had seen it, alive and, yes, desperate, in Beatrice's eyes—eyes that were, at the time, looking at Anne.

She wanted to say that she, Karen, had times of calm and times of chaos, that she did, when chaos came, breathe desire into her roses and into her drawings, that she *did* love herself with it and torture herself over it, that Beatrice had, in a most passionate and un-Beatrice-like way, said, ten years ago, that she must never do it violence because without it this life was nothing. She wanted to say that sometimes (maybe because she had tried not to do it violence) she, Karen, wanted her, Anne, desperately and passionately, not often, but sometimes. Like, Anne, like tonight when we were dancing, when you and Teresa broke away from the circle and I said to myself, damn them, damn them. I said that, Anne, because *I* wanted you, I wanted to throw myself at you and rip off that witch's shirt and—right there on the common room floor—suck your nipples through my teeth until they bled. That's what I wanted, Anne (how do you like that?), that's what I *want.* She wanted to say these things and she did say them. She said them all except for the part about Jan, which she knew but couldn't say and the part about Beatrice, which she didn't know and couldn't say and was afraid of. She said them until the tears were running down her cheeks and until Anne unbuttoned first the witch's shirt and then the witch's skirt and took off the bra and pants underneath and came at Karen naked, her nipples erect, and said in her huskiest voice, "Suck them, Karen, until they bleed."

While Karen sucked, Anne stripped her, not gently, carefully—as she had fifteen years before when that Karen's tall, thin body even breathed must have seemed to Anne a fragile miracle—but quickly, roughly. Karen helped with her jeans, let go of Anne long enough to light a candle to replace the dimming propane lamp. "I want to *see* you," she said. She looked hard at Anne's body, different from the memories but no less compelling. She ran her hands down Anne's hips, felt Anne's hands grabbing her butt, pushed Anne to the bed. They struggled there, not for anything but the struggle itself, and Karen came out on top. She slid herself down until her mouth was again around Anne's breast, and she drew the nipples again through her teeth, in and out, in and out. At the same time she thrust three fingers inside of her and rubbed the ball of her hand firmly against Anne's pubic bone. Anne spread her legs far apart and danced wildly into Karen's hand, whispering, hoarsely, harshly, "Harder, harder," then moaning so loudly that young Karen would have let go at first sound of it, but this Karen didn't, couldn't. She only sucked and pushed and pulled harder until Anne came, almost shouting. She tasted blood.

Without transition, without letting up on the frantic pace, Anne flipped her over and took charge. Suddenly the moans were Karen's and she felt with panicked pleasure the finger that had been aimlessly roaming her belly and cunt work its way slowly into her ass and Anne's thumb on her clitoris. And by the time Anne's mouth closed over her breast she had wrapped her legs around Anne's body and was using them to push her hips forward into the firm flesh of Anne's belly. "What *is* this," she said in a loud voice that seemed to be coming from across the room, "O God, what *is* this?" Anne slid her mouth down Karen's pumping body and with her tongue traced circles in Karen's pubic hair while she pressed her thumb inside her. Karen writhed, trying to get herself into Anne's mouth, but Anne teased on. "Tell me what you want."

"You know what I want," Karen managed to say between breaths.

"Say it."

"Suck me."

"How?"

"Hard."

When she woke up at four-thirty, Karen lay quietly beside the sleeping witch and wondered if what they had done at midnight was make love or do battle. She felt bruised, her thigh muscles ached. She remembered the way they had held each other down, pushed and pulled, teased and scratched, bit and shouted and dared. She remembered it as a dream and she the dreamer but not one of the breathless, violent women, teeth bared, rolling over in the bed, spitting blood out of their mouths. She wished it were light so she could see if she had broken the skin on Anne's breast. Surely not. She tried to say "Damn you" to the body at her side but she couldn't. The words that came so easily last night were gone. And when she slid silently out of the bed and into her clothes, she longed for Anne's fingers on her flesh, not clawing but tracing. She took her shoes to the entry way, and as she bent over to pull them on, she noticed the objects on the table by the door. A glass of water, with a note taped to it: Always drink before running. Two pieces of chocolate on top of another note: Don't run away altogether. Anne must have written the notes, blind as she was, in the night, while Karen slept; Anne had known she would run, though she hadn't run for years; Anne, Anne, Anne.

Karen loved her with every sore muscle in her body, with every drop of her blood, with every cell of her brain. She had loved her, not since the day they met, the two young newcomers, wary of the women, of each other, wondering, separately, about this strange step their lives seemed to have taken without them, not since then but since the day Anne appeared at the side of her bed, asked by Louise to be her nurse, though she had never nursed, and stayed through the long and frightening illness that so suddenly claimed her. Though the doctor had answered her questions patiently enough, the diagnosis of Karen's driving pain paled in explanatory power beside the dark, troubling pieces of her life that worked their way like shards of glass to the surface of her skin. It was Anne who took tweezers to them, held them up to the light for her, safely disposed of them when she was finished. Likewise, the doctor's account of Karen's recovery bore too little resemblance to her own sense that cells healed under the tips of Anne's fingers, that every time Anne's hands rubbed her neck, her shoulders, her sides, they rubbed off death.

Outside Anne's door, Karen stretched and reached and fell without thinking into her old pre-running routine. It was dark and it was cold, but Karen thought that in a couple of miles it would begin to get light and she would begin, even sooner, to get warm. And so she ran, trying at first to ward off the cold by singing some of the songs, what she could remember of them, that Anne had sung to her the weeks of nursing. Quiet, kind weeks. Anne had sung while she stroked Karen's face, blew cool breath on her hot forehead, traced soft circles on her cheeks. First there were folk songs—it was 1972—lullabies, labor songs, songs from the civil rights movement, songs from some long ago summer camp. "From the hills I gather courage/ Visions of the days to be/ Strength to lead and strength to follow/ All are given unto me." Karen looked out the window when Anne sang that one. "Nuns," Anne explained. "It was a camp run by the Sisters of Social Service. They wore grey wool and were into the inspirational stuff." But she sang it purely and Karen's arms got goose bumps. They were so young.

"O gay is the garland and fresh are the roses/ I've culled from the garden to bind on thy brow." Karen had liked the roses in that song. Some days she imagined them yellow and warm, other days, when her fever raged, lavender and cool. And then there was the song in a minor key, so slow and mournful. How did it go? "Come all ye fair and tender maidens/ Be careful when you court young men/ They're like a star on a summer morning/ They'll come in view, then fade again."

"And, Sister Karen," Anne had said, after the first time she sang it, "let that be a lesson to you." Karen had been too sick to laugh. And there were days when she was so sick that she only wanted one song, but she never told Anne that, she just let her sing and hoped she'd come to it eventually. "When you wake, you will find/All the pretty little horses/ Dappled and grey, pinto and bay/All the pretty little horses." Karen's mother had sung that song, but never the part about dappled and grey. Had Anne made it up?

She was already at the apple orchard when she remembered the Irish songs. Anne had thought of them late, when Karen was already mending, so she associated them with the best days of the illness, when she and Anne could talk and laugh, and she could eat, and Anne took such touching pleasure in bringing her food, always carefully arranged on the plate, trimmed with bits of parsley, accompanied by slices of apples, from neighbors' orchards, in whose restorative properties Anne firmly believed. An apple a day.

"You may take the shamrock from your hat and cast it on the sod/ But 'twill take root and flourish still though underfoot 'tis trod." Once Anne had figured out all the words, she sang it almost every day. A fighting song, she said to Karen, good for you. "And if the color we must wear is England's cruel red/ Sure Ireland's folk will ne'er forget the blood that they have shed." Anne's English father hated that song, she said, so she sang it often, especially in March, especially when she couldn't get his attention any other way. He hated that song most, but he hated all Irish songs. Maybe, she said, maybe that's why she knew so many.

Anne used to say good-night with "Danny Boy," which, as often as not, she changed to "Annie Girl." After a while she'd make Karen sing the last two lines—while she kissed her: "For you will bend and tell me that you love me/ And I shall sleep in peace until you come to me." The better she felt, the more lines she would sing, the more Anne would kiss her, her forehead, her cheeks, her ears, her neck. And, when the song was over, her lips. The kisses got longer, and one night they kissed so long and it was so dark and cold that Anne asked if she could stay. She could, oh yes, she could.

Karen picked up the pace, partly because she was running downhill, partly because she couldn't bear to remember what happened the night Anne stayed. The sweetness of it, the youthfulness of it, the carefulness of it, the wholeness of it. Whole and healed she had felt afterwards, lying in Anne's arms. She didn't want to sleep because Anne was asleep and she wanted to watch her, so small, so lovely, so delicate, so unlike the vigorous woman who had cared for her so competently, day after day, for almost three months. Sweet gum leaves were falling all around her, red and orange and yellow, she knew, though they all looked alike in the dark. She wanted to see a real fall someday, a Vermont fall, for example, a New Hampshire fall. Anne said that you had to see it to believe it but that they deserved it, the New Englanders, to compensate for the cold and the dark.

By catching leaves and giving them colors—pomegranate, persimmon, pumpkin, grape, mustard, ocher, olive, chestnut, aubergine—Karen could stave off exhaustion for a while. She stuffed them into her pockets so she could see, after sunrise, if they lived up to their names. She ran and ran. At quarter to six she reached Sheep Ranch. It was still dark but you could feel dawn. She knew she should stop because she'd been running an hour after years of not running and her knee ached. She knew she should stop because she had gone too far already, mostly downhill, and it would be a long hike back. She knew she should stop because she was too old for this, not the running but the running away. But she kept going because Anne's taste was still in her mouth, Anne's smell in her nose, Anne's fingers on her breasts, Anne's leg between her legs, Anne's eyes everywhere. Run, Karen, run.

When Helen saw the two young nuns kissing by the pond, she called her name. "Karen." She called it sharply, scoldingly, pleadingly. She walked away. She didn't say "Anne," only "Karen." "She's given me up," Anne said. "I have a temper, I jump in too quickly, too adamantly, I have too many opinions. I argue. Karen, you've been missing my performances. Now that you're well you'll see them. Sometimes I even say 'Oh fuck.' An old habit but I could break it if I wanted to. I just don't want to. Do you understand?"

Karen hadn't understood. Not altogether. And Helen's voice had hurt her; Anne shrugged it off. They were different, Karen and Anne. Anne had seen New England falls. Anne had slept with Patrick. And Maureen. The years Anne had worked for the *Chronicle* Karen had taught first grade at Holy Trinity and lived at home, as she had all through college, and watched her mother die. "Asshole," Anne said, when Helen walked away. "Did I scare her off?" Anne asked when Beatrice announced that Helen had gone back to Mt. Carmel. Beatrice had looked at her for a long time and then said, "Yes, I think you did." It wasn't a judgment, just a statement. "Yes, I think you did," but it frightened Karen. Karen hadn't liked Helen, but Helen was there first. Helen was a real nun, from the mother monastery. She hadn't taken to new ways. She never wore jeans or work boots. She didn't like meetings. She always wanted Beatrice to do something. "Beatrice, you're the abbess. *You* decide if we're going to be vegetarians." "Beatrice, you're the abbess, *you* decide if Louise should keep working at the hospital." Beatrice, Karen imagined Helen saying, you're the abbess, *you make them stop or I will leave.*

On the way back, less than a quarter mile out of Sheep Ranch, Karen's knee collapsed. She felt it coming, she pretended it wouldn't happen, she hadn't finished running. It was cold, it was dark, she was seven miles from Julian Pines, she couldn't stand up. She dragged herself to a tree and sat down against the trunk. She cried for a while, whether because of the pain or because of her night with Anne or because of Helen long ago saying, "Karen," she didn't know. But it felt good to cry. Anne hardly ever cried but tears came easy to Karen. Mostly she fought them off, but sometimes she knew enough to give in. Anne gave her an article once that said crying was good for you, it flushed out a brain chemical that caused depression.

Karen had cried when Helen left. "Beatrice," Karen said, "I love Anne."

"Yes," Beatrice said, "I know."

"If I say 'No more,' I will hurt her."

"Yes," Beatrice said, "you will."

"If I don't," Karen said, "I will hurt the rest of you."

"Maybe," Beatrice said. "Maybe not."

Karen stopped crying and stretched her arms and her good leg. She tried to stretch her bad one, but pain hit her hard and fast. "Fuck," she said, "oh fuck." She thought of home. Sitting down to a hot cup of coffee after Matins and Lauds. Matins and Lauds, special today for All Saints. They had prayed without her. They were breaking their fast without her, warming up for the day without her. Anne would say, "She's running." Or maybe Anne wouldn't say anything. Breakfast was a silent meal. "The chief advantage," Anne said once to a shocked young woman thinking of nunhood, "of living in a monastery is that no one talks to you before your second cup of coffee." Karen laughed at the vision of Anne in a rumpled, worn out, flannel shirt (it was black watch plaid, she remembered, just right for Anne's gray eyes), looking up from her second cup of coffee at the earnest aspirant and saying that. "Oh Anne," Karen said. "Oh Anne."

There was a house not far away, she didn't know the people but there would be a phone and she could call and someone would come and get her. Maybe Anne. On the other hand, her knee didn't hurt if she kept still and the tree was friendlier than she thought at first, and warmer, and very near the road. Eventually someone she knew would come along and she could hitch a ride. Yes, she said aloud, that's what I'll do. Wait. With luck it would be Kat or Skip on the way to pick up their mail. Without luck it would be Jim Kroner and she'd have to sit next to a rifle in the front seat of his pick-up. He'd insist on driving her all the way to the common house and he'd roar up to the porch, clouds of dirt flying up from his fat wheels. He'd ask her to marry him and laugh heartily at his own ready wit. "Where were you twenty years ago?" she had disgusted herself by saying on a similar occasion. She imagined saying instead, "Fuck off." "All these broads," he had said once to her and Anne, "I'm in hog heaven just thinking about it. You got some real lookers up there." He looked confused when Anne agreed so wholeheartedly.

Karen shifted her weight because her good leg was falling asleep and her tail bone ached. She thought of Anne's hands, generously covered with almond oil, cinnamon scented, starting with her feet and massaging their way up, every muscle, large and small, succumbing to their warm pressure. Thanks, she was convinced, to those daily rubs, her limbs had worked admirably when she left her sickbed. Louise had been surprised and pleased. "So I picked you a good nurse, did I?" The best, Louise, the very best. Years later Jan brought professional massage skills, but Karen had never asked for them, had, in fact, refused them when Jan offered, even when her back was tight from chopping wood, even when her legs were sore from Sunday hikes. Perhaps, she thought, her body preferred memories to relief. A perverse preference.

She leaned against the tree, almost warm against her back. She listened for cars, heard nothing for a long time, thought again about the house, then fell, briefly, asleep. She dreamed. A vague woman, a half seduction, a windowless room, a cup of coffee she tried to smell but couldn't, a heart—hers—beating fast, hard, loud. She caught herself before she toppled over onto the ground, dream suspended. She was cold, her bladder was full, her knee hurt. She wondered why no one came.

Finally she heard a car approaching the curve around her tree, more slowly than she would have expected. She was relieved that it didn't sound like a pick-up, disappointed that she didn't hear the barking that would signal Kat or Skip. She wouldn't ask a ride from a stranger, but there were, she reminded herself, other friends in the mountains. Dave, Shirley, Maggie, Dawn and Henry, for example, maybe still sticky from the caramel apples. It was, however, none of the Halloween guests who was driving the car. It was one of the witches. "Anne," she shouted. "Anne." Anne parked the Toyota in a small clearing on the other side of the road from Karen's tree. She got out slowly and walked, just as slowly, across the road. She sat down next to her. "Hi," she said. "Hi there."

"Hi there, yourself," Karen said.

"You forgot your chocolate." Anne held out the wrapped balls. Karen shook her head.

"I picked an apple on my way through the orchard."

"Looks like it's still in your pocket."

"It is," Karen said, "minus a bite." She took it out along with the leaves, most of them disappointingly brown, which she tossed in Anne's direction. Several landed in her hair. "Happy fall."

"Happy fall," Anne said, "O happy, happy fall. When did you do it?"

"Do what?"

"Fall."

"How do you know I fell? Maybe I'm just resting. Waiting for the sun to rise over the mountain peak."

"You're facing in the wrong direction."

"And what are you doing in these parts, Sister Anne Stratford?"

"Looking for a runaway nun," Anne said. "Tall, thin, brown hair, wearing jeans and a green jacket. Early forties, very attractive, bum knee, answers to 'Karen.' There's a reward."

"What is it?"

"Oh, a cup of steaming hot coffee. Scones and boysenberry jam. Me."

Karen licked her lips. "I had a dream."

"Was she beautiful?"

"Very."

"Did she look like me?" Anne asked.

"Not a bit. She was tall, elegant, dressed in some sort of smoking jacket. When she was dressed."

"Nice dream. Did you run away?"

"No," Karen said, "I woke up. And I was cold and my knee hurt."

"That's the trouble with dreams," Anne said, reaching out to help Karen to the car.

"But maybe," Karen said, "maybe that's the trouble with sex."

And so the conversation went, predictably enough, all the way home, Anne wanting, it seemed, to go over every inch of the night's territory, describing the warmth of it, delineating the loveliness of it, dwelling on the usefulness of it. "We have been talking for fifteen years," she said, "arguing away our lives. I feel as though we've settled something, come together, loved each other again in some significant way." Absorbed in the eloquence of one and skepticism of the other, they missed the sunrise.

"I tasted blood," Karen said.

"How did it taste?"

"Bitter," Karen said, "and strong."

Anne one-handedly unzipped her jacket and unbuttoned her shirt and lifted her breasts, one at a time, out of her bra. "Look," she said, "whole and pink. If you tasted blood it was your own. Maybe you bit your tongue." One at a time, Karen tucked the breasts (they were soft, smooth, tempting, unmarked by teeth) back into the cups; she buttoned the shirt; she zipped the jacket. She exaggeratedly examined her tongue in the visor mirror.

"Tongues heal quickly," Anne said, as she turned into the abbey entrance and drove slowly up the dry dirt road to the common house.

"Maybe breasts do, too," Karen said, "on the feast of saints. You know, a sort of miracle in honor of Agnes, who lopped off her breast to save her hymen. Or did the Romans lop it off?"

"The Romans. And it was Agatha. Or maybe you're thinking of Lucy who plucked out her eyes," Anne said, "or Apollonia who jumped into the fire. They were bloody and savage women, our virgin martyrs."

"I smell coffee," Karen said.

"Well," Anne said, "let's drink to them: St. Agnes, St. Lucy, St. Agatha, St. Perpetua, St. Felicitas, St. Apollonia, St. Cecilia, St. Anastasia, St. Catherine, St. Bibiana, St. Christina, St. Ursula, St. Dorothy, St. Barbara, St. Emerentiana, St. Margaret, St. Martina...."

"Anne," Karen said, interrupting the litany, "sometimes you exhaust me."

Chapter 8
 Unbecoming a Nun
(Louise: 1988)

"YOU can't just leave," Jan said. "You can't."

Louise, not by nature or profession inclined to sympathy for the well (for the sick, yes; she was, after all, a nurse), snapped back a bit heartlessly, it might have seemed to an observer, it did seem to the several observers, even though they knew that Louise, unless she was having a bad day with her back, did not snap without provocation. "I can leave and I'm going to leave, and there's really no point in getting all worked up over it. Life will go on much as usual and you'll soon forget I was ever here."

"Tell yourself that, Louise, but you know it's not true," Jan said. "You've been here for twenty years. It will change everything. *Everything.*"

"Yes, I've been here for *over* twenty years and I've seen plenty of comings and goings. They hurt for a while, I'm not saying they don't, but then they're over and you go on with your life. I guarantee it."

"Well," Jan said, now worked up to great wrath, "maybe I'll leave, too, maybe Anne will leave and

Karen. Who knows, maybe Beatrice will leave. And then just life as usual, right?"

Louise put her hands on Jan's shoulders. "Honey, you've got to stop. We've had this conversation three times in the last two days. There's no point to it. I don't want to talk about it anymore."

"Fine," Jan shouted, backing off from Louise's hands. "Don't talk about it. Just walk away from me. That's a very helpful way to work this out."

"But there's nothing to work out and I'm not walking away from you. I'm just trying to end this pointless, irrational exchange. Let's do the dishes." She led Jan to the kitchen and the noises there, louder than usual, muffled their voices.

Beatrice, still at the table with Karen and Anne, sighed. "Trouble in paradise," she said.

"We could do it," Anne said to Beatrice. "We could leave, you and I. Go to San Francisco. Hang out in the women's bars. I hear they're fun. Dance every night, nights we aren't at the opera, of course."

Karen watched the conversation attentively, tensely. It worried her. Anne was trying too hard to be funny, she thought. Her notes were flat. But Beatrice smiled and squeezed Anne's hand. "Don't tempt me," she said. "Not today."

Anne laughed at the prospect, she said, of tempting the abbess, but all of them (Anne, Karen, and Beatrice at one table, Kathleen, Donna, Teresa, and Sharon at the other) looked sad. Louise was leaving. They let Jan—the youngest among them though Sharon had come to Julian Pines a year later—pester Louise and torture her and try endlessly, tiresomely, to change her mind. They let her because they all felt the same way she did—abandoned, betrayed, angry, frightened, bewildered, exhausted—but were too mature, civilized, reticent, wary, and sophisticated to cling so obviously.

Louise's leaving meant starting over again. It was hard even when Bernadette left, who had only been with them for three months. They had loved Bernie, so intense, so sharp, so wry, so fragile, and, in the end, so determined to go back to Detroit, though they had asked her to stay, had wanted her to join them, had wanted to protect her from her twelve hour days in the inner city. "I'm only a shrink," she had said, catching the concern, not wanting to hear it, loving it, hating it, "save your tears for the nuns who run the soup kitchen. Better yet, save them for the folks who eat there."

Beatrice knew that Bernadette's bitterness hid her fear of another collapse and her attraction to life at the monastery; Anne and Karen, who had talked to her less, suspected the same; Jan, though, who desperately wanted Bernie to stay, took hard what seemed to her Bernie's anger at their life, the life that had, Jan thought, saved her own sanity and would have saved Bernie's if only she hadn't left. And that was only Bernie. This was Louise.

Louise had been at Julian Pines from its beginning. Through her, in fact, the already-nuns Beatrice, Patricia, Helen, and Kathleen found the land. Jan knew by heart the story of the finding and the founding, and since Patricia and Helen had left long before she came, Beatrice, Kathleen, and Louise seemed to her the firmest and finest among them (though it was Anne she loved most).

Sobs came from the kitchen and then Louise's voice, loud and angry, "For God's sake, Jan, I'm not your mother." And then there was the silence during which they all remembered (though Beatrice had been thinking about it all day) that Jan didn't have a mother. Louise led her tenderly from the kitchen and sat her down next to Beatrice. Louise rolled her eyes, Beatrice nodded, and they both understood that Louise couldn't take it anymore.

"I can't take it anymore," Louise said to Beatrice, later, in Beatrice's cabin. "I'm going tomorrow."

Beatrice closed her eyes. "You said the end of the month. It's only the fifteenth. We need time."

"You need, Jan needs, Karen needs, Kathleen needs—what about what I need?"

"What do you need, Louise?"

"I need peace and quiet. I need to stop arguing with all of you. Why can't you let me go?"

Beatrice looked at the stranger sitting across from her, sitting, in fact, in Beatrice's rose brocade chair. She spoke slowly, sadly. "Your leaving seems so sudden, so strange. For twenty-two years you've been one of us. You've seemed happy and productive and, well, here. I mean, if Donna announced that she was leaving, I'd be surprised but not shocked. Donna is one of us but she keeps herself apart. She has a world of her own that none of us touches. We know that. But it has always seemed to me that *we* were your world."

"Well, Beatrice," Louise said matter-of-factly, as she said everything of late, "you were wrong. I've been happy enough here. I like all of you. But the hospital has always been more real to me than Julian Pines. And Jane has been my friend all these years. A closer friend than any of you, frankly."

"You hardly ever talk about her."

"There are lots of things I don't talk about."

"Are you lovers?"

"Good heavens, no. We're friends. All these young women falling into one another's arms has warped you. Women can be just friends."

"It was only a question," Beatrice said, "asked because I thought I knew you and now I know that I didn't, that I don't."

"I've known Jane since nursing school. Kenneth's death last year left her lonely, free, and well-off. We're going to Hawaii first. I've never been."

"Nor have I. To me Hawaii has always been Molokai where Father Damian kept his lepers. No matter how many times Sister Mary Assumption explained to us third graders that leprosy was a disease, I persisted in picturing Damian roaming a vast, craggy island in the company of large, spotted cats."

Louise smiled. "I'll send you a postcard if I see any."

"But not otherwise?"

"I'll send you a postcard if I don't see any, too."

"We'll miss you," Beatrice said.

"Is that the royal 'we,' abbess?"

"No, it's a collective 'we.' But let me rephrase. *I'll* miss you."

"Will you?" Louise asked. "Will you really miss me or will you miss the free nursing I provide, the extra income when times are rough, the skills that keep this place marginally self-sufficient? Have you ever really liked me, Beatrice? Loved me? The way you loved Patricia? The way you love Karen and Anne and Teresa?"

Beatrice took a long time to answer. They sat there, silent, Beatrice sorting out, in an attempt to respond to Louise's questions, her feelings about the sturdy, middle-aged woman whose harsh words she found as shocking and painful as the leaving itself. Louise crossed her legs and leaned back into the chair, quite prepared, it seemed to Beatrice, to wait.

"You deserve honest answers," Beatrice said finally.

"Yes, I do," Louise said. "Take your time."

"I will miss your nursing and your managerial skills and your financial contributions, which have been generous, Louise. More than generous. We could not have done this without you. You could have gone to Hawaii long ago and lived a comfortable life if you hadn't given us that chunk of money for the land in the first place. But I will miss *you,* too. I like you, I respect you, I love you—if love means that I happily spend time in your presence, that I would offer a kidney if you needed one, though not a heart. That I would empty your bedpan if you were sick, that I have never spoken ill of you, that I think of you with affection and good-will. That I make excuses for you, even to myself, when you are harsh or judgmental or cranky or mean, as you sometimes are, as we all sometimes are. It's true, though, that I'm not drawn to you the way I'm drawn to Patricia and Anne and Karen and Teresa."

Beatrice stopped there, stopped knowing that she could say much more. She could say, for example, that even among those four to whom she felt so drawn, there were distinctions to be made. Patricia had been her best friend, friend from Mt. Carmel, co-conspirator, albeit reluctant, in the leaving. Patricia was, perhaps, her "Jane." "Come to San Francisco," Patricia said whenever she talked to Beatrice on the phone. And afterwards Beatrice envisioned life with Patricia. A good life with a companionable woman with whom she could share both pleasure and pain. They would work hard all day and come home to one another. They would go, once or twice a week, to a favorite restaurant, and over candles and hot soup say things to each other that they couldn't say over breakfast coffee. Patricia's pager would often interrupt their evenings, and she, Beatrice, would no doubt feel momentary irritation, followed by concern for her friend, growing older and refusing to slow down. But she wouldn't mind too much, knowing that Patricia belonged more to her patients than to her.

And there were so many books to read and concerts to hear and plays to see and letters to write that she'd like the time alone. Yes, it would be a good life—she couldn't imagine such a life with Louise—but it didn't tempt her much. San Francisco was not, after all, Julian Pines.

Karen had come back to them from the dead. Karen had taken on death, Anne, Fr. George, and the bishop. Beatrice cheered the courage and intelligence with which she had done the taking on. Beatrice loved the contrast between Karen the indomitable and Karen the gentle grower of roses and painter of plants. Beatrice admired Karen the priest, admired most, perhaps, her perspicacity and tact. It was she who had come to know Beatrice best, observe her most closely, inform her with courteous indirection that she sensed her secrets and kept them safe. Karen loved Anne.

Teresa she loved as a daughter. Teresa could have been her daughter if she, Beatrice, had married young. And she would have married young if she hadn't entered Mt. Carmel. One did marry young then, there, if one was a woman. Teresa saw visions, Teresa dreamed dreams, Teresa painted hearts. Teresa had come to them battered and broken and let them heal her. Teresa loved Anne.

And Anne? I would, Beatrice thought, offer her a heart as well as a kidney.

Louise, though, had named Patricia and Karen and Anne and Teresa in the same breath. Beatrice had admitted she loved them most; that was enough.

"I have taken you for granted, Louise," Kathleen said when Louise told her she was leaving the next day. "I'm sorry."

"You have all taken me for granted," Louise said. "But you least. I will miss you."

"I have been thinking a lot about what life will be like without you. It will be hard for me. You know, I wanted very much to come here with Beatrice. I admired her spirit. She was alive and I was dead. That's how I put it to myself and that's how I put it to Sister Lucy and to Mother Abbess when they talked to me about heading west. I was nervous, I held back, but I wanted to come as much as I have ever wanted anything. And then when we arrived, we found you. Beatrice and Patricia had been friends at Mt. Carmel; Helen I had never liked; when we were five, I thought of you as *my* friend, though you were younger and more world-ly. And then Helen left and Patricia, and the new ones started coming and they seemed so different, so strange, not like nuns at all. I was afraid of them, but Beatrice seemed happy, almost exultant that they were differ-ent. She breathed their air. I never could. I don't now, even though I love them dearly. But you and I, Louise, we seemed not so different from each other. I will be alone tomorrow."

"I'll write," Louise said.

"Better yet," Kathleen said, "come back. Bring Jane."

Louise laughed. "Jane is a Protestant and a Republican. And quite attached to hot running water and barbecued steak. Even if I got her past the beans, rice, and outhouses, she'd run off screaming during the first political discussion."

Anne walked up noiselessly behind Louise, put her arms around her waist, and said, "Are we talking about Jane, the mysterious Jane, Louise's girlfriend? All these years, Louise, you've been holding out on us."

"Beatrice asked me if we were lovers."

"I could have told her, " Anne said, "that you weren't."

"And how would you know, Sister Anne? Intuition? Or maybe you think I'm too old for sex. Not so attractive as the women you sleep with."

Kathleen picked up the garbage pail and hauled it out the back door, leaving Anne to maneuver the latest conversational turn. Anne sat down on a kitchen stool and motioned Louise to the other. "Blackening your breasts?" Anne asked.

"What?"

"You know, the way mothers used to wean their nursing young. Making yourself as unappealing as possible to lessen the pain of parting."

"I have no idea what you're talking about," Louise said.

"I come to you prepared for a loving and tearful farewell and you pick a fight. Save your tactics for Jan. I'm a grown-up. I can handle your leaving. I'll only be devastated for a few years."

"A few minutes maybe?" Louise asked. "Be honest, Anne, you're the advocate of honesty around here, wanting everyone to say what they think. Say what you think. That I'm a dried-up spinster, not overly bright, replaceable."

"Louise, you can't be serious."

"*I* can't be serious? You're the one who can't be serious for more than five minutes a day. You're the one who turns everything into a joke and doesn't care who she's hurting. You're the apple of everyone's eye, the abbey's princess, the abbess's golden girl, who can say anything and do anything because she's bright and cute and clever with words."

Anne would have shaken the woman beside her but she was afraid to touch her. Instead she pounded her fist on the work-table. "Louise, it's me. Anne. We've lived together for seventeen years. You taught me to cook. You like my green enchiladas. 'Dried-up spinster' isn't a phrase in my vocabulary—or even a concept in my head. And if it were, I would never apply it to you. Louise, are you there?"

"You hounded Lynn. You drove her out. She was a good young woman. She tried her best. But that wasn't good enough for you. She wasn't smart enough for you. She wasn't well-educated. She wasn't beautiful. She didn't fall all over you. And she was Teresa's friend. That was the last straw for you, wasn't it? You wanted Teresa for yourself."

She's leaving, Anne reminded herself. She's leaving and it's hard and she needs to distance herself from us and I'm staying and I won't have to deal with this after tomorrow. For a few minutes I can be patient, I can be kind. "Lynn was five years ago, Louise. Why are we talking about her now?"

"Because I was too cowardly to fight for her then. Because I didn't want to make waves. Because I don't like to argue with you. You and your words that you twist and turn until we're all confused. And then you win. Always."

"My problems with Lynn had nothing to do with the way she looked or how many years she had gone to school. Lynn was manipulative and judgmental, and she didn't have a clue about what was going on inside her."

"She didn't approve of your relationship with Teresa and you wanted her out."

"Louise, that's absurd. Lynn was in love with Teresa; she followed her around like a puppy. She hated me because Teresa loved me and because my being a lesbian scared the shit out of her."

"And we all know," Louise said, "that when someone doesn't like Anne—Lynn didn't hate anybody—she has to leave, right?"

"You are re-writing history," Anne said. "I didn't make Lynn leave. It was Beatrice's suggestion, I believe. And Lynn made the decision."

"But she *decided* because you were making her life here miserable and impossible."

"Not because of anything I did, Louise, but because of who I am."

"Of course, you never thought that maybe you should leave, that maybe you were the one who didn't belong here, did you?"

"Actually," Anne said, losing the steady voice she had sustained only with great effort, beginning now to raise it, "I thought of nothing else for several weeks. But finally, after great anguished soul-searching and hours of agonizing conversation with my confessor and tormented consultations with the abbess, I realized that there was in fact, a good reason for her leaving and my staying."

"Tell me the reason, Anne, because I'll never figure it out on my own."

"The reason was, the reason is," Anne said, shouting now, *"that I was here first."* She kicked the table before walking out the back door and slamming the screen.

"Louise," Donna said, breathless from running up the road, "Beatrice told me that you're leaving tomorrow. I'm sorry."

"Don't be. It's what I want. It's what I've wanted for a long time."

"Why did you stay then?"

"Waiting for the opportunity to leave, I guess. Waiting for Jane. Why do *you* stay, Donna?"

Donna smiled. A large smile that drew hundreds of lines on her round face. She laughed. Such a funny question, she thought, no one has ever asked it. "Because I love the animals."

"Donna, that's crazy. There's only Kiera and the chickens now. One dog, twelve hens."

Still smiling, Donna looked hard at Louise. "I love *all* the animals," she said.

"Oh," Louise said, "I see. And what animal am I?"

"No," Donna said, "you don't see. But when I woke up this morning, you had turned into a porcupine."

After dinner Teresa walked Louise back to her cabin. "I'm sorry you're leaving," she said.

"Don't be," Louise said. "It's what I want. It's what I've wanted for a long time."

"You hurt Anne," Teresa said.

"I might have known she'd go whining to the members of her fan club."

Teresa knew what would follow. She didn't like it. She wanted to believe Anne's theory of the blackened breasts; it was, Teresa thought, a kind theory, kind but stubbornly blind to something she had been watching for a while now, something Beatrice and Anne and Kathleen, who had known Louise much longer didn't want to see, but what she, Teresa, couldn't help seeing. Donna saw, too. Donna, admirer of the great draft horses, used to refer to Louise as a Clydesdale. But Teresa hadn't heard that name for at least three years, maybe more, maybe, it occurred to her, since Lynn left. Armadillo, Donna called her now, and Teresa had sensed the armor growing thicker, month by month. She didn't like what was growing underneath the armor either.

"Anne didn't whine," Teresa said. "I found her swollen eyed in her room. I've been here a long time and I've only seen Anne cry once before. I made her talk."

"I'm not really interested in discussing Anne. I'm leaving tomorrow. You came to say goodbye."

"Yes. But there's something I have to tell you. Anne didn't make Lynn leave. I did. And Beatrice."

"Beatrice suggested that she leave for her own good," Louise said. "She couldn't flourish here, not with Anne around. And you were Lynn's friend. She told me that. You were kind to her. Always."

"I tried, but it was hard. Maybe making her leave was my last kindness."

"A kindness to whom? Anne?"

"No. To all of us. To Lynn. She didn't belong here."

"Anne's line," Louise said. "Anne's line from the beginning. We fell in with it. I did. You did."

"Can I come in," Teresa said. "I need to tell you something. I don't want to do it standing on the porch." Louise's cabin was almost bare, stripped of everything but the furniture (two chairs, a desk, a bed, a small oak table). "There's more than enough furniture at Jane's," Louise said. They sat down.

"Life accumulations of a nun," Louise said in response to the silence. She indicated two bookshelves and six variously-shaped boxes stacked compactly near the door. "They will all fit in Jane's car."

Teresa knew that Louise didn't want to hear what she had to say, and she didn't want to say what she had to say. But she said it anyway, in part out of loyalty to Anne, in part because, as she explained to Louise, she had never told anyone, not Anne, not Beatrice, what had happened the night she told Lynn that she, like Beatrice, thought she should leave. She had told them parts, maybe the important parts, but not the whole, not the details that now seemed unreal, sordid scenes from a bad film.

"She followed me around," Teresa said, "she hounded me about Anne. She said Anne was my special friend and that we shouldn't have special friendships, she said Anne was a bad influence on me, on everyone, she said without saying it that before I came Anne had slept with some-one named Lisa—which I already knew. She said Anne would hurt me. She knocked at my door, Louise, sometimes in the middle of the night. Sometimes she came in without knocking. She was angry, all the time, so angry. I didn't know what to do. I didn't want to hurt her. She didn't know that I was sleeping with Anne. She wouldn't look. And then, that night, the night after Beatrice told her she should leave, she came to my cabin. She wanted advice, she said. But what she really wanted was to tell me again about evil Anne. That she did things in bed with women. That she'd do things to me if I weren't careful. She wanted me to tell her that I didn't love Anne, but I couldn't tell her that. She said, will you pray with me, and I said yes, and we prayed, and then she said we must do penance for Anne, and I said what do you mean and she said penance, real penance, and she pulled a little whip out of her pocket. It was made with thin leather strips, from the moccasins she used to make, with tiny stones tied to the ends. She told me she used it during Lent and that it was Lent and I should use it too, nuns did, she said, real nuns did."

"They did, you know," Louise said. "Even at Mt. Carmel. Beatrice told me once that they had whips for penance. Little ones."

"I know," Teresa said. "And so did the saints. But that was then and this is now, that was Mt. Carmel and this is Julian Pines. Besides they did it alone, or they were supposed to. Lynn wanted to do it with me. Don't you see? She took her shirt off and showed me how and I said no, Lynn, no, and she said Jesus shed his blood for us and she said I should do it to her and I said no, Lynn, no and she said she would show me how, take off my shirt and I said no, Lynn, no, and she begged me, she cried, please, Teresa, please. I said no. She beat her back again. I had to stop her, she was bleeding. I washed her off. I held her all night in my arms. I told Beatrice about that, I told Anne, but I didn't tell anyone about the whip because she was leaving, she promised me she'd leave, and I thought there was no reason, but now there's a reason."

"O God," Louise said, "I gave her a book. She saw it on my shelf, a book about saints. And it had pictures in it, one of some holy nun using the discipline, that's what the book called it. It was a little whip. My cousin gave me the book right after I came here. I don't even know why I kept it. Such an awful book. I asked Beatrice about the whip. That's when she told me that they had whips at Mt. Carmel. Lynn must have gotten the idea from the book. It was stupid of me to let her have it. I didn't think."

"Lynn was thirty years old," Teresa said. "Not a child."

"In a way, she was a child. So earnest. She wanted so much to be a good nun."

"But her idea of a nun," Teresa said, "came out of a book. I don't mean the book you lent her. She probably noticed it because she knew others like it."

"She was impressionable," Louise said. "I should have realized."

"She was impressionable," Teresa said, "because she was stupid. I know that sounds harsh and callous, but it's true. She was a very stupid woman, she took everything literally, she had no sense of humor, no imagination. I tried, Louise, I really did try. But she wore blinders, she never looked, she never saw. People like that are dangerous. They step on snakes they didn't notice. And the snakes bite. St. Teresa said that she'd rather have a confessor who was worldly but intelligent than one who was holy but stupid. Much less dangerous. And there are rattlers in these hills."

"I came to apologize," Jan said.

"No need," Louise said. "Leaving's hard on everyone."

"My mother left me. My shrink said that makes me terrified of other people leaving me. It's true. I cling. I've done it all my life. I'm sorry."

"It's okay," Louise said. "Let's just forget about it."

"She never told me why," Jan said. "She just woke me up one morning and said she had to leave and I should go to Hazel's after school and she never came back. Hazel said she didn't know why either. I asked her every day. She knew but she wouldn't say. I thought for years that it was me, but it wasn't. It was men and it was drink and it was drugs. I was twenty before I figured it out."

"Well, honey," Louise said, "it's not men and it's not drugs and it's not you. So relax."

"But what is it? If you could just tell me *why.*"

"We've talked about this before, Jan."

"And every time we talk about it you say you just want to leave. That you've been here nearly a quarter of a century and you want to do something else. But *why?* Something must have happened to make you feel that way."

"Something did happen," Louise said. "Jane's husband died, she's lonely, he left her money, she wants a companion, she wants to travel. It's as simple as that. Don't try to complicate it."

"So you're giving up everything you've loved for twenty-two years to go to Hawaii? Beatrice said you're going to Hawaii."

"First we're going to Hawaii. Then maybe a cruise. Then maybe Europe. I've never done any of those things."

"But you could do those things and then come back. You could take a leave of absence. Beatrice said you could do that."

"This has nothing to do with Beatrice," Louise said. "I'm not coming back. I don't want to come back. This part of my life is over. It's been nice. I've learned a lot. I like you all, but I want to move on."

"But this is *home*. You can't just leave and not come back."

"Yes, I can. I can and I'm going to. This is the fourth time we've had this conversation. Aren't you getting tired of it?"

Jan started to cry. "I'll never get tired of it. Not until you tell me why."

"Why? Because I'm almost sixty years old and I'm tired of being cold in the winter and hot in the summer. Because I'm tired of getting up before dawn every morning. Because I'm tired of Thanksgiving without turkey and Christmas without ham. Because I'm tired of seeing the same faces day after day and hearing the same voices and washing the same shirts and saying the same prayers and having the same discussions. I'm tired of being surrounded by women. We've filled our library with books by women and our record rack with music by women composers, women singers, women guitar players and our walls with paintings and prints and photographs by women artists. We have a woman doctor and a woman dentist and a woman lawyer and a woman mechanic for God's sake. We have a woman priest. And endless women visitors. When I say to Beatrice that I'm going to live with Jane, she says, Are you lovers? No, we're not lovers. We like men. Men. You know, half the world. But maybe you don't know. Maybe you're all too busy looking at each other. Looking to Beatrice like she's some sort of sage, to Teresa like she's some sort of saint.

Well, they're not, honey, they're just flesh and blood women with faults sticking out all over the place for anyone to see who has eyes. And I don't know what's with all of you and Anne. Anne this. Anne that. Frankly, I think you all want to go to bed with her. I haven't got the faintest idea why, but I wish you'd just do it and get it over with. I'm sick to death of her. Say a bad word about Anne in this company and everyone acts like you've committed a sin. I'm sick of the whole business. So that's why I'm leaving. Stop crying. That's another thing I hate. Someone is always weeping."

"Anne says that you're being mean and spiteful so we won't feel so bad about your leaving," Jan said, weeping still.

Louise grabbed her by the shoulders and said, "Fuck Anne."

"Louise," Karen said before Compline, "could we have a little ceremony after Lauds tomorrow, you know, a rite of leaving or something like that?"

"No," Louise said. "I'm not coming to Lauds, I'm not coming to breakfast, Jane is picking me up at eight and we're going out for bacon and eggs and croissants. And coffee without chicory."

Karen laughed. "Your quills are showing, Louise. They don't become you. We'd like to say good-bye."

"You've all said good-bye and good-bye and good-bye. I'm worn out with your good-byes."

"But this would be different and more satisfying. Communal. A way for us to end things."

"More satisfying for whom, Karen? Not for me. I just want to get out of here. And I'm tired of re-arranging my needs to suit yours. Just let me go."

"I will miss you," Karen said, acknowledging the depth of Louise's stubbornness, recognizing her partial truths.

"Yes," Louise said. "I've heard all about how all of you will miss me. I'm tired of that, too."

"You have known me for seventeen years," Karen said. "That's a long time. Nearly a third of your life. More than a third of mine. We have been good to each other."

"I'm not complaining," Louise said, "I'm leaving."

"You're leaving a lot of bad feeling behind. Jan told me what you said."

"Look," Louise said, "I have an idea. After I leave tomorrow you can have your little ceremony and you can all tell each other the horrible things I said before I left and you can all have a good cry and then Saint Anne can elaborate her theory of my blackened breasts and you can all nod and say 'poor Louise, dear Louise, she didn't really want to leave us' and then you'll all feel much better and you can get on with your life."

"It's Anne you've hurt the most, Louise, and it's Anne who's taking care of Jan and defending you, even to Beatrice."

"Anne's a snake," Louise said, "and you're well rid of her."

"What are you talking about?"

"I'm talking about you, Karen, you and Anne. You know, your special friendship, your affair, whatever you called it."

"I don't think you understand," Karen said. "I don't think you understand at all. I love Anne. I have loved her since the day she appeared at the side of my bed—sent by you, Louise. She saved my life. Sometimes I think I wouldn't last a week here without her. It scares me to think that, I don't want to think that, but I wake up in the morning saying her name. Do you really think that because I don't sleep with her anymore—I did recently, by the way, I haven't even stopped wanting her—that our "special friendship" has dissolved? You couldn't be more mistaken. Well rid of her? Oh Louise, I'll never be rid of her. I'd rather be rid of my arms and legs."

"You are crazy," Louise said. "I had hopes for you but you're as crazy as the rest of them."

Louise's place was empty at prayers, at breakfast. No one spoke, but breakfast always was a silent meal. Afterwards Beatrice sat, alone, wrapped in a heavy coat, on the porch. She listened. When she heard the car, she began her walk, slow, thoughtful, down the hill. She met the car before Louise did. The car stopped.

"You are Jane," Beatrice said to the driver. "You can park here."

"Yes," said the driver. "And you are?"

"Beatrice."

Jane looked around. "Have you been here long?"

Beatrice answered simply, though she was puzzled by the question, "As long as Louise."

"Yes," Jane said. "I think Louise has mentioned your name. You are very isolated up here. Louise said less than twenty miles, but she didn't say how hard the miles were. You'd think I'd know these mountains better. I've lived in San Andreas all my life."

"And now," Beatrice said, "Hawaii."

"Hawaii," Jane said. "Yes. Maybe Hawaii."

"We will miss Louise," Beatrice said.

"Louise," Jane said. "Yes, I'm sure you will. Kenneth always said you were very lucky to have Louise. Have you found another manager yet?"

Beatrice began to explain that Louise was not so simply replaceable, that she was manager by choice and by acclamation and by virtue of her own conviction that Julian Pines needed a manager, that they would miss her not because of that but because she was one of them, that she, Beatrice, was the abbess and Louise's old and dear friend. But before she got to the first point, she saw suddenly that Jane was so confused, so idiotic, about Louise and Julian Pines not, perhaps, from innate idiocy but from misinformation, misrepresentation. Before she could register the implications of this insight, Louise, wearing a skirt and carrying two boxes, emerged from behind a pine. And then Anne, Donna, and Karen with boxes and bookshelves. Donna packed the trunk first, then consulted Anne about the back seat. Louise introduced them to Jane.

"Coffee?" Beatrice offered.

"Oh no," Jane said. "We're off to breakfast at the Mark Twain Hotel. Best bacon in California, Kenneth used to say. Thick and lean, that's the way we like it. A good breakfast, I always say to my patients, is the best way to start the day."

Sharon came running down the hill. "Louise, Louise, I haven't said good-bye. I hate good-byes. I've been avoiding you for two days. I'll miss you."

"You will miss my quiche," Louise said.

Sharon laughed. "Not at all. I watched you make it. I wrote down the recipe."

"Sharon, this is Jane," Louise said.

"Jane," Sharon said. "Happy to meet you. We will miss Louise."

"Oh yes," Jane said. "But you know she's fifty-eight years old and still doing some nursing and this job, too. It's a lot."

"This job?" Sharon asked.

Beatrice put her hand on Sharon's arm. "Managing a monastery is full-time work," she said. "Hard work."

Jan walked uncertainly toward the car from the craft house. Anne went to meet her. The others watched a short drama, Anne holding Jan back, expostulating, Jan crying, struggling. "Leave her alone," Louise shouted from the car window. "Let her say good-bye."

Anne shrugged, took Jan's arm, and led her to Louise. "She's drunk," Anne said quietly to Beatrice. "Very, very drunk."

"Good-bye, Jan," Louise said. "I'll write to you."

Jan leaned on the car door and kept sobbing. Louise pried her hands from the window. "Now you get a hold of yourself," she said. "I'm leaving now. You'll be fine." But Jan continued to cling to the car.

"Bitch," Jan said. "You're a mean, ugly bitch. And I'm glad you're going. Go. Go. Drink and fuck if that's what you want to do, that's all you've ever wanted to do, you've never cared about me, never. You said I was an ugly baby, you said you couldn't stand me, you said they didn't like me either, I'm such a crybaby, stop crying. I tried not to cry, I tried, I tried, but they hurt me. It wasn't my fault, you fucking bitch, you fucking bitch."

Anne pulled her from the car while Louise rolled up the window and Jane drove off down the hill. Jan struggled in Anne's arms. "Fucking bitch," she said, over and over, hitting Anne's arms with her fists. "You fucking bitch. You could have stopped them."

Chapter 9
 The Abbess Clears Her Desk

(Beatrice: 1989)

FEAST OF ST. AGNES

Dear Jesse,

A cold thick rain, a sore throat, and a sudden need for solitude keep me in my cabin this Sunday afternoon. You were here in January, you know what it's like, though, if I remember right, we had a few days' break that year, with temperatures in the seventies and soft winter sun. On one of those days you cried so hard and long that I wondered in a flash of irrational panic if such profusion of tears and resultant loss of liquid could induce dehydration. I asked Louise later, and she laughed at me.

Louise, you probably haven't heard, has left us, but I will pass on your message when next I write to her, which may, in fact, be this afternoon. She lives now with a widowed friend in San Andreas, though a recent postcard gives a temporary address in Oceanside. Bacon, she said when she left, was what she wanted, bacon, men, and a reliable supply of hot water. Who can blame her? We do, by the way, have a great deal more of the latter than we did when you were here, thanks to Jan, a young woman who joined us shortly after you left by way of meeting Anne at a solar energy conference. Jan has been taking courses in sustainable energy technology at Calaveras Community College and thus do we progress, albeit slowly. Now I even have a shower and a compost toilet in my cabin. Not to mention a rose brocade chair that I inherited when Faye died.

Lynn left not long after you did, unhappily, as you predicted she would. But you were so unhappy yourself and so very young that we didn't pay much attention to your occasional Cassandra-like pronouncements.

There have been, speaking of Faye and Lynn, more goings than comings. Or perhaps it only seems so because the goings have been permanent, the comings transitory.

But I shouldn't let musings borne of winter blues and advancing age distort the facts: Teresa, with whom you shared the guest room when it became too cold for tents, has stayed. She names you faithfully in her litany of sisters. Two years later, Sharon, a high school teacher in Hemet, came for a retreat and never left. And Bernadette, a sister of St. Clare, has come so often that we think of her as one of us.

I'm pleased that you felt you could finally write, pleased that you found someone to help you through. No, I've never met Edith but Patricia speaks highly of her always and assured me many times that you were in good hands. I wouldn't worry about loving her too much, but I would tell her your concern. She'll know what to do. I announced at dinner last night that you had not only gone back to Sonoma State but were pulling A's in all your classes, and there were cheers, even from Jan and Sharon. I'm not surprised that environmental science is your favorite class and probable major; it was, after all, you who insisted that we learn to compost the garbage, cut down on our paper use (your apology to Louise is, I presume, for that awful shouting match over her private store of toilet tissue), and plant vegetables outside the kitchen door so we could recycle dishwater. Kathleen remarked once that an advantage of being in her sixties was not having, like the younger women, to defend her use of disposable sanitary supplies. You were relentless.

Of course you can visit and of course you can bring Else. It's lovely that your therapy group has brought you friends as well as health. Your circuitous and theoretical description of your relationship to her left me muddled, but if you mean you are lovers, please be assured that that in no way affects your welcome. It occurs to me that you were here during some of our more celibate months and so did not perhaps understand that we, too, work at love. Let us know when you will arrive.

Love,

Beatrice

P.S. We are expecting some visitors you might be interested in meeting—Clara, a sister of St. Joseph, in serious trouble with the diocese for her gay ministry, and Carol, an ex-Maryknoll who worked for many years with Rigoberta Menchú in Guatemala and other human rights activists in Central America. They're both lovely women, who've never met but who are, coincidentally, both en route to the House of Peace for a thirty-day retreat.

FEAST OF ST. AGNES

Dear Lisa,

Congratulations on your show. We received the announcement and the note with much pleasure, Anne especially since she has been a barker for your talent. She asks me to tell you that she and Jan (whom you don't know but who now uses the photographic equipment that you left behind) had hoped to drive to San Francisco for the opening but that Jan's winter flu and Anne's then-approaching deadline for revisions prevented them. (The article that occasioned the revisions, called "Food for Thought: The Theory and Practice of Monastic Cookery," is, by the way, my favorite of Anne's now substantial store. She wrote it for *Religious Life Journal* but sent it as well to the *Journal of Gastronomy,* where it will appear sometime during the summer. *RLJ* was "disturbed" by its "subtle irreverence." "Subtle?" Anne said. "Hardly.")

I'm sorry that the marriage isn't working out and gratified that you think Julian Pines would provide the perfect place for a few weeks withdrawal from the post-divorce trauma. Unfortunately, we have no room at the moment. For many years now we have been a last resort shelter for battered women in the area (which extends as far as Angels Camp and Mokelumne Hill). We have averaged only three or four a year, but we have a woman here now and are expecting as well another of our former members (after your time) and two other guests. Were it spring you would, of course, be welcome to pitch a tent, but in January that's not an option. There is, however, a retreat house near Mt. Shasta that you might try. It's called House of Peace and is run by a small group of Trappistines who practice Buddhist meditation. They're engaging women (and quite photogenic), adequate cooks, excellent housekeepers; the guest rooms are lovely in their utter simplicity, and the views of Shasta are quite spectacular. Tell them I sent you.

Fondly,

Beatrice

FEAST OF ST. AGNES

Dear Patricia,

Thanks so much for the hazelnut truffles; I spent a good hour sitting in my chair, sipping a cup of tea, letting the chocolate coat my mouth, remembering—as you no doubt meant I should—the day you and I left Sister Helen saying her rosary in St. Patrick's to explore like giddy teenagers the streets of San Francisco. Fisherman's Wharf. North Beach. Stella's bakery. And that chocolate shop whose owner waxed eloquent, or as eloquently as she could in her halting and heavily-accented English, on the glories of Italian chocolate hazelnuts. Is she still there?

The package said "Perishable," so of course I opened it immediately, even though I knew it was a birthday gift and my birthday still several days away. So, sitting here, counting how many years it has been since that first sighting of the West Coast, reminding myself of just how long I've been a nun, I began to suffer the birthday syndrome, seeing my life moving inexorably toward its end. Oh, yes, if my health holds—and why should it not in these ideal conditions?—I have thirty or forty years left. A long time. But my parents and all four grandparents were dead by their late sixties, so the genes don't promise more than a dozen.

And as I age, I wonder what happens to my relationship with the women here. I have been steady and strong. I have been The Abbess.

Our rhetoric about the position of abbess is that it exists for "the others," for the outside world, for the institutional Church; at Julian Pines, we say, it's only a convenient fiction. But I have known since the beginning that the notion of the abbess as a fiction is *our* fiction. The title itself carries stature with it. To use the word is to put me in charge. And I have acquiesced in that charge; I have conspired with language and tradition. Being "Beatrice" instead of "Reverend Mother" perhaps mitigates but does not obviate the conspiracy.

Add to this the fact that I am, like Kathleen, older than the others and one of the founders. And the fact that—now a part of the abbey's etiological narrative—Julian Pines was originally my idea, my vision. And that you, who first shared that vision, have been gone so many years that, Louise gone, only two of us remember your time here. And that next to quiet and self-effacing Kathleen, I seem a "natural" leader. Thus do personality and position conspire to compound my authority. Now, as I age, do I fear losing that authority I said I never wanted? Fear losing status? Do I think that when I am no longer abbess (and in a few years my sisters and I should certainly talk about my "retirement") the abbey will fall somehow into chaos and factiousness? Have I, that is, come to believe in our fiction?

Worse, I find myself, the abbess of a monastery, afraid of death.

In keeping with these Morbid Reflections on the Occasion of an Impending Birthday, I'd like to tell you something, a kind of confession,

I guess. You are the only one to whom I can confess because you still remember the long, slow dying that was our postulancy and novitiate and early years at Mt. Carmel; because our setting out together to found a new monastery meant, to us, that we hadn't quite succumbed to that turning to ashes; because you will understand, I think, the conflicting needs I have had all these years both to kindle and to extinguish the remaining flames.

Before Louise left she accused me of never having loved her, at least not the way I love you, Anne, Karen, and Teresa. I admitted not to not loving her—because in many ways I did—but to being drawn to the four of you (and to Bernadette, I might have added) in quite a different way. And who has ever been able to explain that drawing? What I did not admit (what I have long thought, in my false sense of my own self-sufficiency, I could and should keep from everyone), is that it is Anne who, like the abbey itself, burns in me and has burned in me since she visited here twenty years ago. I, abbess, am afraid and embarrassed to be weak, ill, old, and un-abbess-like in her presence. I'm afraid, too, that she would want to take care of me, visit me, hold me, rub my back, massage my feet. I'm afraid that if she did, all those years of teaching myself not to want her will have been wasted and I will want her desperately. I'm even afraid that I have taught myself all too well and that I won't want her at all.

I am, Patricia, afraid of death in all its insidious forms.

Love,

Beatrice

FEAST OF ST. AGNES

Dear Louise,

I was puzzled by your Oceanside address; are you wintering there? Just after your postcard arrived, we received a long letter from Jesse McMahon, whom I assume you remember from the stormy months she spent with us. She has been seeing a psychiatrist—one of Patricia's recommendations—for many years and feels, she says, finally sane. The doctor had her on drugs for a while but she's off them now, back to school, working part time at the Sonoma Inn, and wanting to visit for a week or two. She mentions you specifically, asks your forgiveness for her "inexcusable outbursts," hopes you are well. I just replied to the letter and informed her that you had left but did not give her your address. I enclose hers in case you should want to write.

Two other pieces of surprising mail that might interest you. Helen writes from Mt. Carmel that she is well, that the community there grows smaller "in these godless times," and that she keeps us in her prayers. Bernadette writes from her office in Detroit that she has been given a year's leave and wants to spend it with us. Presuming, she said, on our acquiescence in her plan, she has already begun the process of weaning her clients and hopes to be able to join us in mid-February. I'm delighted, of course, that she's coming and immensely relieved that we'll have extra hands for the next few months. Donna and Sharon have been talking about some goats and a very small goat cheese operation; Anne says "handcrafted" cheeses are all the rage and the monastery label would suggest cheesemaking secrets handed down through the centuries. Sharon has volunteered to take a cheesemaking course at a farm in Sonoma County. As you predicted, we are financially shaky without your income from the hospital work, Donna being, quite rightly, reluctant to raise her fees in these foothills where, as you so well know, incomes seem never to be adequate. But this new money-making venture has everyone's approval and enthusiasm, and it's good for us to remember what it's like to live a little closer to the edge.

I still, after all these months, expect to find you sitting at the small table in the common room with a book and a mug (one of the striped ones you favored) of black coffee. The first sunny day after several recent cloudy ones, I looked out the kitchen window after breakfast thinking you'd be hanging laundry in the breeze. Yesterday I almost shouted your name when I saw someone, built like you, climb out of a car near Anne's cabin, but it was a nun from Reno whom Anne had met on her tour of monastery kitchens.

A Novel by Susan J. Leonardi

A wonderfully amusing woman, by the way, full of entertaining anecdotes about West Coast convent characters, her favorite being the principal of a conservative and exclusive girls' school in Los Angeles, who spent a cold December night (does it get cold in L.A.?)—in a sleeping bag—in line for Grateful Dead tickets. She explained to a surprised parent, also in line and seeming chagrined to be found there, that the coterie of school troublemakers were Dead heads and she thought their teachers should be able to converse intelligently on that phenomenon. Informed by said parent that the limit per person was four tickets, Sister Anonymous opined that surely *she* would not be so restricted—and she got the seven tickets she came for. Sister Margaret, the storyteller, affected a British accent in imitation of Sister Anonymous, born and raised, Margaret assured us, in San Diego. This narrative was by no means one of the more scandalous or salacious in Margaret's repertoire.

Anyway, Louise, I do miss you and hope that you and Jane are enjoying balmy evenings on your ocean-view balcony and thick slices of bacon with your morning toast.

Love,

Beatrice

FEAST OF ST. AGNES

Dear Bernadette,

In my junior year of high school I developed a monstrous crush on my chemistry teacher, Sister Mary St. Daria. She was new to St. Elizabeth's, young, fragile, passionate, pale, and enormously intelligent. She wore glasses. Unlike most of the other sisters, who had gotten their degrees (when they had them at all) at their mother house in Chicago, Daria (we all called her that, of course) entered with a Ph.D. in chemistry (at least that's what I seemed somehow to know; given the reluctance of those women to reveal anything whatever about their pre-conventual lives, I cannot imagine that she or any of her sisters actually revealed that detail. Now that I think about it, it's more likely that Susan, Marianne, and I, her three admirers, invented it to explain her superiority), no small achieve-ment, in 1950, for a woman. I was in awe of her. I followed her around asking questions about metals and molecules, questions I formulated late at night while fantasizing her pleasure in my smart enthusiasm. And she did seem to like me, especially since, except among my cohorts, she was not a popular teacher, requiring as she did more theoretical sophistication than her students had anticipated. "But last year," ran the refrain, "all they had to do was memorize the periodic table."

That fall I woke up cheerful in the morning—chemistry was my first period class—and made not only my own bed but that of whatever sib-ling had waited longest for the bathroom. My mother suspected some furtive amorous adventure and asked so many bewildering questions that I began keeping under wraps my newfound joy in the incredible com-plexity of molecular structures. I was hard hit.

Christmas vacation lingered mercilessly, sweetened only by the used college chemistry text that Daria had given me, almost shyly, the last day of class. "In case," she said, "you get bored over break." "Break," she had said, not "vacation." A college word, I thought, and immediately made it my own. "What are we going to do for the rest of break?" became my daily question to Susan and Marianne. "How's your break going?" I asked the friends whom I saw Christmas Eve at the parish vigil.

When I entered the lab on January 2, I attached no sinister signifi-cance to the fact that the periodic table had been moved from the side board to the front and none of my classmates, lost in admiration for one another's pink angoras (I, too, got one that year) seemed even to notice. My disappointment—that's all it was, at first—was deep when Sister Carmella Mary walked to the front of the lab and picked up the pointer. Just my luck, I thought, Daria's sick. Or spent Christmas at the mother house and hasn't returned. But before Carmie even opened her mouth, my heart started jumping around in my chest and I could feel the flush rise from my neck to my temples. Something was seriously wrong here. "Sister Mary St. Daria," Carmie announced, in response, it seemed, to my premonition, "won't be coming back to us. She was transferred to a teaching position at the college level—where she really belongs—and I'm sure we all wish her well."

Tears ran down my face the whole class period and I decided during the following forty-five minutes that I would not be a Sister of the Holy Rosary or of any other order that would pick you up and put you down on a whim. I would be a nun in a monastery, where you went and you stayed.

All this (I hadn't intended to tell the story in such detail; I have, in fact, told it only once before) in response to your dilemma over discussing your imminent departure with the postulants and novices. I think, as I always do, that openness is preferable to secrecy. You are tired, you are becoming less effective in your work, more impatient, more bitter, more cynical. Tell them that. Postulants and novices are not children; they need to know that you are human; they need to see confusion and see, as well, mature options for confronting it. Sister Jean would no doubt feel more comfortable if you simply disappeared and she could announce a transfer, an illness, a family crisis. But it would be unfair to those young women, Bernadette, unfair and harmful. My friends and I speculated endlessly on Daria's fate. Had they lied to us? Was she really teaching in a college or had she left the order? had a nervous breakdown? been sent away for inciting students to a passion for chemistry—or, as I feared in some psychic recess but never voiced, even to myself, for inciting students to a passion for her? Ten years later, I told the story to Sister Lucy, my spiritual advisor at Mt. Carmel, and I cried. I admit that my reaction was extreme; as far as I know none of my friends, not even Susan and Marianne, were permanently scarred or even upset for very long. But you're a wonderful woman, Bernadette, and one of the young sisters perhaps loves you, and you must take care for her.

Lucy looked grim when I told my tale. She had always opposed our order's policy of spiriting off leaving sisters in the night and, without saying anything to me, she initiated an inquiry among her network of nuns to find Daria. She had indeed left the order, but the Sisters of the Holy Rosary had lost track of her entirely. Her real name, they told Lucy, had been Jeanette Anderson, but the only Jeanette Anderson Lucy's check in the directory of college teachers (I hadn't known such a thing existed) turned up was a professor of art history. Daria might have married, Lucy said, when she told me about the search and its outcome. I'm sorry, she said. The simple apology and the obvious compassion that motivated it made me Lucy's fan for life. But that is another story altogether.

And here I am many pages into this letter, and I have not told you how truly happy I am that you are coming back. We're all happy. Jan beamed the whole evening after I read your letter and Anne proposed a toast to you with our after-dinner coffee. The idea that you have nothing to offer us is, you must know, ludicrous. You can plant the garden, work on the craft catalogue, tend the chickens, help build Sharon's long-over-due cabin (she's in Louise's right now, but we're hoping to use that one as a permanent guest space, so our guests aren't always housed above the common rooms). And soon, perhaps, you can milk the goats. But we'll tell you all about that project when you come. If you feel eventually that you want to use your professional training there's always work at Mark Twain Hospital or, if you prefer not to leave the abbey, phone counseling for the battered women's center in Angels Camp.

No, I won't interpret your decision to return as in any way vitiating your arguments against our contemplative existence, and I look forward to the restorative powers of the inevitable skirmishes.

Love,

Beatrice

FEAST OF ST. AGNES

Dear Helen,

It was thoughtful of you to send a Christmas card. You can imagine my surprise, hearing from you after almost seventeen years. I did write to you on occasion after you left—I assume you received the letters—but without replies my motivation dwindled. I kept Mother Agnes, and, of course, Sister Lucy, apprised of our progress for several years and they us of yours, but after Lucy died and after you elected Mother Henrietta abbess, I submitted only the annual report. Since Henrietta and I exchanged harsh words at a conference for superiors several years ago and she made clear to me that events at Julian Pines were of no concern to Mt. Carmel (in fact, she said we should regard ourselves as disowned and disinherited), I have had no contact at all.

I am, however, pleased to hear that all is well, even if your numbers have fallen off "in these Godless times." We grow slowly and have at this moment eight: Karen, Anne, Teresa, Kathleen, Donna, Jan, Sharon, and myself. Louise left only recently, tired, she said, of vegetables and women, so Kathleen and I are the only remnants of the first group. Karen and Anne you know, of course, since it was they who precipitated your leaving. (I gather from your comment on our moral tone that their sexual involvement still rankles and from Mother Henrietta's fury that you complained in bitter, bony detail about my failure to expel them from our midst. You will perhaps be comforted to know that the two of them, now in their mid-forties, have for many years not slept with each other, and discomfited to hear that we all find Anne's on-going experiments with sexual love of great interest and educational value.)

Teresa is an art historian and painter, Donna a veterinarian, Jan a former employee of a prostitutes' rights organization and a massage therapist, and Sharon an ex-high school teacher. They're wonderful women, smart, warm, funny, thoughtful. You wouldn't like them. Sometimes they make noise, sometimes they cry, sometimes they fight, sometimes they kiss, sometimes they shout obscenities, sometimes they see visions. Messy women; they would annoy you, irritate you, exasperate you. They would rub against your skin like raw wool in an overheated room and you would twitch at first, then scratch, then writhe in your straight-backed chair and run to the nearest shower (we have four now besides the one downstairs in the common house) to wash them off. Your cabin has made me a perfect home to which I am inordinately attached. Sometimes, in fact, I think that I was so willing to see you go because I loved your little house and knew it would be mine when you left. I made new curtains just a few weeks ago, bright blue and yellow. They clash with the rose brocade chair that Faye left me when she died, which clashes in turn with the red Persian rug Anne found me several years ago in a San Francisco thrift store. But it's a cheerful space, marred only by periodic hauntings of its previous tenant, so often sour, petty, and joyless. O Helen, you hardened your heart against us and seventeen years, if I read you correctly, haven't changed you at all.

You ask about our priest. Because you have heard rumors? They are no doubt true. Karen has for many years now taken that role for us and I cannot begin to tell you what a difference it has made. She cares, she listens, she watches, she is one of us. Kathleen, who used, you may recall, to make vestments at Mt. Carmel, made the garment for Karen's first official mass, a garment she still wears. I don't know what happy demon inspired Kathleen to such heights of dramatic elegance, but Karen garbed in yards of appliquéd silk, mostly blue and plum, looked—with finches and dolphins and morning glories climbing up her front and back—like some breathtakingly strange angel. When she lifted her hands we wept. For me, the daily liturgy, familiar as my heartbeat but belonging to "The Church," became suddenly, clearly, spectacularly mine, ours. The spirit had at last pitched her tent among us.

Helen, you frown, you shake your head, you roll your eyes, you take my letter to Mother Henrietta and you say, see, see, they're worse than before. What I wish for all of you are Karen's hands in blessing. Peace, my sisters, she would say, and you would be at peace. You would have to love her. She isn't noisy, she doesn't cry, she doesn't fight, she doesn't shout obscenities, she doesn't see visions. She sings her sorrows to her roses and stretches out her hands to us all. But sometimes, Helen, I wonder and I worry when and where she aches for Anne.

Love,

Beatrice

Chapter 10
The Erotic Adventures
of a Lesbian Nun

(Anne: 1989)

CATCHY title, isn't it? I think I'm pretty good at titles, though I haven't been altogether happy with the one I gave my Beatrice-the-sleuth story (a story I have yet to show to said sleuth). This one is meant, of course, to evoke the long, dark, secret tunnels of anti-Catholic gothic and the sweet forbidden-ness of sex under the habit. Though I suppose the tunnels would be superfluous if you were a lesbian nun, since they supposedly connected convents of women to monasteries of men.

Alas, there aren't any tunnels here and there aren't any habits, unless you count the robes we wear in chapel, and most disappointing of all, there aren't any edicts. I used to try, when I was young and foolish, to get Beatrice to forbid my sexual experiments, to threaten me with expulsion, to do something about the chaotic passions that seemed to promise both ecstacy and annihilation. She refused. But more about all that later.

What I'm trying to convey here is that, contrary to the lure of the title, all you're getting is a rather prosaic summary of a fairly ordinary sex life. And that's the point of writing this in the first place. Like Teresa (of Avila, that is, not the Teresa who is one of my great loves and whom you've already met many times, unless you make a habit of reading chapters out of order), who wrote her visions and other spiritual adventures, yes, for her confessors, but also for her daughters in religion to make them understand that such were signs not of her reputed holiness but of God's mercy and were part of the everyday blessings of a serious prayer life, so I write to deny the perceived glamour and/or horror of my sexual adventures (though they have been, for me, signs of mercy and part of the everyday blessings of communal life) and to reject them as signs of my reputed promiscuity. Okay, the sentence is long and the parallel weak, but I'm sure you see what I'm getting at.

I'm Anne, by the way. And, as you have probably gathered, I'm fortysomething years old (I say that not to be trendy or coy but because I often forget just where it is in my forties I am), entitled therefore, it seems to me, to a sexual history consisting of—if you don't count the mild flirtations which I can't imagine why you would, though I am going to tell you about one of the steamier ones—five affairs-of-the-heart-and-body. Five in forty-odd years is positively abstemious in some circles, but I suppose in a monastery it might seem excessive, though two of them have nothing to do with the monastery and occurred before I came here, but I'll explain all that in a bit.

Five is actually a generous estimate, because the second was just a one-time thing, though of vital importance to this narrative, which accounts for its elevated status as one of the five. And another of the five was my first serious sexual relationship, which was with a man and so, strictly speaking, outside the parameters of the adventures of a lesbian nun, since I was neither a lesbian nor a nun at the time. Nevertheless, I'm including that, too, for reasons I think you'll appreciate as the story approaches its climaxes, so to speak.

I'm going to try to tell this story, or, more accurately, series of stories, in chronological order, though I know that's unpopular in postmodern literary circles (I will say here that I have nothing against postmodern literature or postmodern anything. I mean, I'm never altogether sure what postmodern means, but I interviewed an English professor some years back, who let slip that as a postmodern post-structuralist, she saw the self not as a given-at-birth, but as a social, and so somewhat artificial, construct. I was enormously relieved to hear it. I felt as though the burdens of a lifetime had been lifted from my shoulders, that the elusive, painful, and so far futile search for my true self—in which I had been engaged since my freshman year of college when I discovered existentialism—could be abandoned on sound philosophical principles. I've been much happier and more productive—it was after that interview that I started writing fiction—since. Looking for your true self takes a lot of time and energy. No wonder, if it's not even there to begin with), because I used to be a journalist and chronological order was one of the big things, right after the lead. But sometimes I'll jump ahead a little or go back a little in order to add to the eroticism of the piece, which so far at least—I admit this freely—has been somewhat tenuous.

The other thing I'd like to say about these, what shall we call them? erotic vignettes, is that some of them have appeared in print elsewhere. But only one at a time, so here I'm pulling them all together, all the juicy parts, which seems to me a great service to a certain kind of reader, of which you may be one, who goes right for the juice. I suppose there could be some copyright trouble because it's not as though I wrote all those parts myself, but they're my stories and my life and if someone else has written them up and described them a little more elegantly than I might, well, that's her problem. If you go around borrowing bodies and love affairs and crises and arguments and encounters, your own rights to the material seem a little ambiguous, too. Besides, if I sell this story, I'll only get maybe $400, which might sound like a lot to people who don't write stories (or even to people who do write stories because sometimes you don't get anything at all except for a couple of copies of the book or magazine) but, trust me, that works out to a lot less than minimum wage. So, if I can recycle, I come out ahead. And finally, this sort of borderline plagiaristic pastiche seems to have a fair amount of currency in contemporary literary circles, so you could, if you wanted to help me out here, claim that, in spite of the chronological order, I'm being avant-garde.

Here goes. You'll probably have a hard time believing this, especially if you're under thirty, but I graduated from college a virtual virgin. By that I mean that I'd done a little necking and petting—those were the current terms, indicating, respectively, heavy kissing or other above-the-neck activity and below-the-neck-but-not-including-the-genitals activity. Inclusion of the genitals would have constituted heavy petting or worse and I wasn't into it, unless I was by myself. Then I met Patrick, a cute curly-haired Irish-American (though at the time it wouldn't have occurred to anyone to add the "-American") who worked with me at the *Chronicle* and who assumed me a woman of—I was, after all, twenty-three to his twenty-two—vast sexual experience. Are you wondering, by the way, *why* I was still a virgin at 23? There's no reason really. I just was. I mean I was raised a Catholic, and the Church, as you no doubt know, severely frowned upon pre-marital sex, but I knew lots of other Catholic girls, and you probably do, too, who didn't let even the severest frown inhibit their sex lives. My best friend in college, for example, Carol Mason, who was from Chicago and moved back after we graduated, was definitely not a virgin and she went to communion just as often as I did, which was not, I admit, all that often. She said I was probably a late bloomer and subsequent events have certainly lent credence to that hypothesis.

Patrick was short, slight, smart, and funny. I fell in love with him right away. Now I had been in love before, at least seventy-five or eighty times, from Chuck Hollerman in fourth grade to Sister Mary Agnes in fifth, to John Shell, my sophomore econ professor, to Vanessa Redgrave whom Carol and I saw bare-breasted in *Blow-Up,* to, now that I think about it, Carol Mason herself. But I didn't date much and when I did, I counted the number of kisses, just to make sure I didn't go over the mortal sin limit, a limit I set at seven kisses when I was a sophomore in high school (with Johnny Stegmaier), twenty-two as a senior (that was Bob Gomez) and fifty-seven as a college student. The numbers were purely private ones and purely arbitrary, corresponding vaguely perhaps to how long it took for my clit to start throbbing, though I never used that term at the time. In fact, I never referred to it at all except in my head where it was "down there," which I understand is common to women of my generation. Anyway I figured that if my clit was throbbing I was just about to go too far. Counting helped keep it quiet.

But back to Patrick, who kissed me seventy-three times when he walked me home after our first beer together. The next day I didn't count at all. And by our sixth after-work beer-drinking session, he took me to his cubby hole in the Mission district and played with my breasts a lot (which got the clit throbbing pretty fast) and finally said he loved me too much to hold out any longer and would I please take my pants off and I said I loved him, too, and I did as requested and he floundered around with his penis in the vicinity of my vagina and came all over the bed before he could get it in. Which was a blessing, since we weren't using any birth control and since, as I subsequently discovered, it would have been pretty obvious that he was my first and that would have been unbearably embarrassing.

So the next day I found a doctor who not only put me on the pill (when I decided to abandon my Catholic principles, pre-marital chastity was merely the *first* to go) but gave me a set of graduated inserts to stretch my hymen, which she told me was very tight indeed. I managed to put Patrick off for a few days while I spent long hours in my bathroom, one foot on the toilet seat, wiggling the inserts—considerably plumper than the tampons I had only recently and with some pain started to use—up my cunt. I told him I was working on a story and sex distracted me.

I had some bleeding on the fourth day, so I guess I broke the hymen, and then I was ready for Patrick's Penis.

Now I know you're wondering what all this can possibly have to do with the erotic adventures of a lesbian nun, and I can understand why you might be confused by these preliminaries. But you see, it was while Patrick and I were having regular sex that the lesbian part, though not the nun part, happened. Regular sex, by the way, was Patrick's term. He thought our sex life lacked a certain drama (I found it pretty un-earth-moving myself and not so interesting as the inserts) but made up for it by being companionable and regular (twice a week, usually on Tuesdays and Thursdays for reasons that I can't honestly remember but that had to do with the rhythm of the *Chronicle's* demands and the timing of late night phone calls from Patrick's mother).

Patrick had a sister named Maureen who lived with his parents in L.A. After he and I had been together for about a year—I had moved into his cubbyhole by this time and we were talking about getting married—she started graduate school at UC Berkeley and hung around a lot. She was taller than Patrick, two years older than I, and, like her brother, smart and funny. We started to spend a fair amount of time together, and when she went home for Christmas vacation I called her every night. Patrick and I argued over the phone bill. That was our first big fight. Later I did a story on a local rape and I got pretty involved with the two victims and they were not in good shape. I won't go into it because this is supposed to be an erotic story and this rape had nothing remotely erotic about it, quite the opposite, which is why I begged off sex for a while and slept on Patrick's couch. I was, in fact, so unhinged that Maureen took to staying over, on a sleeping bag on the floor next to me. She would wake me up when the nightmares got too loud.

By the end of the fourth week, Patrick was pissed. I'm pissed, he kept announcing every morning at breakfast. Companionship and regular sex my ass, he kept mumbling before bed at night. Maureen and I smoked dope a lot and Patrick didn't like that either. You two are turning into goddamn hippies, he took to yelling. He started eating dinner at The Camel's Back and met Ceci and thought he might be in love. The real thing, he said. Not just companionship and regular sex. One night he called about eleven and announced firmly, as though he had spent many hours working himself up to the phone call, that he was spending the night elsewhere. Maureen and I decided to be comfortable for once and we slept together in the double bed and did a bit of kissing and exploring sometime in the middle of the night.

We got to kiss number three when my clit started throbbing. By five it felt swollen to bursting. When she put her hand on my breast, it did burst. Or something. I tried to be cool, to pretend that I wasn't breathless with surprise and unfamiliar passion. I slid my tongue between her very dry lips and my finger into her very wet cunt. She panted, she writhed, she moaned. I knew that something spectacular was about to happen. And then she made me stop.

She would always love me, she said a hundred times in the next few days, but we were good Catholic girls from good Catholic families and that was that. Well, speak for yourself, Maureen. I thought about her and her warm wet body all day, every day. It was distracting me from my work. I cried a lot, every day, and I've never been much of a crier. Finally, I told my mother and friends that I had broken up with Patrick—I told Patrick, too—and was going to take a few days off for rest and recreation. I was gone for a month. I had heard about a women's monastery with guest accommodation in the Sierra foothills. It sounded restful and you paid what you could and I thought I might get an article out of it. Well, Beatrice, whom I thought the most intelligent and holiest person I had ever met, nixed the article idea but told me I could stay as long as I liked. I went to all the prayers, I gardened, I cleaned, I cooked, and I thought about Maureen. I remember deciding, in what I perceived as a particularly poignant moment, that if I couldn't have her, I'd give my life to God and the great outdoors, which was the extent of the guest accommodations in those days.

At the end of a month, which made it late June, Beatrice called me into her office for a chat. Another woman was planning to join them in September, she said, and they needed time alone to prepare for her coming. I could return then, if I wanted, but she thought I should go home, go back to my job, make some new friends, think about it. You can come, Anne, she said, but not to run away. Now, you have to understand that by this time I had told Beatrice the story of my life—all about my affair with Patrick and about my dear friend Maureen, Patrick's sister, who had practically lived with us, and about my grouchy father, dead in a small plane accident when I was thirteen, my chronically disapproving mother, my ten-years-younger sister Carolyn and my even younger brother, born after the accident, whom I hardly knew. I had told her about high school and college and trying to get a job and my work at the *Chronicle,* and the rape case. The only thing I held back was the night in bed with Maureen. What possible importance could it have? I asked myself. It was nothing. It was once. It will never happen again.

So I said to Beatrice, "Running away? What do you think I'm running away from?" She didn't hesitate, she just looked at me and said, "Maureen."

I came back to Julian Pines in September, much to the incredulity and horror of family and friends, especially Maureen and Patrick, whose incredulity and horror was, as you can imagine, the most gratifying of all. Well, my arrival at the abbey and my first months here and the other nuns and all that are a novel in themselves, but I promised eroticism, so I have to do some quick summary. Besides, I don't remember those first months very clearly. I guess I was a bit dazed by the sort of shocking thing I had done. I was not, by the way, one of those Catholic girls who decides when she's five that she wants to be a nun. Frankly, in spite of sixteen years of Catholic education, it had only occurred to me once and that was, as you have probably guessed, in fifth grade. The phase was exactly as short-lived as my crush on Sister Mary Agnes.

So there I was, trying to be a good nun, succeeding fairly well in putting Maureen out of my mind (except when she'd write me one of her long letters in her stilted and convoluted prose, which I secretly admired and which, inexplicably, set my clit a-throbbing. Maybe you'd like to read one, just to give you an idea of what I found erotic in those days. Skip it

A Novel by Susan J. Leonardi

otherwise. It has no bearing on the plot and only tangential thematic relevance:

Dear Anne, Your letter of 1 June proposed a utopian vision of sexual freedom which though perhaps more Christian than that advocated by gurus in the Haight seems to me nonetheless irreconcilable with the teaching of the Church. While, as you know, I'm quite sure that that teaching is historically conditioned—refer to our argument of last January—it has independent merit and serves as an important antidote to the execrable view of sexuality, equated as it so often is with the appetite for nourishment, rampant on this campus. The potential for exploitation, in this view, especially of women and children, is immense. Admittedly, your own more conservative proposal in which sex, firmly allied to friendship and limited, if I understand you correctly, to same sex relationships unless the sacramental bond is present, is, of course, less subject to such exploitation and does, as you suggest, dissipate some of the concern about birth control which has been, unfortunately, the Catholic issue of the decade. However I don't think we can so easily dismiss the natural law argument for the teleology of the sex act. Performed under conditions other than normal heterosexual intercourse, its morality continues to seem to me problematic though, of course, at least partially excusable under circumstances of reduced consciousness. We can discuss this further if you like, but only if you agree to keep said discussion theoretical. I'm rather surprised you aren't struck dead for unorthodox thoughts in that holy place; I do wish you'd stop hiding yourself there and rejoin the human race. Patrick is no longer seeing Ceci and would doubtless take you back. I would write at more length but the fall exams necessitate a summer of fairly constant study. Fondly, Maureen).

The other new woman at the monastery was just a year older than I and her name was (and still is) Karen. At the beginning of our second year at Julian Pines, she got deathly ill with some liver ailment that none of us, including, I suspect, her doctors, ever fully understood. Anyway, someone had to take care of her and I, completely without nursing skills but easily the most expendable member of the community, got chosen. So, of course, we spent a lot of time together, Karen and I, even though at first she was too sick to talk or do much of anything besides lie in bed and smile wanly, which I think she thought she had to do because she was a nun and therefore supposed to bear suffering with equanimity and/or joy. Offering it up, we called it in grammar school.

After a few weeks, though, she started to mend, and then we talked a lot and laughed a lot. I should warn you that there are two versions of the next step in her recovery, her version and mine. She claims that she was singing the last two lines of "Danny Boy" to me (I taught her that and hundreds of other songs to pass the long bed-ridden days)— "For you will bend and tell me that you love me/ And I shall sleep in peace until you come to me"—when I reached down and kissed her lips. *My* memory is that I had just come back from a particularly vituperative community meeting and was yelling at Karen about this fucking-asshole place when she started to laugh and kissed my bad mouth to shut it up. Well, no matter. One of us kissed the other and the other kissed back and that's how it started. Of course, she was still pretty weak, so a little lite kissing (I'd say we got up to ten or twelve and, yes, that was enough for my clit to throb) was all we did for several days. And then one night I got a bit carried away and I kissed her long, thin neck (Karen is a very tall woman, almost six feet), and the dear sweet indentation made by her collarbone, and the tiny mound of flesh on the trunk side of her armpit, and the firm soft skin at the top of her breast. She moaned a little. That encouraged me to take her nipple into my mouth and suck on it ever so gently and by this time it was way past the hour of night prayers and silence and I asked her, a little breathlessly, if I couldn't just spend the night, and she answered, a little breathlessly that oh yes I could, I certainly could.

By the end of the next week she was up and moving and my newly expert nursing was no longer needed, but by then we were inseparable and very much in love. And very indiscreet. I'd kiss her when we went for walks, rub her shoulders in the dining room after lunch, things like that.

We talked about leaving together, building ourselves a cabin in some other part of the Sierra's or going to Sacramento to get jobs, anything, we said, even cleaning toilets, so that we could stay together. Of course, given our college degrees and a decent economy, there was little danger that we'd end up maids in a Sacramento motel, but you have to allow for the desperate romanticism and subsequent hyperbole of the young.

One morning we woke up early and I said that maybe we should talk to Beatrice about our plans to leave and I put my head on her breast and started to make love to her and she pulled my mouth to hers, kissed me sweetly and said, "I love you, Anne, but no more." She said it so firmly and so sadly that I never doubted for a second that she meant it and not just for that day. So I got out of bed and got dressed and went back to my room and cried for three months. But I stayed. We both stayed.

Beatrice, when I talked to her about the affair, only reminded me with a sympathetic little laugh that she had warned me that I'd find life among women "not without its difficulties."

I was celibate for several years after that. Maybe just to prove Beatrice wrong. I didn't even fall in love with anyone, except Beatrice herself, but that didn't count, I thought, because, well, everyone was in love with Beatrice. I didn't flirt with visitors. I didn't get turned on by Maureen's letters (which had by this time become increasingly domesticated as had Maureen herself, a recent wife and even more recent mother of a small daughter named—what else?—Anne). I honestly thought I had conquered my lust, but as subsequent events suggested, I seemed to have been storing it up for the big explosion. Her name was Lisa.

She arrived one day in a red Corvette after announcing by letter that she planned to join us. I guess Beatrice must have talked to her on the phone or maybe she had paid us a surreptitious visit, but I can't recall ever seeing her before she unfolded herself from the driver's seat. Though the beginnings are murky, I remember clearly that first glimpse of her thin, wiry body that seemed always in motion even when she was standing still. After we moved her belongings into the recently finished guest room,

Beatrice asked me to show her around our modest acres before vespers. She had a camera, a very good one, and she shot juniper and madrone and outhouses and gardens and me and talked non-stop the entire time. Stories. The adventures of an intrepid photographer. I thought she was amazing and beautiful, long curly red hair, green eyes, baggy twill trousers with a soft chamois shirt in sage. Before I even knew there was such a color. A *good* photographer, she assured me, she couldn't wait to show me her pictures, and my cabin, could she see that, she was burning with curiosity to see the living space of such an obviously intelligent and passionate woman as myself (yes, she really said that and in precisely those words. I was so smitten that it didn't occur to me to wonder how she knew about my intelligence and passion, since I myself had contributed almost nothing to the conversation).

I walked her around the pond—the last leg of our tour—and then, to oblige her (it was getting dark, I worried we'd be late for prayers), to my cabin, which is not really a cabin at all but a two-and-a-half room apartment in back of an old barn, here before the place was seized by a small band of unarmed nuns and named Julian Pines Abbey. I opened the door and gestured to the sitting room, so tiny that it only holds a chair and a lamp, my thinking room, and then to the bedroom that also serves as my study. She nudged me a little to suggest, I thought, that she wanted to see more. I took her further inside, into the bedroom. The air was as hot and heavy as Florida in August (I'm speaking metaphorically here; the actual temperature and humidity were about average for the season). But, I laughed to myself, as I motioned her to my chair, what could happen? She has just entered a monastery. I myself have been a model nun for five years. It's cool. I was cool (I'm speaking metaphorically here; my actual temperature must have been somewhere around 109). I even reached into my desk drawer for a cigarette. Stale, of course, since I only smoke when I'm nervous or horny, but cool. I offered her one.

"No thanks," she said. "I'll just take a puff of yours." When she reached up for it, she managed to brush her hand across my cheek. When she put the cigarette back into my mouth, she ran her fingertips down my neck. Down my breast. Down. And then she got up from the chair and nudged me to the bed. I sat. She pushed me over and started to kiss me. Serious kisses. Wet kisses. Lip-sucking, tongue-licking kisses. (Yes, of course, my clit was throbbing, but then it had been since about three o'clock in the afternoon.) I didn't once protest. She ripped my shirt in her eagerness to grab my breasts and I thrust my tongue inside her mouth while I wiggled out of my boots, bra and jeans.

By the time I tore her clothes off, she had three fingers inside me and then four and I was thrusting my hips at her and screaming so loudly with pain and pleasure that I was sure the whole group would come running to see what bloody accident had befallen good Sister Anne. We missed vespers, we missed dinner, we missed compline. We must have had twenty orgasms between us—or maybe twenty each. Who was counting? No one interrupted our orgy because, I found out later, Beatrice had, in fact, come to my cabin after vespers and glanced in my candle-lit window. I did not find out what she saw and heard but I can imagine. Lisa licking her fingers, Anne crying for more.

The next few days were almost exact replicas of the first, though we did try hard to make prayers and meals. She started taking pictures of me, close-up shots of my cunt mostly, murmuring all the while about what she was going to do to it with her mouth when she finished the roll of film. I thought I might die of an overdose of orgasms. I didn't care.

Karen and I fought. She's obnoxious, Karen said, disruptive, careless, intrusive, self-centered, totally lacking in self-control, immature, completely ill-suited to life at Julian Pines, and—most damning of all—not your type. I yelled at Karen that she should mind her own business, that I was in love. I knew all the time she was right. I just didn't care.

The third week, Lisa started to talk about leaving, and she wanted to take me with her. She pleaded, she sobbed, she rubbed her tears all over my body, while we made love yet again. She told me she would die without me. And she told me a lot of other things, too. A gypsy mother. A near brush with the Olympic Gymnastics team. Aborted months at four different colleges, including the Naval Academy and Julliard (the French horn her instrument, since abandoned), two years on Crete trying to make a film, photographic assignments in Saudi Arabia, Vietnam, Sri Lanka, a week-long affair with an unnamed prince whose penis looked like a bull's. We were experimenting with a carrot at the time of this tale. She liked sex and vegetables.

In those few days I guess I heard close to a hundred stories about her lives, which had been diverse, and her loves, which had been many. She had wondered (Oh, so many times, Anne darling) in the midst of them what it would be like to fuck a woman. And now that she knew (Now? I was almost sure there had been another woman somewhere, Baghdad? Jerusalem? Amsterdam?), Oh, please, Anne, please come with me, Tuscany, Provence, Sicily, the Gold Coast, Thailand.

It must have been the stories—effortless but exponentially inconsistent—that began to penetrate the haze of craziness that seemed to have enveloped me at that first kiss. I said no. For your penance, Beatrice said, you must promise to talk to me next time before anything happens. Oh and happy birthday. I was thirty.

Do you think it was a deep-rooted fear of that penance that so curtailed my erotic adventures for the next six years?

This is, if you've been keeping track, number five. Actually I'm not altogether keen about telling you this one. Not because there's anything kinky about it. Nor was its beginning either so sweet and tender as that of my time with Karen or so spectacular as that of my affair with Lisa. Maybe I'm afraid it will just sound boring. I mean, Teresa had been here for a year, we were good friends, she was recovering from a brief and brutal marriage. We talked a lot sometimes and then sometimes we went for weeks without talking much at all. She visited me in my barn suite once in a while, but otherwise we were just nuns together. When we drifted slowly into a daily routine of chatting by the pond, exchanging books, walking up to Faye's together, I honestly thought nothing of it. Six years is six years, after all. I was pushing forty. I'd been a nun a third of my life. And then one day I put on a new shirt that my sister Carolyn had brought me. It was blue with a peacock embroidered where the pocket should be. Carolyn says my flannel shirts make me look like a dyke. She worries that I'll be a bad influence on my niece and nephew. She doesn't know the half of it. Or at least she didn't then. I decided two years ago that the only thing more complicated than being a lesbian nun was being a closeted lesbian nun.

Anyway, I was wearing the shirt and Teresa walked up to me on the middle of the path that leads from the barn to the common house and she touched the sleeve of the shirt and said, Nice, that's a very nice shirt. And that's when I knew I loved her. Weird, isn't it, the way something like touching the sleeve of a blue shirt embroidered with a peacock can trigger so much—affection, passion, a twitching clit.

Telling this story is a lot harder than I thought it was going to be. Maybe because I still sleep with Teresa sometimes or maybe because there hasn't been anyone else. Or at least not anyone new. I may as well admit, since you may know it already, that Karen and I had sex again not so very long ago. It was a very strange event, sudden, passionate, and almost violent. Did we make love, we asked each other, or war? We only did it once and it seemed to suffice; we still look at each other in surprise when we remember it. We blush, avert our eyes, like nineteenth-century brides the morning after. "Maybe you should write it down," she says, "for your confessor." Most of you will get the joke: Karen is our priest now and "confessor" to all but one of us.

But it's one thing to write about involvements ten and fifteen years old, which by this time have become mildly amusing, and quite another to write about what still makes you tremble. Teresa still makes me tremble. Maybe this is the time for that steamy flirtation I mentioned, even though it occurred more recently than the blue shirt incident, which wrecks my chronology, but then I already wrecked it by telling you about Karen, so I guess it doesn't make any difference.

I wrote an article about the abbey (finally), and the journal sent a photographer to take some pictures of us. Her name was Marta. I don't know what's with me and photographers, but as soon as I saw the camera (body memories, do you think, of Lisa's camera between my sweating thighs?), I knew it was going to be a long day. She wore a hat and riding boots. She took a lot of pictures. She told me that she had a lover but that she also had affairs sometimes. By the time she left, we were looking longingly at each other. And at this point in the narrative I probably don't have to tell you about the condition of my clit, which seems to respond similarly, you might even say predictably, to certain stimuli. She kissed me good-bye.

To avoid resuming my Teresa story, I thought of writing up a second flirtation, this one with the lead guitarist in a black women's rock group, but the plot is complicated and she wasn't into sleeping with the oppressor so I'd use up a lot of exposition, fast-paced and fascinating though it would doubtless be, for scant erotic yield. So, on to more fertile territory.

With a little nudging from Beatrice ("Anne, why don't you come by this evening and have a glass of wine with me. We haven't talked in ages"), I kept my promise to tell her before it happened with Teresa. She sensed, I guess, that I was barely hanging on. I told her how desperately I had begun to want Teresa, and that I didn't know if I could go through the emotional turmoil again and that maybe I didn't belong here after all and that I wish she'd just tell me to leave or deliver an ultimatum or something. Anyway there were a lot of tears shed—mine—and a few angry outbursts—mine—and finally she shoved me out of her office, quoting Saint Teresa at me: "The body understands only one kind of love." I've thought about that a lot, both then and now, and I read some of the French feminists, hoping to get a handle on it, but I have to tell you that so far I haven't made much progress. (Beatrice and I have had other enigmatic and epigrammatic exchanges on this topic. "Without passion," she said once, "this life is nothing."

"Passion for *God*," I said, "not for women." She shrugged.)

A Novel by Susan J. Leonardi

It was a planned seduction. I even wore the blue shirt with the pea-cock embroidered where the pocket should be. I plied Teresa with wine. We told stories. I told her I loved her. "I love you, too," she said, and then just sat there on my bed, all calm and peaceful, obviously not under-standing the full import of my declaration. "I guess I better go," she said, looking at her watch. It was past our bedtime. "No," I said. "Not yet." We had another glass of wine. We told more stories. Finally when I was shaking so hard that I was afraid she'd notice, I kissed her. That and the faint taste of wine on her lips made my clit throb like a terrified heart.

She kissed me back.

And that's the best I can do. Readers need to work a little anyway, don't you think? Color the eyes, skin, and hair. Add an apple scent to the freshly shampooed head. Choreograph the kisses. Linger over favorite parts. Suck and savor all the juices. And if we're good together, you and I, decide what to do with a throbbing clit. May you have a hungry lover or a young zucchini still moist from morning picking or a warm bath scented with oil of sage.

Teresa has visions, by the way. Did I tell you that?

Chapter 11

Wild Thyme

(Donna: 1989)

THE thrust-by-thrust sex scenes so casually ubiquitous in the novels left lying around the common house should have prepared her for the heedless frenzy of the man fucking her. Should have. She was not a giggler, not even someone who laughed easily, at least not in human company, but she had to turn her head into the hotel pillow (linen-cased, down-filled) to stifle the weird noises she knew were working their way up and out—possibly provoked by the unwonted sensations in her crotch but more likely, she thought, by the contrast between his current compulsive energy and the soporific delivery, several hours earlier, of his paper, "The Failure of Vitamin E Therapy in the Treatment of Canine Degenerative Conditions."

A sharp bark escaped her, more chipmunk, she decided, than dog, but he didn't seem to notice.

When all was spent and done (she could have faked an orgasm; she had certainly watched enough rutting animals to do a credible imitation, but honesty intervened), she asked him what seemed an obvious question, frustratingly unaddressed in his twenty-five minute presentation and cagily evaded in the restaurant where they'd had dinner (he a veal something, she herbed vegetables over polenta): why didn't he use d- rather than dl-Alpha Tocopherol, since the former had better results in the anecdotal evidence from human patients?

"Donna," he said, "whether it's extracted from so-called nature or cooked up in the lab from so-called artificial ingredients, Vitamin E is Vitamin E. And anecdotes are anecdotes." She didn't say anything, though she could have. She could, for example, have referred him to a recent and, she thought, persuasive piece in the *Journal of Veterinary Medicine* and an approving mention of said article in last month's *Journal of the American Medical Association*. She could have cited her own success with d- Alpha. But she wasn't even a talker, much less an arguer.

He filled the silence, as she knew he would. "I must," he said, with the smile that had charmed her earlier, in a voice not unkind but vaguely pitying, "be in bed with a New Age Veterinarian." "No," she said, and then, the second concession in five minutes to habitual honesty, "I don't think so, anyway."

What she didn't say (she had been a quiet child and was, at thirty-nine, borderline laconic) was that she had spent the last nine years of her life in a monastery and had little contact (until this weekend when the contact was more intimate than anticipated) with other vets, New Age or otherwise. So how would she know? But, of course, she read the journals, traditional and alternative, so she began to see what he meant by "New Age Veterinarian."

"Well, maybe."

He wanted to do it again, hoping, she guessed, that he could please her the second time around, when his own need was a little less urgent. He seemed a nice enough man. He nuzzled her breasts, he slurped her belly, he mounted her leg. But he was clumsy and a stranger and a little patronizing (she hoped it wasn't genetic) and almost annoyingly young, so she didn't want to waste her first orgasm on him. She vaguely hoped that there would be another, more compelling, opportunity. She was middle-aged, yes, but monasteries were strange places, at least Julian Pines was. You sometimes found yourself alone in a sunny meadow with a particularly interesting guest who held your hand to her cheek, or you got kissed by a grateful cheese-maker for healing her prize cow, or someone you'd lived with, quietly, for years, handed you a second glass of wine and your fingers touched and your heart started beating very fast and you wouldn't at all object to her nuzzling your breasts and maybe one day she would. But it was hardly an urgent issue. She had time. There was always time at Julian Pines.

Dinner had seemed an easy continuation of the after-panel discussion, to which she had contributed several nods and frowns. The others in the small group—three vets, one student researcher—had already made reservations at San Diego's trendy cafe, Wild Thyme it was called, and she would like to have gone because it was mostly vegetarian and the owner had written a cookbook, *Wild Thyme, Wild Thyme!,* and Patricia, who was once a nun at the monastery, had sent them a copy, and they used it a lot, and it would have been fun to announce, "I had dinner at Wild Thyme." Teresa would have coaxed details, and she liked being coaxed occasionally. Teresa had a talent for it. But when David (David Messaline, DVM, the stud at her side), asked if he and Donna could join the party, the waiter laughed. Not a chance. At least she could describe the bar. Crowded. Green.

Her second choice on the conference's annotated "Recommended Eateries" was Rosemary (she wondered if Parsley and Sage languished, un-recommended, on fringy side streets), which offered, the list promised, a wide choice of vegetarian entrees, as well as meat and fish, in an intimate, casual setting with friendly if sometimes sluggish service. "Casual" was reassuring since she hadn't anticipated nightlife and packed only two changes of underwear, two long-sleeved t-shirts, and clean jeans.

"Come with me," she said to David, pointing to Rosemary on the list, and he had. She was not at all an attractive woman, she knew that, with her big-boned body, thin, curly, colorless hair, round face, small eyes. Neutral enough, though, for the present project. He, short and slightly chubby, wasn't terribly attractive either, but he had Kat's dimpled chin and Skip's receding blond hair and when he smiled he reminded her of a Yellow Labrador, her second favorite breed (second out of loyalty to Bjorna, a Samoyed, her faithful companion throughout college, vet school, grad school, first real job—Attending Physician at the Sacramento Zoo—and first months at Julian Pines. A trusting beast, but she shouldn't in her old age have trusted the rattlesnake. And to Kiera, half-Samoyed, who was just a puppy when she arrived). She thought that he probably had decent genes, pedantry not being, as far as she knew, inheritable, although it did seem to occur more frequently with the Y chromosome.

She liked the polenta, but it wasn't any better than Bernadette's. The dessert, however, a bittersweet chocolate cup filled with hazelnut cream and topped with toasted nuts and mascarpone, had never been, to her knowledge, on the monastery menu.

When he asked her to come to his room afterwards for a drink, she knew what he wanted. And she wanted it, too, though perhaps for different reasons. But it was all too complicated (especially for someone who seldom spoke unless coaxed) to explain, the late nights at Katrina and Skip's farm nursing Gretel, their pregnant goat, the sweet, body-long pleasure of Kat's calloused hand so gently pushing the hair out of her face while she delivered the recalcitrant kid, the way the two of them, she and Kat, leaned into each other after the birth, spent, exultant, Kat crying because she, turning forty in less than a year, couldn't conceive, when even Gretel, an inexperienced two-year-old, was already a mother, Kat fantasizing her 40th birthday party, the nuns all invited, of course, they were practically neighbors, the unhurried thank-you-good-bye kiss, Donna's own sudden vision of a perfect birthday present.

Besides, David didn't ask for explanations. Why would he? When he kissed her, she put her arms around his neck, and rubbed her hair on his cheek. Yes, she said when he asked her, politely, if she wanted to, ah, have sex. They only had to move two feet, from the tiny table to the bed. Hotel rooms were clever that way.

The conference hadn't even been her own idea. She had tossed the announcement on the breakfast table with the rest of the throw-away mail, and Beatrice had glanced at it and said, why don't you go? It's only for the weekend. You haven't spent a night away since you arrived. This was not the literal truth. On occasion a neighbor's cow, horse, pig, goat, or—once—peahen needed round-the-clock care. There was, for example, the night at Kat and Skip's. But that's not what Beatrice meant. Beatrice meant recreation, fun, relaxation, a chance to be with other vets, and Beatrice was the abbess and Donna's all-time favorite member of the human species, so why not? It was pure and happy happenstance that the dates coincided so precisely with the time of her ovulation.

Five weeks later, on a Sunday, she almost lost her breakfast. It was only the third time in her life she had been nauseous and there was no flu going around and she hadn't eaten anything out of the ordinary, certainly nothing that commonly harbored salmonella or E coli. The nausea recurred morning after morning, and then she started to crave grapefruit, heretofore her least favorite member of the citrus family. And so she knew. That Friday, after dinner and clean-up, the eight of them were in the common house, Beatrice on the couch with a novel, Anne, Karen, Jan on the rug talking about building a bigger solar oven, Teresa at the small table, sketching, and Sharon, Kathleen, and herself at the large table playing Scrabble. Just before evening prayers, she suddenly felt so tired that she thought death itself would be preferable to the short walk to chapel, so she stood up—Kiera stood up with her—and said flatly to the group as she walked out the door, "I'm pregnant." Well, there might have been a better way. She had meant to tell them, Beatrice at least, about Kat and David and the whole serendipitous, providential confluence of need and desire and birthing goats and despair and ovulation and inspiration and over-booked restaurants and fortieth birthdays and Vitamin E and the tendency of men to follow the inclination of their crotches. But she was not a woman of that many words.

Epilogue
First Installment of the Autobiography of Sierra Wolf

(2000)

ANNE says I've been on the agenda for eleven years even though I'm only ten. As soon as I learned to read, she said I should have my own copy of the agenda. I only knew a few of the words then, I was only four and a half, but now that I'm reading at eleventh-grade level, I usually know them all. Most days there's no written agenda anyway, only for the Big Meeting on the third Saturday of the month at 4 o'clock. Mornings someone just says, "Well, what's on the agenda for today?" It's funny to think that eleven years

ago, someone said, "Well, what's on the agenda today?" and someone else said, "Sierra Wolf." Or maybe they just referred to me as "the baby," even though Mama says she gave me the name as soon as she knew. But she might not have told. She doesn't talk much.

When I started school, I had to explain about the agenda because most of the kids just live with a mom and dad or a mom and a couple of brothers or something and don't need to figure out every morning after breakfast who's doing what when. But with eleven of us not counting visitors I guess we do or things could get pretty chaotic. Anne says "chaotic" is from a Greek god named Chaos who was the confusion of the world before it got to be the world.

Anne says that I might be a writer when I grow up. With a name like Wolf, she said, you almost have to be. Beatrice said, "Christa, Thomas, Tom, or Virginia"? and Anne said, "All the writing wolves," but she gave me a book called *Thrush* that Virginia Woolf wrote about a dog. I don't think I could write a whole book about a dog, but Mama could. Anne says that if I want to be a writer, I should have my own agenda. For my birthday, which was February 1, she gave me a list of fun things to write about. She said making lists has a long literary history even in Japan and there's a book called *The Pillow Book* which she showed me (she's going to give me a copy eventually) that a woman wrote a thousand years ago and is *filled* with lists like "things that fall from the sky" and "things that gain by being painted." One of her "things that should be short," is "the speech of a young girl," but Anne said that if Sei Shonagon had known me, she could never have written that. Here's my list of lists from Anne:

SIERRA'S OWN AGENDA: PART I
    items on Beatrice's desk
    smells after a rain
    chocolate desserts (see Sharon's recipe file for a good start)
    varieties of lettuce
    books you want to read before you're fifteen
    insects in the garden
    countries of origin of kids at your school
    words that make your heart beat faster
    ways to cook overgrown zucchini (no help from Sharon on this one)
    jokes that start with "why" or "how"
    things to do in San Francisco (the other half of your birthday present is a trip to SF in the spring—your agenda, not mine)

gross words

herbs in Ming's herb garden

one-sentence biographies of visitors

kinds of soup

animals your Mama has treated in the last six months

colors in Teresa's palette

animals that you feel close to

kinds of massages that Jan can do

words of more than four syllables that your Mama knows

cars neighbors drive

days of celebration

spices Kathleen uses in baking

presents you'd most like to have for your next birthday that don't
cost anything except time, effort, and maybe an unusual ingredient

words for colors on the purple-blue spectrum

songs you can play on the piano

flowers in Karen's greenhouse

one-sentence biographies of neighbors

one-sentence biographies of nuns you know

your own list of lists

Calling it "Sierra's Own Agenda" was a joke because she wrote it even though it was a present for me. But she said I could officially adopt it, in part or in its entirety, and then it would be really mine, no joke. I started working on the lists right away. I tried at first to do them in order but it hasn't rained for a long time, so I had to skip that one, and I know there will be a lot more insects in the garden in spring than there are now, so I just made a page for those and will fill them in later. I had the idea of making a page for every list and putting them in a 3-ring binder so I could add pages, because I can see that some of the lists might turn out really long, like Mama's words or one-sentence biographies of nuns I know, which will overlap with biographies of visitors, but Anne said it gives me a challenging categorization problem. I think I'll just change it to biographies of visitors who aren't nuns.

When I made the label for the last page, the list of lists, I started to laugh because what if I put on my list of lists a list of lists and then on that list of lists I put a list of lists. It could go on forever. When I told Anne, she laughed, too, and said it was a mise en abyme (she wrote it for me) which is French and means plunged into the abyss because it's funny but also kind of scary. I wonder if "abyss" is related to "abbess."

Mama says that Anne has a word for everything.

Like when I read *How the Crocodile Got Its Tail* and Anne said it was an etiological tale. She said I should write my own etiological tales like how I got my grandparents.

Well, how I got my grandparents is a funny story, but when I started school and the other kids had grandmas and grandpas who gave them presents and took them on trips I felt bad. Not right away. Maybe when I was seven or eight. I mean everybody here gives me presents and they take me places, too—once Beatrice did, even though she doesn't like to drive and doesn't often leave Julian Pines except that she said she'd come with us on my birthday trip to San Francisco and visit Patricia while Anne and I were off gallivanting. "Gallivanting" is probably the funniest word I've ever heard.

Kathleen never leaves. She says she just likes it here and there are plenty of places she can walk to that are trips in themselves and well worth visiting. Anyway, I needed some grandparents, so we put it on the agenda. I think it was number 4. "Grandparents for Sierra." There was a long discussion about it and a lot of laughing because Mama was forty when I was born and then was forty-eight, so Karen said maybe grandma should be in her late sixties and only Kathleen and Beatrice were that old, but Kathleen said she could easily be my great-grandmother and everyone but Ming was at least young-grandmother age so she didn't see why Donna's delinquent pregnancy should have any bearing on the matter. It seemed like she and maybe Karen and Anne were getting frustrated or something.

Finally Anne said, "Sierra, why don't you just pick a grandma?" But then I didn't want to pick because it seemed silly to have Anne or Sharon or Karen or Beatrice suddenly become my grandma. And besides that still left me without a grandpa, which I wanted, too, even though not all the kids have a grandpa and some have two or three. So I said I'd think about it some more. After a couple of days I hiked to Rita and Ted's, which is the farm next to ours further up. I've already written their one-sentence biographies under "neighbors." The one-sentence part was hard because I knew a lot about them from listening and also from asking questions myself. "Born in Mississippi and raised on Navy bases all over the world, Ted had a wild youth as a leather worker until he was thirty-five when he met Rita at a wild party he wasn't invited to and he hasn't moved a single time in five years which is a record." "Rita originally came from St. Helena which is in Napa County but she spent a lot of time here because her grandmother Faye owned the farm she and Ted live on now and she never thought she'd want to be a farmer but she got tired of nine-to-nine and keeping corporate felons out of jail."

Rita and Ted said sure, no problem being my grandparents if it was okay with the nuns. So I asked if we could put 'grandparents for Sierra' back on the agenda and then I just announced it—I hadn't even told Mama—and they all laughed again because Rita and Ted aren't even as old as Mama even though Rita has grey hair. But I didn't know that. And we all decided it didn't matter one bit.

Rita and Ted are pretty good grandparents. I heard Rita tell Teresa that she's really getting into it. She said she sort of forgot to have kids herself and she would have made a lousy mother but this seems more manageable. They come to visit, which they did anyway, but more now, and they bring me presents, like the fountain pen I'm writing with, which they didn't. And they've taken me on two trips, one to Sacramento where Rita's parents live and where there's a zoo my mom used to work at before she came to Julian Pines. She doesn't take me there because she has ambivalent feelings about zoos. Anne says that there are other "ambi" words, like "ambidextrous" and "ambiguous." She showed me the page in the OED, which is a huge dictionary that you need a magnifying glass to read unless you have really good vision which I do. But I like to use the glass anyway because it makes me feel interesting and the small print hurts my eyes if I look up a lot of words at a time. Maybe I'll make a list of words with "ambi" that I hear people use. Would "Bambi" count? That's a joke because I know Bambi has nothing to do with "both," which is what "ambi" means, but I don't know how to make jokes when I write except by using a smiley face, which Anne says is trite, which means used too often, but if I keep saying "that's a joke," then I would be using that too often, too. Trite. It seems like it should be an object like a slide or a sled or even a stream. "Grandma, can we go wading in the trite?"

I never did call Rita grandma because I starting thinking about my real grandma who died a long time ago when Mama was a little girl. Her name was Marcy, but Mama called her Shining Wolf. She was part Chumash and part Mi-wok. Those are American Indian tribes that lived around here, though we didn't learn about them in history class the week we talked about American Indians. Mama doesn't know how her mother got to be living in Southern California, which is where Mama grew up, because she died before Mama could ask her and my real grandpa didn't talk much. I'm named after her. The Wolf part. But Shining and Sierra both start with "s," so we have the same initials. If you write "shining Sierra sings" it's called "alliteration." I heard Mr. Chavez say to Anne, "Sierra sings spendidly."

Grandpa died when Mama was in high school. I hope Mama doesn't die. Or Anne or Beatrice or any of the others. Anne says that we'll all live to be 100 because we spend so much time working outdoors and we grow our own vegetables and grind our own flour and make our own bread. Plus, Ming came. Here's my one-sentence biography of Ming: "A child in China for eleven years, she immigrated to Sacramento with her parents, but because she had been picked out from age five to be a doctor, she went back to China for medical training before returning to the U.S.

and eventually settling at Julian Pines Abbey in 1997 after visiting us seven times and trying to talk herself out of it." Anne is teaching me to get as much information as possible in a sentence by using dependent clauses and conjunctions and semi-colons. She says I'm getting really good at it, except for the semi-colons, which seem like cheating to me. Soon, she says, we'll get to work on parentheses, which is the plural of parenthesis, because it comes to us from the Greek. "Parenthesises" would be very awkward anyway.

Ming teaches us Tai Chi and Qigong which will also help us live longer and healthier lives like some of the masters she knew in China who lived to 120. One of her teachers was a 125-year-old Taoist nun. Kathleen said just the thought of teaching at 125 exhausts her, and she's only seventy-six. Ming knows all about herbs, too, but only Chinese ones, so she has been trying to learn about native herbs. She says that some of them were used by the Mi-wok and Chumash and maybe Shining Wolf knew about them.

I think Mama must have been lonely when she was little, but a teacher at her school sort of adopted her for a while after my real grandpa died. She smiles when she tells me the story but I still think it's a sad story. I have a sad story, too, that I never tell anyone at school because it's too hard to explain. Anne says that complications make people squirm. My whole story is complicated, and even though I'm only ten, I haven't been able to write my one sentence biography. When you write your own biography it's called autobiography because auto means self, like an automobile gets around on its own. But that's not really true because not only does it need a driver but it also uses gas which is made from oil, a precious natural resource. We try not to use the car unless it's really important like when Mama has to get to a sick animal right away or when Sara is sick and can't drive me and Molly and the others to school or when Ming goes to Angels Camp to teach Qigong.

The sad story is about my other mom and dad. Kat (her real name is Katrina) and Skip. They lived on a farm near ours but in the opposite direction from Rita and Ted. Allegra and Chris live there now. Mama was their vet. They really wanted to have a baby, but Kat didn't ever get pregnant and she was almost forty which means that it gets harder and harder to have a baby. Mama thought that if she got pregnant with me, I could live with them part of the time or we could all live together or something and then they wouldn't be so sad, but after Mama got pregnant with me, Kat got pregnant, too. And that was really good because I would have a brother or sister just a few months younger than me. But Kayla had something wrong with her called Down's syndrome and some other things. Mama says it was hard for Kat and Skip to see me every day because I was always laughing and crawling around and learning to talk and Kayla couldn't do any of those things. And then Kat and Skip decided she would live in a place with other children who had Down's. Mama didn't agree because she thought Kayla should be with me, and she wanted to bring Kayla here, but one day Kat and Skip just packed up and drove away. They didn't even say good-bye to me and Mama; they just left a note asking her to find good homes for the goats and sheep and chickens. They took their sheep dog, who was named Paco and who helped them take care of Kayla. Mama and Anne tried to find out where they had gone but they couldn't find them anywhere, not even on Jan's computer. When I was in second grade, Kat sent Mama a letter from Boston, Massachusetts. She said that Kayla died and Skip was in Arizona, and she was working in a boring office and also selling her jewelry at craft shows and she was going to be at a craft fair on Union Street in San Francisco and would like to see us. Mama and Teresa and I went to San Francisco for the weekend of her show, and Mama was so excited, but Kat wasn't there. And the letter Mama sent afterwards came back with a stamp that said, "addressee unknown." Twice. Mama still has that letter in her desk drawer, right on top. I think she worries about Kat, but she doesn't tell me. I don't think she talks to anyone about it, even though she says that you should talk to someone if something is bothering you because if you don't, the worry will get all globbed up inside of you like peanut butter,

which depresses your immune system, which means you might get s
I asked Ming if she had any herbs for when this happens and she saic
in China they call it "stagnant chi," and she showed me Qigong exercises for unsticking. I didn't tell her that it was for Mama and not me.
But sometimes I do the exercises anyway, because they make me feel
like I'm floating.

Another thing besides grandparents that all the girls at school have is
best friends. Everyone knows that Molly and India are my best friends
because we come to school together and eat lunch together every day.
Their mom, Sara, picks up Daniel and Jacob, too, but they don't eat lunch
with us, because Jacob's only six and boys can't be your best friend, even
though Mama says that's a silly assumption. An assumption is when you
take something for granted, but then what about the Feast of the
Assumption on August 15 which we celebrate with lots of singing at mass
and cake and dancing afterwards just like New Year's and the Feast of Our
Lady of Mt. Carmel and the feast of St. Teresa of Avila because we are sort-
of Carmelites. Well, I'm not a sort-of Carmelite because you have to be
25 to come to our monastery, and I'm only ten, but this is my home, so
I'm sort of a sort-of Carmelite. When I grow up I'll have to make my own
decision about whether to stay at Julian Pines Abbey or not. I'm going to
be a singer and a gardener. Kathleen says I have a green thumb but that
doesn't mean that your thumb is really green, only that plants grow when
you talk to them. Also a writer, of course. Maybe I will write for a newspaper like Anne used to do before she came to Julian Pines, which was a
really long time ago. I might like to live in Davis and work for the newspaper there which is called *The Davis Enterprise,* and I would ride my bike
to work every day because Davis has more bike paths than any city in the
U.S. And because cars are very polluting, but Bernadette says by then
there's sure to be an environmentally responsible automobile. Anne says,
"Dream on, Bernie." That's sort of a joke because Bernadette doesn't like
to be called "Bernie," but she laughs when Anne does it.

Every year as many of us as can fit into the Toyota and Sara's van go

Earth festival in Davis, which has games and crafts and food and it's always sunny and warm. There's a big university Mama went, and Molly and India and I may go there, too, and then we could rent a house together. Maybe in Mama's old neighborhood, even though it has gone upscale, which means that it costs a lot of money to live there and they don't take pets, which Molly wouldn't like because of Prima, her Rottweiler, who is also part Lab. Anne says that if I want to work at a newspaper I have to cut down on my digressions. Digressions, she says, were her own journalistic downfall and she'd hate to see me succumb. Also her visit to Julian Pines. I'm pretty sure I'll come back home after I work at the *Enterprise*. I can sing and garden and write here and Teresa says we'll need a new abbess by then because she isn't going to spend the rest of her life with that superfluous title and I will be the only person not in her dotage with an extensive institutional memory, which is handy for an abbess. Beatrice was the first abbess of Julian Pines.

Mama said the Feast of the Assumption is about Mary being assumed into heaven but she didn't know much else because she wasn't raised Catholic. She likes the singing and dancing part. She said I should ask Anne. Anne said that assumption means to take to yourself and you can take to yourself an idea like that boys can't be best friends with girls, or God can take to herself Mary or Elias or anybody else whose company she thinks she might enjoy, which is what the Feast of the Assumption is about. I said I guess that means God doesn't think she'd enjoy any of us, and Anne said, "That's the plan." Anne understands all my jokes and I understand most of hers. Mama says that's why we get along so well.

Molly and India don't celebrate the Feast of the Assumption because they're Methodists, and Daniel and Jacob are Jewish. Molly is ten and India is nine, but they're both in fifth grade because India learned to read when she was only three. India wants to be a foreign correspondent like her grandmother, and Molly wants to be a vet like my mom, which you can learn to do at Davis and not many other places. Molly likes to go with Mama when she helps with a birthing cow or horse, so if she has time,

Mama picks her up even though it's usually out of the way. Sometimes she drops me off and India and I work on *The Mountain Newsletter,* which we started last year and planned to put out every month, but so far we have only finished two issues. I write a column called "Mountain Profiles"—we're doing one in every issue—which means that I interview all the people who live around here, if that's okay with them. I wanted to do Anne first and then Ming, but India said it might be seen as favoritism and I should do other people for the first few issues, so I did Daniel and Jacob's mom, Rachel Cummings, who came here from Los Angeles and works as a real estate agent in San Andreas but is planning to open a bagel store because she says that outside of L.A., you can't get a decent bagel in the state of California. She's going to call it "Hole in the Wall" because bagels have holes and she can't afford more than 400 square feet. She's going to refuse to make blueberry walnut or dried tomato bagels because they're trendy and not authentic. And she won't put sugar in them either because she says the slightly sweet taste of a good bagel comes from malt. Last month Kathleen tried to make bagels but they were a disaster. Once a monk visited us from New York City and he brought us a bag of bagels and I loved them, especially the poppy seed, so maybe I can work in Rachel's store when I'm in high school.

Then I interviewed Molly and India's mom, Sara Tribach, who teaches seventh grade at my school. India didn't even know until the interview that her mom tried to make a living as a potter but couldn't, which India says explains a lot but she didn't tell me what. Sara's mother was born in New Zealand but she lives in Sacramento now and is an appliance repair person. She taught Sara to fix things, which is why we call her when our washing machine breaks down. Then when Prima is sick, Mama treats her free, which is called bartering. Jan said we should have a "Barter" page in *The Mountain Newsletter* so our readers can list skills or goods they want to trade. India and I voted to do it for the next issue. And I'm going to write about Carlos Chavez, who teaches music at my school and comes to Julian Pines for feast days because he likes to sing with us and he usually stays for dinner because he says Julian Pines kitchen is the best vegetarian restaurant in California and he should know because as a callow youth he worked at the Greens Restaurant in San Francisco and cooked with Deborah Madison, who wrote Bernadette's favorite cookbook. Mama doesn't much like to cook and when it's her day we usually have sesame noodles, which are delicious and so easy that if she gets called away, I can make them myself. Also the baked tofu she serves with them. The recipe is from a children's cookbook, which she says is just her speed. But Kathleen says Mama is good at using up aging garden surplus and making the noodles taste different every time. Now that I'm ten, I'm going to get my own cooking day once a month. Also, we're going to talk more about building me my own house because Mama's is so small that we bump into each other a lot. Jan has a friend named Jeff who said he would teach us to build a straw bale house, which is just what I want because they're very energy efficient and I like the way they look. Jan showed me pictures.

When kids at school ask about my dad, I think of Mr. Chavez because he's very funny, and when he plays the cello I feel the strings vibrate inside my stomach. Every year we have a visitor named Sojourner Truth. When she comes, she likes to play the violin with him and I stay home from school because I want to listen to them practice together. Last year it was the only day I missed, but it was definitely worth it. I know Mr. Chavez likes me. He's gay but I'm not supposed to tell the other kids because their parents could get him fired. I know for a fact that the kids would do other things too, because two years ago an eighth grader said he was gay and some boys from his class beat him up and he had to transfer to another school. All of us at Julian Pines were very mad when that happened and we talked about if I should transfer too, but the next closest school is far and I get carsick. I didn't tell Mama that the kids tease me and once Jared hit me, because I live at the abbey. Sometimes they call me Sister Sierra. Anne said that there's a very long monastic tradition of raising the occasional foundling, not that I'm a foundling but she's pretty sure some of the foundlings weren't foundlings either. Daniel said that his uncle told him that nuns aren't supposed to have children. Anne said that may be the case at most monasteries but we've broken every other rule so why shouldn't we break that one, too. She has a big word for rule-breaking but I can't remember it. Anyway when Daniel said that, I knew the next question would be about my dad. Anne said I could just claim Virgin Birth. Mama said, "Close." I hardly know enough about my dad even to write a one-sentence biography. He's called a birth father but Mama says a conception father would be more accurate because he wasn't around for my birth. Which was not his fault, she said. Mama met him at a conference and they had sex because she wanted to have a baby for various reasons. He doesn't know about me because the custody issue could be a real mess because some people, like Jared, don't like the idea of growing up in a monastery. Mama says I can write to him when I'm seventeen and a half and see if he wants a ready-made daughter. She said he was a very nice man but a bit unimaginative. And she doesn't agree with his research methods. I looked him up on Jan's computer and found some articles he wrote about animal experiments. I couldn't understand the titles; Jan said they were very technical and she didn't understand them either. His current address is Las Vegas, New Mexico, and he has two children, both girls. Amy is thirteen, which surprised Mama, and Laura is eight. I'd like to find my birth sisters someday and meet my dad, but I sure wouldn't want him to try to take me away from home. Mama says that's unlikely but why invite trouble? I can wait. I have enough biographies to write.

I have barely even started on visitor biographies and we have a lot of visitors. One is named Louise; she lived here before I was born. She only came once. I remember because she wanted to walk everywhere on the property, but she used a cane and it took us a really long time. When we got to Ming's herb garden, she asked me a lot of questions about Ming and how she got here, and then lots of other questions, too, about everyone here. Then she said, "You know, Sierra, you say 'Anne says' a lot." She said it in a scolding way and I felt bad. For a while I tried to catch myself before I said, "Anne says," but Anne's my friend (she's my real best friend but the kids at school would *assume* that you can't be best friends with someone 45 years older than you are) and she says a lot of things that are interesting to me.

Before we got back to the common house, Louise said, "This is no country for old women." She didn't really say it to me, she just said it, so I didn't say anything back, but I think she's wrong because Kathleen is pretty old and she says she loves every inch of this crazy place.

Bernadette used to be a visitor. She stayed for a long time whenever she came and then when I was in third grade she moved here for good, because when she went back to her old monastery, which is nothing like Julian Pines, and back to her own job as a psychiatrist, she kept breaking down, which means that she cried a lot and didn't want to do anything like go to work or ride her bike or talk to people. Sometimes she still doesn't like to talk to people, but she says it's a lot easier to hibernate here without being badgered. She says she and Jan should go into the depression business because they know it inside and out. Jan never drinks wine at special dinners because she says it can set her off. They both work on the suicide hotline and they get a lot of calls at this time of the year from people who are breaking down from the winter.

When I started to write the one-sentence biographies of nuns I know, I found out that being a regular visitor is usually the way they get here to begin with. Except for Beatrice and Kathleen, who came a long time ago from another monastery. That was in the sixties, which we learned about in history class. Ms. Clavell, my teacher, said that she wasn't even born then. Beatrice and Kathleen and Patricia bought this land and named it Julian Pines after Julian of Norwich who was a writer, too, hundreds of years ago in Norwich, which is in England. Someday I'm going to go there. I have a book she wrote, but it's not very interesting to me yet, and it's not the real book she wrote because you can understand it pretty easily, which you can't if you read it in Middle English, which was a lot different from the English we speak now. But when I get older I'll want to learn Middle English, so I can read Julian in the original and also *The Canterbury Tales* which is one of Beatrice's favorite books.

I should ask everyone I know what their favorite book is and make a list. I already know that Anne will pick either *The Inferno,* which is a very long poem written in Italian but it has the English right next to it, or *Middlemarch,* which is a very long novel that I'm going to read before I'm fifteen. Definitely. Mama says she'd probably come up with something like *Understanding Equine Physiology.* She says she doesn't read much literature, but when she read me the *Earthsea Trilogy,* she kept reading even after I fell asleep, and she picks up the books Anne or Sharon are always leaving around the common house and reads them, too. Sometimes she even reads the adult books I bring home from the library like *C is for Corpse.* Karen says she likes to read novels with flowers in the title like *Daisy Miller* and *In the Name of the Rose* and *The Girl in Hyacinth Blue* and *Lily in the Valley.* She says it's as good a way as any to sample the world.

Patricia visits us once or twice every year. Beatrice said she hoped Patricia would move back here after she retired from her gynecology practice. Gynecology means the study of women and it's related to misogynist, which means someone who hates women, but I don't see how you could hate women. That would be silly, just like hating men, which there isn't even a good word for, Anne says. I think it would make more sense to be a misanthrope, which means someone who hates everybody. At least that's fair.

But Patricia decided to stay in San Francisco and keep doing her volunteer work in a storefront clinic. She says we're too isolated up here. Sometimes she and Beatrice argue about that, but I don't think they're really mad at each other like when Patricia and Ming had an argument and Patricia slammed the door and got into her car and drove back to San Francisco. I heard them because I was in the kitchen making myself a cup of ginger tea with lemon and honey because I had a sore throat. Beatrice had a cancer in her breast and Patricia wanted her to go to San Francisco for an operation, but Ming said it was hardly a cancer at all and wanted Beatrice to try herbs and Qigong first. Patricia said that Beatrice was her oldest friend and Ming would kill her with quackery, which means bad medicine. Ming said it was Beatrice's decision to make and she had made it, but Patricia said she should have been consulted. She was crying. I asked Mama if Beatrice was going to die and she said eventually but not in the next quarter of a century. She said that if Ming's herbs work on the goats, there's no reason they won't work on Beatrice. Ming made Beatrice herbs every day and she did a lot of other stuff and Mama helped and after a year the cancer was almost gone and now it's altogether gone. Patricia and Ming made up. Anne says that people usually do when they have a commitment to civilized behavior. When we go to San Francisco we can all spend the night at Patricia's house because her roommate is in Guatemala for a year.

Last year Bernadette's sister died of breast cancer. Bernadette was really mad about it, and she talked a lot about leaving Julian Pines because she thought she should be working for better health care instead of staring at her navel. Anne said that means just thinking about yourself all the time and some people think that's what we do here, but it's not true and Bernadette knows that but it's a persistent issue for her.

I think everyone must have a persistent issue because India told me that her mom and dad used to fight about the same thing every day, but she didn't tell me what. And I've noticed at meetings that some things keep coming up like whether we should eat our old chickens or not and whether we should buy our wheat from a local farmer who sometimes uses pesticides or go further afield for organic. India says my issue is words, and that I get obsessive about them. Pretty soon, she said, you won't be able to talk at all because you'll be too worried about etymologies, which means where words come from. But that doesn't make sense because Anne's just as obsessive as I am and she talks a lot, and Mama doesn't ever worry about words and she hardly talks at all. She's like a deer in that way.

I think my persistent issue is animals because maybe Mama is disappointed that I don't like animals as much as she does. I mean, I like them but I can't talk to them like she can. And Molly. I just never have anything to say except baby things like, "good dog." I don't know why that is, because I can talk to plants just fine. And people, of course. But animals look back at you and then don't say anything. Not to me. But they do say things to Mama and Molly. Mama said maybe I need to listen harder, but nothing happens when I try, so she said to let it go. When I started to make the list of animals I feel close to, the first one I wrote was "dragon." And then griffin and phoenix. They don't really exist, so why do I think about them more than the animals here or the ones I saw in the Sacramento Zoo? My favorite real animals are the marsupials, which don't grow around here at all. When Mama asked me if I wanted a dog of my own, I said no. Clementine is the monastery dog. Before that there was Kiera but she died when I was a baby. Clementine's a mutt but probably part Shepherd and part Collie and part Retriever. She was very sick when Mama found her on Sheep Ranch Road, but now she's fine and I like to run with her but I never cuddle with her like Mama does or like Molly does with Prima.

Sharon taught me to milk the goats. She spent almost a whole year in Canada with some Benedictine nuns who raise goats and make all kinds of goat cheese and yogurt, and so she knows a lot about them. She says they have a very good sense of humor. I like them more than I like Clementine because even though they don't say anything to me directly, sometimes I can figure out what they mean. We have nine goats now: Agatha, Agnes, Anastasia, Apollonia, Bibiana, Cecilia, Dorothy, Felicitas, and Perpetua. Karen likes to name them. She said St. Perpetua and St. Felicitas always go together, so she skipped from "F" to "P," but we'll fill in if we ever get more goats. We used to have a few goats left from Kat and Skip, but the last one, Gretel, died before Christmas. She was really old. Agatha and Agnes are LaManchas and Anastasia and Apollonia are Nubians. Molly says we should call them Stacy and Polly for short. The

A's look funny together because Nubians have really long ears and LaManchas don't have ears at all. Bibiana, Dorothy, Felicitas, and Perpetua are Alpines, which is what Kat's goats were. My favorite is Cecilia who was a present from Rita and Ted. She's an Oberhasli and is sort of red with a black stripe down her back. St. Cecilia is the patron saint of musicians. Milking is okay but I like the cheesemaking better, and Sharon says if I didn't already have so many careers lined up, I could go into business. We sell the cheese to restaurants in Sacramento and the Bay Area, but Sharon's planning to expand soon because Allegra and Chris just bought a dozen Alpine and Saanen kids and we're going to buy milk from them when they start producing. As soon as Sharon figures out how to get around some petty restrictions, we'll put goat cheese in our catalogue and Jan will make us a web site. Teresa is designing a label. Anne says there's a long tradition of cheese-making monasteries and every Christmas Sojourner Truth sends us a big wheel of cow cheese from a Trappist monastery in the Midwest and everyone likes it but me. It's very stinky. She also sends us a case of red wine, which I do like. Sharon and I are making a special blue cheese using only Cecilia's milk. We haven't decided yet whether we'll call it Cecilia Blue, Red Goat Blue, or Sierra Blue. If it turns out to be my favorite cheese, I'm going to vote for Sierra Blue. India says I'm the only girl she knows who would be flattered to have a smelly cheese named after her. She's going to write about it for *The Mountain Newsletter* and put in a photograph of me with Cecilia.

Bernadette doesn't like dogs at all. Mama thinks she was attacked by a dog when she was a very small child. I'm pretty sure that Bernadette is Mama's best friend, which seems strange because Mama is so fierce about animals. Mama's dog was named Bjorna, which means bear. She sometimes calls me Little Bear, which is fine because after the marsupials and goats, I like bears and wolves the most. Sometimes I worry that Mama would rather have a daughter like Molly but when I asked her once she said I'm definitely perfect and her favorite animal on earth. Anne said that if Mama said that to *her*, she'd feel loved for all her life and then some.

Mr. Chavez has a dog named Calla. He's a Greyhound and used to race but he hurt his leg and then nobody wanted him so Mr. Chavez adopted him. The calla lily is his favorite flower but some people think Calla was named after Maria Callas who was a very famous opera singer. Mr. Chavez says that he thinks she's overrated and he much prefers Dawn Upshaw and Kathleen Battle. He gave us one of Dawn Upshaw's CDs which I like but is strange. I'm learning the first song, "Sleep," to surprise him on his birthday which is December 12, so I have several months to work on it. He told Jan he'd marry her if he weren't gay and she weren't a nun, and Jan said, "Carlos, you just want to live at Julian Pines." And he said, "Well, it's the gayest place I know." She said, "What makes you think I'd want to marry you anyway? Marriage is an oppressive institution." He said, "Not for men." Jan says he chose her because of a remarkable coincidence: they were born on the same day in the same year, although she was born in the morning and he's pretty sure that he was born after cocktails. Usually we don't invite guests to our birthday celebrations but we're going to invite Mr. Chavez for Jan's since it's his birthday, too, and it's the feast of Our Lady of Guadalupe, which is a very special day for the Chicano community. Jan said she never heard of it until she came to Julian Pines, and Mr. Chavez said she's a cultural illiterate. Illiterate means you can't read, but cultural illiterate means more like you can't speak Spanish and don't know feast days or the names of opera singers. Mr. Chavez said that at least I won't be a cultural illiterate when I grow up. Anne said, "Depends on what culture you're talking about. What do you know about Chinese medicine?" She thinks we're all cultural illiterates in one way or another. Anne told Mr. Chavez that he was Eurocentric and he said it's only another manifestation of his general narcissism. Narcissism is sort of like gazing at your navel. Molly said that some seventh grade girls saw Mr. Chavez out running one Saturday morning and were talking about his cute navel. Molly said they have sex on their brains.

"Manifestation" means "showing," which is the title of Julian of

Norwich's book. It also means the same as "epiphany," which is another name for the Feast of the Three Kings, January 6. It's called that because it was Jesus's first showing outside of his nuclear family. But you can't just substitute one word for another even if they mean the same thing. Like you couldn't say Feast of the Manifestation or Mr. Chavez couldn't say that being Eurocentric was just another epiphany of his general narcissism. Well, he could but it wouldn't sound right, Anne said. She said I should ask Sharon if I needed a more detailed explanation. Sharon used to teach high-school English in Hemet, which is in Southern California. The whole area uses way too much water and has serious smog problems.

Sometimes Mr. Chavez talks to Teresa in Spanish which makes them both laugh a lot because they learned to speak it when they were growing up but haven't for a long time, so they get mixed up and use a lot of English words, which they pronounce in a Spanish way like "los blu jeans." They say they're speaking Spanglish. Molly and India and I are going to take a class in beginning Spanish next summer and then Molly and India are going to Mexico with their dad for three weeks. Mr. Chavez has been to Mexico six times. He has cousins in Mexico City but he says it's very polluted from too many cars. Sharon says that she should study Spanish along with us, because her mother was from Mexico but her father didn't like it when she talked to Sharon in Spanish, so Sharon never learned, even though she took it in high school and college. Then Anne said it's ridiculous to live in California and not speak Spanish and she wants to learn, too. And then Beatrice said let's start a class here, maybe we can get a teacher from Sierra's barter column.

In school we can start learning Spanish in sixth grade. Sixth graders also get to write a big paper. They're supposed to work on it all year and then hand it in in April. They look up facts in the library and on-line, like Anne does when she writes an article. I've already decided that I'm going to write about environmental pollutants in the Sierra Nevada foothills. It will keep me very busy and so it will probably be a bad few months for cheese-making and one-sentence biographies. But India and I promised

And Then They Were Nuns

that we wouldn't neglect *The Mountain Newsletter.* Anne says that writers have to have clear priorities, which are the things you put on top of your agenda.

Anne says before you stop writing for the day you should make a list of things to write next time so when you start you don't have a blank page staring you into paralysis. For next Saturday:

> my second trip with Rita and Ted
> my own favorite books so far
> one sentence biographies of Karen and Kathleen
> more history of Julian Pines Abbey
> Anne's best friends besides me
> how I learned to swim
> the Julian Pines craft catalogue
> the chickens, especially the Araucanas which lay blue and green eggs

If I write this much every Saturday, by the end of the year I'll have enough pages for a whole book. That's what Anne says.

And Then They Were Nuns

Reader's Guide
Questions for Discussion

1. The author, Susan J. Leonardi, writes: "I grew up with nuns. I want-
    ed to become one. I entered a convent when I was eighteen (and left
    at nineteen). When I graduated from college (taught by nuns), I
    taught for several years in a high school run by nuns. I've visited
    monasteries all over the country. But while this is a book about nuns,
    I don't think of it as a 'Catholic novel' or even a particularly religious
    novel." One reader disagrees: "This seems to me a *deeply* Catholic
    novel." What do you think? If you had to categorize this novel would
    you call it a "Catholic novel"? A lesbian novel? A women's novel? Or
    something else?

2. Ruth Ozeki, author of *My Year of Meats* and *All Over Creation,* wrote
    "Without the power of the imagination, we lack the ability to envi-
    sion better outcomes, and if we can't envision better outcomes in a
    better world, we certainly can't act to achieve them. In order to cre-
    ate change, we must imagine it first." In what ways does *And Then*

They Were Nuns envision a better outcome in a better world? Asked if she thinks of Julian Pines Abbey as a sort of utopia, Leonardi said no, but that she thinks it is "A small glimpse of a small-scale possibility of a better world." What do you think of this claim? What elements of the novel work to undermine Julian Pines Abbey as a utopia?

3. Sierra says that everyone has "persistent issues." So, too, does the novel. One of them is the tension between being in the world and being apart from it, between action (or activism) and contemplation. This tension climaxes in the scene in Chapter 6, in which a burned-out Bernadette accusingly asks Beatrice, "You sit up here on your mountain and do what?" Is Beatrice's answer adequate? What other "answers" does the novel provide?

4. Another of the novel's persistent issues is the place of the erotic in the life of the spirit. When Anne goes to Beatrice for help in dealing with her sexual relationship with Karen, Beatrice says, "Without passion this life is nothing." What do you think Beatrice means? Why, given all the the turmoil it was causing, does Beatrice not demand (and thereby reassert the age-old opposition between flesh and spirit) that Anne "control" her physical passions? How does the refusal of this opposition get carried out in "Wild Thyme"? Why, in light of this refusal, are the novel's scenes of physical passion so explicit? What other (nonsexual) passions drive these women?

5. Literary theorists sometimes talk about "multi-vocality" as a characteristic of fiction. What purposes do the many voices and/or points of view in *And Then They Were Nuns* serve? How would the novel have been different if it were entirely narrated by an "objective" narrator? By Anne?

6. The monastery is placed in a rural area, in the foothills of mountains, near the California gold country. What is the significance of this setting? Why mountains? Why the West?

7. Asked about the prevalence of food in this novel, the author quotes anthropologist Amy Shulman: "Virtually nothing else we do in our daily lives speaks so loudly of our sense of art, aesthetics, creativity, symbolism, community, social propriety, and celebration as do our food habits and eating behavior." How do the Julian Pines food choices and food debates "speak loudly"? Speak loudly of what?

8. Donna's mother was Mi-Wok and Chumash. Donna herself is a very silent woman who seems to have an almost mystical relationship with animals—just our stereotype of the American Indian. Yet the novel suggests that her silence and even her relationship to animals are rooted in her relationship to her white father. What other stereotypes does the novel both play with and then undermine?

9. Anne is a wordsmith and Donna a woman of very few words. Yet in some ways the two of them anchor the novel. How does this tension between speech and silence work throughout the book?

10. Teresa says in Chapter 4 that Anne is writing a story that features Beatrice as a detective. Chapter 5 seems to *be* that story. Teresa also says that she's uncomfortable with Anne's mixing up fact and fiction. How does the possibility that Chapter 5 is a fiction within a fiction blur that boundary? What difference does it make if we read Chapter 5 as written by Anne rather than by Beatrice as it claims to be? What is the significance of Beatrice's being cast as a Sherlock Holmes sort of character?

11. A conversation in Chapter 8 suggests that Lynn was asked to leave the monastery. Teresa says that "her idea of a nun came out of a book" and implies that Lynn's rigid, conservative, and unimaginative notion of religious life made her a bad fit for Julian Pines. How does the novel play with our stereotypes of nuns and convent life? Lynn's notion of nunhood is based on austerity, sacrifice, and physical suffering. What are the values of the Julian Pines nuns?

12. The letter is one of the most intimate kinds of writing. What effect does a story-in-letters have on readers? What difference does it make that the letter chapters (3 and 9) contain only one side of the correspondence?

13. As she leaves the monastery, Louise unloads her pent up frustration with Julian Pines and with monastic life in general: "I'm tired of being cold in the winter and hot in the summer....of getting up before dawn every morning...of Thanksgiving without turkey, Christmas without ham...of seeing the same faces every day....of saying the same prayers and having the same discussions. I'm tired of being surrounded by women." How do you feel about this outburst? Does she have a point? Why, after all Louise's vitriol, does Beatrice protect her and cover up her lie to Jane?

14. Sierra's chapter begins and ends with "Anne says." Why is what Anne says an important motif througout the novel?

15. Sierra's chapter is called an "Epilogue" and takes place 10 years after the action of the rest of the novel. How is it, despite its marginal position in the book, central to *And Then They Were Nuns?*